DEAD

IN THE

WATER

BOOK ONE

DEAD IN THE WATER

Donna Collins was born at home in Romford, Essex, England. Five minutes later she was a 100% bookworm, her favourite being Enid Blyton's *The Children of Cherry Tree Farm* - bought by her parents and the most worn book on her bookshelf.

It was this book, and her love for the 70's and 80's TV shows such as *Hart to Hart*, *Charlies Angels*, and *Dempsey and Makepeace*, that lured Donna to the dark side of mystery and thriller writing. Since then, Donna has wracked up many favourite authors, including Paula Gosling (*A Running Duck* is the second most worn copy on her bookcase), Jonathan Kellerman, Patricia Cornwell, and A.J. Quinnell.

But, although Donna loved to write, she also loved crime - and her career proves it. At school, Donna founded the school magazine, and her professional career includes OK! Magazine, Essex Police, Ormiston Prison Services, and Essex Offender Services. With publishing credits for freelance and commissioned magazine articles under her belt, Donna has now turned her attention and imagination to what she is best at - storytelling.

In her spare time (what spare time?), Donna loves anything scary that will get the adrenaline pumping, including storm chasing, fright nights, zombie-infested shopping malls, and seance panic rooms - with her all-time goal including the open sea, a cage, and a whole heap of great white sharks. Donna also proudly boasts finishing the 2010 London Marathon, but you'll have to ask nicely if you want her to tell you where she was placed and who overtook her.

Dead in the Water is Donna's fourth book and the first in the Jason Wade Thriller Series.

Visit her website at www.donnacollins.co.uk
Twitter @donnacollinsUK
Facebook.com/donnacollinsUK
Instagram @donnacollinsUK

Also by Donna Collins

DEAD IN THE WATER

Donna Collins

Willow Books

First published in Great Britain in 2019
by Willow Publishing.

ISBN: 9781068738821
Second Edition

Cover Photography & Design: Paul Waddell

Special Thanks to Dave Riches,

(a.k.a. CSI Dave)

For all your patience, knowledge, hot chocolate, 11pm murder chats, and for generally just putting up with me so I could get this book finished.

Now here's to the second one!

AUTHORS NOTE

The Golden Jubilee Bridge – aka Hungerford Bridge.
I happen to love this bridge – although it isn't my favourite bridge in London. But, whichever way you walk, it leads to two fabulous places: the National Gallery at Trafalgar Square, and the South Bank. I frequent the latter. A lot!

Let's start with the South Bank. Warm summer evenings bring with it pop-up eateries, carousels, and vibrant music. The winter – mulled wine, log cabins full of food, and lots of beautiful lights.

I would highly recommend grabbing an ice cream or a bite to eat and then taking the riverside walk from the London Eye to Tower Bridge.

The second place I have to share with you is, as I just mentioned, the National gallery. It's totally free to enter and it's where you'll see the Chalet of Rigi (at least it was there when I wrote this book). Walk the halls, admire the artwork and, outside, lean on the stone wall and take a mesmerising glance across Trafalgar Square and the rest of London.

For Pete

Daddy #2
I finally finished it.

PROLOGUE

8 MONTHS AGO
Peckham, London

Jason Wade removed his mask and breathed in the night air.

The April evenings had become surprisingly warm of late and being able to return to wearing only a T-shirt and fleece pleased him no end. He glanced back at the house. One of his colleagues knelt by the open front door. Two police officers appeared from the living area and waited for him to close the lid on his work box, then exited behind him – their questioning of the aggrieved occupant inside complete and the lure of a brew calling them back to the station. For Jason, it was the lure of a pint down the pub.

Jason peeled off his latex gloves and threw them – along with the mask – into the back of the Ford Transit parked beside him. He found dusting for prints monotonous at the best of times, but at the scene of a burglary? Heck, it was bloody tedious. He unzipped his white overalls and stepped out of them.

His colleague, Ben, reached him. He pulled the mask from his face and wore it like a bow tie. "Don't think there's much hope of linking these to anyone."

He referred to the minimal prints they'd lifted from the open window in the kitchen where the thieving bastards had levered their way inside.

Yep. Jason bloody hated burglaries.

Ben slid his box into its niche, placed his gloves on top of it, and pulled off his overalls. "Fancy a beer when we're through?"

Jason closed the van's doors. The guy was a bloody mind-reader.

The radio in the front of the van crackled. "We've got a body on the south side of the Thames. Outside the Tate Modern. We need you to attend."

Jason's ice-cold beer slipped away. A dead body was not what he needed right now. He headed round to the front of the van and leaned in through the driver's side. Swiped the radio from the dash. "On our way."

Jason made it to South Bank in just under ten minutes, which, everything considered, wasn't too bad for the time of evening. He followed Holland Street around the Tate Modern – a route, it soon became apparent, the majority of the London Met had also taken – and parked as close to the river as he could get before two bollards stopped him.

He unclipped his seatbelt, climbed out of the van, and headed to the back doors. Pulling out a kit box identical to the one Ben had put away ten minutes earlier, he grabbed a camera and a clipboard of paperwork.

He leaned around the open door and tossed Ben a fresh set of overalls. "See you up there." Then strolled over to where two officers stood by a cordon of crime scene tape.

Neither of the men looked familiar to Jason so he pulled out his lanyard and flashed his ID. The officers glanced at it briefly. The one on the left scribbled Jason's name onto the scene log and, once done, the officer on the right stepped aside, pulling back a piece of tape and opening up access to the path behind them.

"Cheers, guys," Jason chirped and followed the immaculately trimmed hedge to the top of the walkway.

Police presence was much more visible up here. Jason caught the eye of the nearest officer – a young chap, his shaken demeanour suggesting he was still a probationer who'd just seen his first corpse.

"Which way, fella?"

"She's down there." The officer pointed left towards a tree-lined tunnel that led to the Thames. "It's not a pretty sight."

"Dead bodies never are, pal. Not even the female ones."

Jason wanted to smile to put the kid at ease but, however bad it was up there, a new day always brought something worse with it. Best the kid grew a pair now if he wanted to survive his thirty years of service.

Halfway through the tunnel, Jason saw the rotund figure of a man waiting for him at the other end. "Hey, Ed. What we got?"

But Ed didn't look right. He patted Jason on the shoulder, the same way he always greeted him whether at the station, a crime scene, or even down the local. But this embrace was different. Strained. Something was off.

Ed's hand trembled but remained on Jason's shoulder. "Not much. We have things covered. You don't really need to be here."

He started for the tree tunnel, his unsteady hand urging Jason to move with him.

"What's going on, Ed?"

"Nothing."

His reddened eyes said different and continued to turn Jason from the scene.

Jason halted a quarter of the way in. "What the fuck's going on?"

Ed swallowed. Beads of sweat caught the moonlight. "Jason…" He swallowed again and glanced over his shoulder.

Jason pulled away from his friend's grip. He waited for Ed to finish the sentence.

Ed didn't.

"Tell me."

Ed turned back to him. "Let's just head back down to the car."

"Why?"

"I'll tell you back at the car."

"Tell me now."

Ed shifted his weight. "Not here."

"Not here? What do you mean, not here?" He stared over Ed's shoulder and back through the tree tunnel. Saw the glow of lights, heard the murmur of police. Nothing looked out of the ordinary – at least not for a crime scene. Except Ed. Ed looked like he'd swallowed a pint of green tea and couldn't spit the shitty taste from his mouth. Jason pushed past him. Ed called out and made after him, but Jason quickened his pace to an anxious jog. He exited the tunnel and the open air hit him in the face.

Ed's hand caught his shoulder. "Mate, please, come back to the car."

"Who'd they pull from the river?"

Ed's eyes glazed over. He chewed his lip but no words came.

Jason's grip tightened around his kit box and he shrugged himself free. "Do I know them?"

Ed reached for him again, but Jason stepped back. He looked left to where a crowd of onlookers were held back behind more tape. Then right. Police and paramedics were dotted everywhere. He saw the SIO in charge and then, along the river's edge, the scene tent.

"Fine," Jason said. "I'll go see for myself."

He marched towards the tent, his chest tightening with every heavy step.

"Jason," Ed called out behind him. "Don't be stupid."

Jason didn't stop. He reached the tent and pulled back a flap. Two investigators dressed in white scene suits didn't bother to look up. A body lay on the ground, partially hidden behind them. Female. Only one shoe – a red stiletto. Red-painted toe nails, unchipped and newly applied given the lack of new growth. Dirty, scratched calves showing through ripped tights.

Jason stepped forward, ignoring the distant warning bell at the back of his mind about the risk of contamination.

A black skirt, soaked through and crinkled to her thigh. A small mark, mid-way between her buttock and her knee, the shape of a butterfly.

Jason froze. Bile reached his throat. His shoulders stiffened.

"Jason?" Ed was behind him again, his voice low and soft. "Come with me, mate."

Again, his hand touched Jason's shoulder.

Jason threw the clipboard. He spun, hooked Ed's arm and held him still. "Why the fuck didn't you say?"

One of the investigators stood. "Hey! Take your shit outside."

Jason pushed him back down.

He turned back to Ed, dropped the kit box and grabbed his friend by the scuff of his neck. Disgust filled his veins. Ed mumbled something, and Jason shoved him away.

Ed stumbled out onto Southbank and the flap fell shut.

Jason whirled back to the body. The girl. The victim.

"Jason!" Ed was back at the tent's entrance. "Let them do their job."

Jason dropped to his knees. Now he saw everything. Her dark hair matted with water and grime. Her eyes open, clouded blue and staring up at the fabric ceiling. Her delicate neck lined with bruises. Needle marks dotting her arm. Jason reached for her hand. Ice cold.

He'd touched so many dead bodies. Knew the freezing temperatures they reached when the blood no longer warmed their skin. But to feel Leah like this? His own sister? It was wrong. This was very, very wrong.

Footsteps approached the tent but Jason heard Ed hold the newcomers back.

He cupped his sister's face, her cheeks just as cold as her hands.

"I'm so sorry, mate." Ed's voice was little more than a whisper. "But you need to come outside now."

Tears filled Jason's eyes. He crumbled forward, burying his head into her chest. He wrapped his arms around her neck and pulled her close. He waited for her body to warm. For the next gasp of life to enter her lungs. Instead, she hung in his arms, a dead weight.

"What happened to her?"

"Come outside and we'll talk."

Ed was right. Jason shouldn't be in here. Touching her contaminated the evidence. His falling tears contaminated the evidence. Heck, being in the vicinity of her contaminated the evidence. But you know what? He didn't give a shit. The only way he was going to leave her was if he was dragged out – and Ed wouldn't risk the scene any further by doing that.

A moment passed before Ed spoke again. "She was pulled from the river."

"But what happened?"

Ed sighed. "We don't know. It looks like she may have fallen in."

"How long ago?"

"Less than an hour ago. Some men found her."

Jason glanced up. "What men?"

"Just some passers-by."

Jason gently laid his sister's body back on the ground and stood. "Show me."

Now Ed blocked him from leaving the tent. "Jason, my boys have already questioned them. They don't know what happened. You know better than anyone that it's the forensics that'll give us the answers."

Jason pushed past him. "You don't have to be sodding Sherlock Holmes to see she was strangled."

He glanced around. Four men, suited but dishevelled, stood on the far side of the scene, two officers with them.

Jason marched towards them.

Ed pulled him back. "My men'll handle it."

Jason snorted and shrugged his friend away. The officers beside Ed straightened like two dogs ready to pounce on their boss's command.

Jason turned from them and looked at Ed. "This how you want it to go down?"

"You're leaving me with little choice."

"I'm asking those idiots a fucking question. One fucking question."

Ed swallowed and took a deep breath. When he exhaled, it was long and steady. He glanced first at the copper to his left, then the one to his right. "Take him to the car."

Jason hit out. His first punch connected with the officer on Ed's right. Arms wrapped around Jason from behind and he head-butted backwards. His skull cracked the cop's nose.

The officer released his grip and Jason made a run for the four men. "What happened?" he shouted. "Did you bastards kill her? Rape her?"

He was three or so feet from them when more officers pounced and took him to the ground. Jason struggled. He caught one in the nuts and pushed him away. Head-butted another. He could just about taste freedom when further police joined the heap. Black fabric swarmed him from all sides, and the four witnesses disappeared from view.

"I'll fucking find you!" he screamed as the constables rolled him onto his stomach.

They forced his arms behind him and cuffs swiftly imprisoned his wrists, but the quantity of men around him still didn't lessen. They lifted Jason from the ground, the tips of his shoes scraping the pavement as they dragged him towards a police car. He struggled, but the only place he was going was back to the station.

And his sister, Leah, would be left out here all alone.

CHAPTER ONE

PRESENT DAY
Trafalgar Square, London

The wooden bench numbed her bottom.

Kate Caldwell shifted position. She shouldn't have ventured out today. And now she wished she hadn't. She glanced up at the painting in front of her, the *Chalets at Rigi*. You couldn't miss it. It dominated the north side of the room and was one of her personal favourites – probably because her grandmother had adored it so much.

Kate had been gazing at it since arriving earlier that morning; it was the main reason she'd come to the National Gallery in the first place. A print version – postcard size – sat on the bench beside her. A little keepsake to remind her of a stolen day out.

A woman's voice echoed over the Tannoy system for the second time in as many minutes and announced to the visiting public that the art gallery would soon be closing.

Kate's heels tapped against the marble floor. She wrung her fingers together and took a deep breath, but couldn't psyche herself up enough to stand.

"Are you okay there, miss?"

Kate glanced to her right. An elderly security guard stood by the end of the bench.

"Yes, thank you."

He seemed taken aback by her American accent. He pushed his cap up off his face with the butt of his torch and grinned. "If you don't mind me saying, I had you pegged for an English lass."

Kate smiled. "Are we that different from our neighbours?"

The security man laughed. "No. You just have that English Rose look about you."

Kate stood. "That is a compliment I will happily accept."

She gathered up her coat, the postcard, and a plastic sandwich container – a half-eaten egg mayo on white still inside. The postcard she slipped inside her coat pocket.

The guard collected her bag from the floor and handed it to her. "Don't forget this."

"Thank you." Kate hooked the strap over her arm.

"You must really like that painting," he continued. "I don't think you've moved from this spot all day."

"My grandmother owned an art gallery."

"Back in the States?"

Kate's shoulders tensed. She hadn't meant to reveal anything about her life, and the conversation had suddenly become a little too personal. "She had a love for Alexandre Calame. I guess her admiration for him rubbed off on me."

She started for the door, aware she hadn't answered his question.

The security guard followed. "I'm a Da Vinci man myself."

"Really?" Kate quickened her step through the next hall.

"I know. A bit cliché but, at my age, does it even matter?"

"Not really." They'd made it down the first flight of stairs. "I think I know my way from here."

"That's okay. I have to go this way." He kept up with Kate's brisk pace. "Next time you visit us, you should head down to the theatre. They host a wonderful range of films and lectures."

"I'll certainly bear that in mind." Another flight of stairs and the entrance was in sight. Kate turned to the guard and held out her hand. "Well…"

"Jonathan, ma'am."

"Well, Jonathan." She shook his hand. "Thank you for getting me here safely."

Jonathan smiled. "All part of the service, Miss…?"

Kate stared at him. She thought about lying but not one name other than her own sprang to mind.

"Caldwell. Kate Caldwell."

"Well, Miss Caldwell. You have a yourself a nice evening and a Merry Christmas."

He pushed open the door and a rush of cold air swept in.

Outside, work had finished for the day, leaving Christmas party-goers – some of them merry, most of them drunk – free to sing, sway, cheer, and frolic in the freshly laid snow that surrounded Nelson's Column. The scene brought back memories of Kate's uni days. Good memories that should have warmed her insides. Instead, her stomach knotted. She didn't want to leave.

"You'd think it was Christmas Eve already," the guard said.

Kate forced a smile, but her attention was on the crowd outside. Young, old, male, female. Nobody seemed bothered by her being there. In fact, nobody gave her so much as a second look. But even with that knowledge, Kate still didn't want to leave.

Jonathan chuckled. "When the snow begins to fall again, they'll be too intoxicated to care."

Kate glanced up at the sky. Not one star in sight. It would make the back streets darker and she'd have to rely on streetlights alone.

"Yep, that cloud's getting ready—"

"Cloud?" Kate turned from her thoughts. "Did you say *cloud*?"

"Yes, miss."

Kate pulled him into a half hug and kissed his cheek. "Jonathan, you're awesome."

Jonathan blushed. "I'm not sure what I did…" He glanced at the ground and shifted his feet before looking back up at her. "Miss, you have yourself a wonderful Christmas, you hear?"

"You too," Kate called out over her shoulder.

She bounded down the gallery steps, her half-eaten sandwich still clasped in her hand.

Trafalgar Square was abuzz with Christmas cheer and it showed little sign of fizzling out. Kate buttoned her long coat to the neck and wiggled her cold fingers into her friend Charlotte's thermal gloves. Northumberland Avenue was directly in front of her as the crow flew. The easiest route through the sea of party hats and glow sticks, however, looked to be via the east side of the square.

Revellers littered the pavements and crowded Nelson's Column like an army of ants around a sugar cube. Kate elbowed her way through them all, pushing away the ones who wrapped arms around her shoulders and blew party whistles in her face.

Northumberland Avenue wasn't much quieter. The festivities rolled outwards like a disease spreading across the capital, infecting anyone it came into contact with. Drinkers spilled out through pub doorways, Kate an easy target for their banter.

She pressed her chin into her chest, exposing the back of her neck to the bitter night, and scurried past them. She didn't want to laugh and she didn't want to join in with their celebrations. She just wanted to get home and log onto her cloud account.

The more distance she put between herself and Trafalgar Square, the more Christmas disappeared behind her. Shops turned into office buildings, where no tinsel or fairy lights illuminated the night. In the doorways, flattened cardboard and newspaper covered just a fraction of London's homeless.

She reached the corner of the road and paused by the Playhouse Theatre. In the doorway was the same pair of worn boots she'd seen earlier that morning.

She knelt. "Hey."

The old man looked up, his eyes glazed. Finally, he focused on her, but the recognition wasn't there.

"We met this morning. I gave you money so you'd have a bed for tonight."

His eyes widened. "Ah, my favourite girl in the whole world." He swept the empty beer cans from his lap and patted the doorstep next to him.

"I'd love to, but I can't tonight. I have to get home. Why are you out here?"

The tramp popped open a new can of beer and took a swig. "Nothin' like sleepin' under the stars."

"There are no stars tonight, and it's freezing."

He chuckled and gulped back a long mouthful of beer. A dribble escaped the side of his mouth and ran into his unkempt beard. It was clear he didn't remember her; he was probably drinking the money she'd given him.

"Aye, the stars are a wonderful thing, alright."

Kate took his hand and wrapped his fingers around her leftover sandwich. Grime darkened his fingernails and sores marred his calloused fingertips.

"Please, go get yourself a bed for the night. It's too cold to be out here." She removed her gloves and placed them on his lap. She knew he'd still be there come morning. "Happy Christmas."

She stood and, without another word, turned for the Golden Jubilee Footbridge. She climbed the stairwell, the heavy snowfall clinging to the sides of her suede boots, and started the short walk over the Thames. Few people remained on the street below, even fewer on the footbridge. In the distance, music pumped from a docked riverboat, the slow turn of the London Eye its backdrop. A train headed out of Charing Cross Station and rattled past, momentarily drowning out the sound of the party and whipping the wintery night into a frenzy.

Kate gripped her coat tighter and quickened her step but, even after the train was long gone, the openness of the footpath still allowed the wind to attack her. She continued to walk, the halfway mark not far from her now. A jogger appeared at the other end of the bridge. Hunched over and wearing a hooded sweatshirt and baggy bottoms, he resembled a boxer in training more than a runner. Kate moved closer to the handrail, giving him room to pass.

The jogger's eyes remained focused on the end of the bridge behind her, only stealing a brief glance her way as he passed. The thud of his step as it crunched the snow drifted farther behind her and eventually replaced by the growl of another train.

A procession of carriages thundered past, and the slight footbridge wobbled under its vibration. Lights whizzed alongside her until the last carriage disappeared, leaving her with nothing but the winter night again.

She heard the noise behind her a split second before the impact hit the back of her head. She stumbled forward into the railing and a hand covered her mouth. Behind, her attacker's bodyweight shoved her harder against the safety rail, and an arm scooped her legs off the ground. Kate tried to scream, but the hand clasped tighter around her mouth. She grabbed the railing, but the assailant threw her lower body over the side of the barrier and let go.

The hand left her mouth and Kate screamed. She gripped the railing, her legs dangling from the bridge. Her attacker stood and stared down at her, his hood shading his face. Then he bent for her bag and picked it up.

"Please help me," Kate begged him.

He looked at her again. Then he reached for her hands and grabbed them.

Kate cried out in relief. He was going to help her.

The man yanked her hands from the railing. And released her.

Kate screamed. Her hands clawed the air, but the railing disappeared. Her fingertips hit snow, then the hard iron of a narrow ledge. She screamed again, her kicking legs looking for some footing. The winter night attacked her body. She couldn't look up. She couldn't look down. Her only view was the dark construction beneath the bridge.

Her fingertips numbed. Slipped. And her scream echoed through the night as she fell.

It was only silenced when she hit the water and her body sank beneath the icy surface of the River Thames.

CHAPTER TWO

Tavish Finley threw his keys at the valet and straightened the jacket of his made-to-measure suit.

Light tremors rocked his body and his heart pounded with excitement at what the next couple of hours could bring him. He jogged up the steps, ignored the welcoming nod from the doorman as he opened the door, and stepped inside the foyer.

He was immediately greeted by a young blonde. "Mr. Finley. So nice to have you back with us."

Red-painted lips smiled at him. This welcome he did not ignore.

"I'll have a seat prepared for you at the poker table."

"It's blackjack that's calling me tonight, Nicki."

The red lips widened and the girl mumbled into a tiny headset. Then her eyes met Tav's again. "Follow me, Mr. Finley."

She turned and led him through a pair of doors, across the casino floor, and to the high stakes room on the north side of the building – his favourite room.

A croupier – brunette – waited for him. She glanced up. Only a small smile scratched her lips before her focus returned to the green, felt table in front of her. Tav released the button of his single-breasted jacket and took the seat opposite. Slipping five fifties from his wallet, he placed them on the table. The croupier spread them out. Calling out the total, she replaced them with chips, then slid two sealed card decks towards him. Tav tapped the pile on the right.

"Is there anything I can get you, Mr. Finley?"

Nicki still waited beside him. He glanced down at her slender legs. Wondered how they'd feel under his touch.

"Scotch, please, Nicki."

"I'll have a waitress bring it straight over to you."

She smiled, then turned and left the room.

Now the croupier had his attention again. He watched her break the cellophane wrapping on his chosen deck, shuffle, and slide the top two cards across the table. A ten and a two.

He nodded and she turned over a third card. Another ten. Bollocks.

The door behind him opened and a blonde waitress sauntered through, a small tray balanced expertly on her palm. She smiled and placed a napkin on the table beside him, a tumbler of scotch and soda on top of that.

"Compliments of the house, Mr. Finley." She hovered. "Mr. Corrone assumes his order is complete?"

Tav nodded. "Rubber-stamped it myself, sweetheart."

He didn't know why, but he'd assumed he'd have a face to face with Corrone himself tonight.

The girl slid a marker towards him. "Your winnings have been deposited with the cashier. You may pick them up whenever you are ready."

She turned to leave, but Tav caught her arm. "Bring me another."

He swallowed the drink and placed the empty glass on her tray.

The waitress nodded and turned to leave, but Tav stopped her again. He opened his wallet and placed a fifty-pound note on her tray. "The change is for you."

She smiled and nodded, then left the table.

Tav watched her retreat through the crowd. She looked classy, a black dress hugging the slender figure beneath. He'd definitely have to tap that later.

He glanced at the marker, the voice inside his head telling him to cash in the payment and leave. That payment, after all, was promised to others.

"Deal," he said to the croupier.

CHAPTER THREE

Jason assumed the 'vibrate' option on his mobile was for quietness.

But pulsating across the wooden coffee table, it was louder than a pneumatic drill. He opened his lids, allowing his eyes time to adjust to the sunlight filtering in through the curtains he'd forgotten to shut the night before. He closed his eyes again.

The bloody phone continued to drill inside his head and he reached for it. "Wassup?"

He recognised the voice immediately – the shrink's petite secretary. Looked like butter wouldn't melt but she was scary as fuck.

She went for the jugular. "Mr. Wade, you had a meeting with Doctor Tandy this morning."

"Check your diary again, sweetheart." Jason propped himself up against the pillow and rubbed the sleep from his eyes.

"You had an appointment for nine O'clock this morning. You are already five minutes late."

She was waking him at nine O-fucking-clock? In the morning?

"I have been told to inform you that if you miss this appointment a report will be emailed across to your superiors at ten O'clock sharp."

Bitch. Jason threw back the covers and sat up.

"How long shall I tell Doctor Tandy you'll be?"

Jason ruffled his hair and grabbed his boxers from the floor. "As long as it bloody takes."

He hung up, reached for his electronic cigarette – Karen's idea, not his – and twiddled it between his fingers, his interest in smoking it gone. He put his head in his hands. He was fine just the way he was and didn't need a bloody doctor poking around inside his head. He reached for the chain around his neck. A silver boxing glove hung from it – a gift given him the day he'd made pro. Shit, that was an age ago. Maybe sticking with his current job had been a mistake. Maybe he should have jumped ship eight months earlier – when Leah died and all this shit hit the fan.

He waded through the papers on the coffee table until he found the controller and switched on the TV. Flopped back, arms collapsing beside him, and closed his eyes just long enough to hear the news bulletin: A girl had fallen into the Thames. He turned the TV off again but the image was already with him – Leah. Her dead corpse shaded blue... He shook his head. Slapped his palm against his temple a couple of times. That fucking image would haunt him until the day he died. The aftermath of that night pushed fourth – visions of a man lying at his feet. His arm snapped. His jaw disfigured. His leg crippled. Jason had done what had been required...what was right – what any brother would have done. The guy was a fucking drug-dealing parasite. Scum.

His sister's supplier. Jason's only regret was that he hadn't killed the bastard.

His mobile rang and the pneumatic drill started vibrating through his head again.

Let it ring. This whole scenario was bollocks. His sister had been murdered and yet it was his head on the chopping block. He threw his boxers back on the floor and plodded bare-assed to the bathroom. A shower was his first priority. Then he'd go to the bloody head-shrinker.

Jason was not a morning person.

The alcohol he'd consumed the night before had seen to that.

He rubbed his eyes and glanced at the clock. Apart from the initial pleasantries, which were curt even by his standards, he'd been sitting in silence for the best part of twenty minutes. It was time he could be wasting elsewhere – like in the boozer. He drummed his fingers on his knees and looked around the room. Very clean and minimalistic. Light cream walls. A single orchid sitting centre of a glass side-table. He caught Doctor Tandy's eye and promptly directed his gaze back towards the clock.

"Jason, this would go quicker if you actually spoke to me."

He glanced at her. She would have been attractive if she weren't a head-shrinker.

"I'm required to extend these meetings until you talk."

Jason sighed. "I said last week, and the week before that, there's nothing to talk about."

"You left early last week and, if I remember correctly, you didn't turn up at all the week before that."

Jason sat forward. "Fine. Let's get this rigmarole over with. Ask me a question, doc."

Doctor Tandy tilted her head and glanced at him over the top of her glasses. Very cliché. She probably didn't even need to wear them.

"That's not really how this works."

Jason stood to leave. "Then I guess I don't need to be here."

"Sit down, Jason."

"I'd rather stand."

Tandy pressed a button on her phone. "Georgia, please get me David Carter on the phone."

Jason laughed. "Jesus Christ. Really? We're playing that game?"

The doctor held his stare for a moment. "How we play is up to you."

"You know blackmail's illegal, right?"

The secretary's voice broke the silence. "Mr. Carter is on line one."

Doctor Tandy raised a brow. "Well?"

Jason sighed. Fucking shrinks. He hated them. He sucked back his annoyance and sat.

Tandy pressed the button on the phone. "Georgia, tell Mr. Carter I'll call him back."

She reached for the notepad and pen on her desk then leaned back in her chair. "Why don't you start by telling me how things are at work?"

"Too many early starts."

Tandy ignored his quip. "And your colleagues?"

"They have alarm clocks."

Tandy smiled and tapped the pen against the pad. "You're not the toughest nut I've had to crack."

"You're opening yourself up, doc."

"I hate to burst your manly bubble, but whatever comebacks you have to fire back, I've heard them before. Many, many times." She lay the pen down. "It kind of makes you desperately predictable."

Jason shifted in his seat.

"What would make you unpredictable would be to answer my questions, so you can get out of here."

Fuck. The doc was a ball-breaker – and a good one at that. "I keep myself to myself at work."

"Is that healthy?"

"It's how I prefer it."

"The officers you attacked at the scene, you were lucky they didn't press charges against you."

"My sister's corpse lay three feet away from me. They'd have been labelled arseholes and they knew it."

"Still, making amends would be progress, don't you think?"

Jason sighed. "They hate me. I hate them. Only progress I want is on my sister's murder."

Doctor Tandy eyed him for a second. "Why do you feel the need to disbelieve your sister's death was an accident?"

"You mean, why do I think she was murdered?"

"Okay."

"Because she was."

"Her death was ruled an accident."

"Somebody didn't do their job correctly."

"You think she was strangled?"

"Yes."

"Because of the marks around her neck?"

"Yes."

"It was ascertained that those marks were from her becoming tangled in something not dissimilar to a fishing line."

Jason grunted. "Her body was found in the Thames, not off the end of Southend Pier."

"Jason, she drowned."

"There was no water in her lungs."

The doctor tilted her head again. "And how would you know that?"

Jason glanced at her.

"Jason, you were explicitly refused access to your sister's autopsy report."

"And now look where I am. Parked behind a shitting desk."

"Then open an investigation and deal with it through the correct channels."

"I tired. Every door gets shut in my face." Jason tapped at his knee again. "Have I talked enough?"

Tandy glanced at the clock. They were nowhere near finished.

"Okay, so what now?"

"Jason, you were put on desk duty because you attacked a young man."

"The drug dealer?"

"Still a human being."

Jason laughed.

"You hospitalised him."

"He pushed drugs on my sister and insinuated she was a whore. What should I have done? Told him he was a bad boy and not to do it again?"

"Do you not feel any remorse?"

"Towards him? Only that he didn't die."

"You also lost your driving license because of it."

"I lost my license because I went to the pub afterwards and got hammered before wrapping my car around a tree."

Tandy stared at him for a second, then relaxed back into her chair. "The point I am trying to make is: How much more are you willing to lose on this pursuit of yours?"

"That junkie prick knows something."

"You thought the casino knew something."

"I still do. How else d'ya think I found the junkie?" Jason leaned forward. "She phoned me. Leah, that is. The night she died."

Tandy's expression froze. "You've never mentioned this before."

"Left me a voicemail asking if I'd pick her up from work. Haven't spoke to her in close to ten months and then, out of the blue, she calls."

"Jason, it means nothing other than she was making contact. Extending an olive branch."

"It means something was wrong and she needed my help."

"You are in denial."

"Because I want to know the truth?"

"Because you blame yourself."

"For her death?"

"For not being there."

Jason stood. "I was always there, doc. She just preferred being somewhere else." He turned for the door and opened it. "And FYI: Your clock is five minutes slow."

CHAPTER FOUR

Tavish Finley didn't like the snow.

In fact, he was the only Scottish person he knew that couldn't tolerate any form of cold weather. He dug his gloved hands into the pockets of his lush, Italian coat. The shop assistant hadn't lied when she said the thermal lining would stop even the harshest of weather from numbing his fingers.

He eyed the area around him. A jogger passed by, scratchy music blasting from his earphones. Farther along the river wall, an oriental man directed his young, female companion into a pose before clicking away on his camera. A little way across the paved area, two men sat beneath a tree, each wearing a cigarette and a smile.

Didn't anyone stay at home around Christmas anymore?

Tav propped himself up against the river wall and continued to scan the scene. Although satisfied he hadn't been followed, he still couldn't relax. Farther down, the London Eye – its vicinity crowded with tourists even though the attraction was closed for the day – cast a shadow across the Thames. Jesus, Tav hated crowds. And tourist crowds at that.

His phone began to vibrate and he pulled it from the inside of his coat. No number on the screen, but he knew who it was. He turned towards the water, inhaled, and lifted the phone to his ear.

"We are unhappy," a voice said.

"I have it in hand."

"You have forty-eight hours. After that, the debt you owe us will be payable by other means."

"I understand." Tav hung up. Bollocks. He'd screwed up big time remaining in the casino last night.

He slipped the phone back into his coat and rubbed his jaw.

A man, not dissimilar looking to Johnny Depp, approached the bench – a newspaper under his arm and a slight limp unbalancing him every second step. His clothes hung from his body, either because their previous owner was a big fucker or because the junkie inside them now had become a little too accustomed to the taste of his own medicine. Not really the kind of man Tav wanted to trust but, wherever he got his information from, Jimmy was always accurate.

Jimmy sat down beside the two other men, unfolded his paper – the Metro – and began to read.

Tav turned back to the Thames and studied the footbridge that crossed to Embankment Station. The television news had reported that a female had jumped the night before, but luckily survived. Luckily didn't begin to describe it. The footbridge had to be a good hundred-and-fifty-foot drop – high tide – at least. How the hell she'd managed to hit that water and survive was a miracle in itself. But to then beat the odds of hypothermia, the current, or…shit, just the weight of her clothes dragging her down to the riverbed…it was a fucking phenomenon.

His phone vibrated again – this time just a short beat against his chest. He reached into his coat pocket and looked at the text. Three words: *HEATHER LOOKS TIRED.* Followed by a picture of a woman similar in age to himself, hair scooped back, lying in a hospital bed.

Shit.

He backed out of the text and hit *one*. The call was answered almost immediately.

"Penfield Healthcare. How may I help you?"

"This is David Turrow. I am calling for an update on Heather Turrow's condition."

"One moment please, sir."

Tav reached into his outer pocket and found the plastic bottle of painkillers he liked to carry around with him – just for emergencies. All around him, people still went about their business. Nobody lingered, and nobody caught his eye. He popped the lid off the bottle and swallowed two pills – no need for water. He glanced at Jimmy, still reading the paper, the two men beside him now gone.

Fuck.

His muscles tensed. Why the hell didn't he leave the casino last night when he should have…with his bloody money? Their bloody money. His lips hardened. He rubbed his jaw and tried to think of a solution.

"Mr. Turrow?" The operator was back. "There is no change in Miss Turrow's condition. She remains in a coma but is comfortable."

"Has she had any visitors or any telephone enquiries in the last week or so?"

"One moment."

Tav watched Jimmy uncross his legs and fold up the newspaper. He stood, leaving the paper on the bench. Tav waited until he reached the steps of the bridge, then marched towards the paper and picked it up.

"Mr. Turrow? I can confirm that, other than yourself, Miss. Turrow has not had any enquiries made after her, nor has she had any visitors."

Tav wanted to scream that someone had been in her fucking three-hundred-a-night room taking pictures of her, but instead said, "Phone me immediately if anybody does."

He hung up and wiped the perspiration from his forehead. Things were spiralling out of control. He needed to find that girl and get to her. Quick. He opened the paper and flipped through to somewhere near the back. Found the crossword.

Scrawled in capitals, filling three rows across and two rows down respectively, he read: ST THOMAS'S HOSPITAL. MAGNOLIA. SEVEN.

Tav threw the paper down on the bench.

CHAPTER FIVE

Jason stared at the computer screen.

He clicked on the Queen of Hearts and dragged it across to the King of Clubs.

"Busy?"

Jason glanced over the top of the screen. Ed stood in the doorway.

"Just patience. And it's testing mine."

Ed pushed away from the doorframe. His open jacket revealed the beginnings of a bulk around his waistline. "Still benched?"

Ed knew he was.

"Then I have something for you to do." He held up a couple of clear bags.

"When did you become a messenger boy?"

Ed placed the bags on the desk. "Since I was coming here anyway."

Jason glanced at the bags. Not much inside – a coat and a couple of other items of clothing. "Whose are they?"

Ed scratched some life into his balding hair. He seemed reluctant to answer. "Some girl who was fished out of the Thames last night."

Jason started to stand but Ed waved him back down. "Hold your horses there, lightning. She jumped."

"Oh?"

"Occupants of a party boat saw the whole thing. Just as well too, or she would have been a goner for sure."

Jason relaxed a little, though not much. "So, what's with the clothes then?"

"She woke this morning with amnesia. Can't remember a thing. And as no bag or I.D. was found..."

"You think her clothes are going to tell you?"

"Hey, you're the forensic expert. I'm just the messenger boy, remember?" Ed pinched his right trouser leg and perched on the desk. "You see the shrink earlier?"

Jason glanced up at him but didn't reply.

"How'd it go?"

"Same as the other couple of times. She asks stupid questions and then we argue about it."

"Stupid questions? You mean about Leah, right?" Ed stood. "Jesus, Jason. Leah was messed up and not thinking straight. Her death was a tragic accident. Nothing more. Why can't you accept that?"

"More to the point, why *can* you accept it?" Jason stood, his height matching his friend's. "You've known Leah since we were all kids. You dated her in school."

"Don't you think I lie in bed at night and wonder if there was something I could have done to stop this happening?" Ed paused and rested his hand on Jason's shoulder. His face softened. "She took the wrong path, mate. She'd lost her job. Was into all sorts. Drugs, prosti—"

Ed stopped.

Jason shook his head but let the comment go. "I've seen the report. I know what it implies. But it doesn't explain why she washed up out the river. And it doesn't explain the marks around her neck."

"Fine. Deny the obvious." Ed released Jason's shoulder and rubbed his head. "But I won't cover up any more fuck-ups for you. And I sure as hell know Carter in there," he pointed to the office on the other side of the room, "won't either. You nearly lost your job and you should've been arrested for what you did to that junkie."

Jason slid the bags of clothes across the table. "I'll call you when I'm done with these."

The drying cabinet room was small. Tiny, in fact.

Jason had never measured it – just like he'd never swung a bloody cat in it – but he still knew it was smaller than it needed to be. Bloody budget cuts.

One by one, Jason opened the bags and sorted through the damp clothes: a white T-shirt, which looked to have a little blood around the back of the neck line; black jeans; black jumper; black coat; one black ankle boot – size 5. Fuck him. The girl certainly liked black. He searched through them, finding nothing but a soggy postcard in the coat pocket. Not a bad picture, but not his cup of tea. He flipped it over. No writing. Just the National Gallery stamp at the bottom telling him the painting was *Chalets at Rigi* by Alexandre Calame.

He draped the items on hangers, hung them in the drying cabinet, and secured the door with a referenced security tag. The process would take anything up to forty-eight hours, but that didn't stop him from sitting back and watching the clothes drying in what was effectively a giant hairdryer in a box for a while. Afterall, he had nothing better to do apart from updating the property systems, and that'd bore him more than solitaire.

He swivelled the chair side to side, his feet tap-dancing across the floor as he moved. His sister's clothes hadn't reached even this early stage of an investigation. As heroin filled every ounce of her veins, and a witness had come forward claiming she'd climbed onto the river wall and toppled into the Thames, her death had been ruled an accident and filed away.

But Jason knew what he'd seen that night – the marks around her neck. She'd been strangled, probably with a cord or rope of some sort, pure and simple. And the witness…they'd conveniently emigrated somewhere nobody knew of.

David Carter banged on the glass wall that surrounded his office. "You finished over there?"

Jason spun the chair to face him. His knee caught the corner of the workstation and he bit back the urge to curse his boss out.

Carter glared at him through the glass partitioning. "Good. I need you to go fingerprint the amnesiac girl."

He had a cock-sure way about him that irked the crap out of Jason. "It's a job for uniform."

"And now it's a job for you." Carter turned his back and retook his position behind his desk.

Jason stood and kicked the chair back. It hit the counter behind him. "This is bullshit."

"Don't start with me, Wade." Carter turned, pulled a pen from the caddy, and scribbled something on a yellow form. "You wanted out of this office; here's your chance."

"But it's a sodding suicide attempt."

"It's an olive branch. Don't waste it."

"It's a piss-take is what it is."

Carter glanced up over the rim of his glasses – the same way the doctor had, only less sexy. "Get down to that hospital now or I'll have you filing shit for the rest of your short-lived career, d'you hear?"

Jason clenched his fists. He glanced at the table in front of him, flexed his fingers, and took a deep breath. Slowly, he placed his palms down and leaned forward. It was that or smash his way through the partitioning and beat the smug look off his dick of a so-called boss. "Then what?"

"What do you mean?"

"I mean..." His lips tightened. "What happens afterwards? I'm shoved back behind that desk out there?"

"It's better than the alternative, wouldn't you say?"

Jason snorted. "I'm not so sure anymore."

Carter slammed down his pen. "Let's not forget, I put myself on the line for you. You'd be suspended if it wasn't for me covering up your shit."

Stealing the limelight like the little weasel he was. Ed had also played a big part in that little cover-up.

"Fucking beating that little shit half to death," Carter continued.

"I was drunk."

"Don't give me that. You got drunk afterwards."

Jason bit his lip and swallowed back the need to set the prick straight. He pushed away from the counter and stormed out of the drying room, grabbing his swab kit and denim jacket from his office on his way to the exit.

Jason walked into the hospital, not bothering to shake the fresh snow from his jacket. Some crap Christmas tune crackled from a speaker and a badly dressed Santa *Ho-Ho-Ho'd* in the corner of the foyer.

"I'm here to see the amnesiac victim." Jason flashed his identification at the young girl sitting behind the reception desk – the spitting image of the head-shrinker, minus ten years and the glasses. "She was pulled out of the Thames last night."

The girl, tapped her keyboard, straightened, and smiled. "She's on the Magnolia Ward. It's on the fifth floor. You can take the lift." She pointed along the corridor. "First on the left."

Jason returned a forced smile and nodded an acknowledgement. He headed along the corridor and, sure enough, found the elevator. When the lift didn't arrive, he thumb-punched the button several more times and waited.

He tapped his leg. What a waste of time it was being here. So, some bird wanted to off herself. Hoo-fucking-ray. Let her do it and move on.

Finally, the numbers above the lift started to illuminate. 5...4...3...2...1. The doors slid apart and he stepped inside, pressed the appropriate button, and let the doors close. When they opened again, he stepped out onto a corridor identical to the one he'd just left. The Magnolia Ward was signposted and led him to a nurse's station.

For the second time, he flashed his identification. "Jason Wade from the police forensics department. Which room is the amnesiac victim in?"

"Room seven."

That was all he got. No smile. No finger pointing him in the right direction. The nurse hadn't even looked up. She simply continued on with her paperwork. Fuck, she was ruder than him.

He turned and looked at the door behind him: Room three – room two was to the left. He turned right and walked. Stopped at room seven. Knocked and, without waiting for an invitation, opened the door.

Partly closed blinds blocked out most of the morning. The young woman was lying in bed, her face slightly turned from him, although not enough that he couldn't see her eyes were closed. She had to be in her mid to late twenties – her age something he hadn't really thought about before.

His chest tightened and a flicker of hatred bubbled to the surface. Why had this woman been deemed important enough for a second chance at life, and yet his sister had been allowed to die? He slammed the door shut, but the girl didn't wake. She didn't even stir. Usually, he'd go and get the shift sister to wake the patient. Instead, he put his swab kit down – loudly – and began to unpack.

When he finished, he turned to the girl again. Partial light lit her sleeping face. Her eyes raced from side to side beneath their lids. Her lips parted.

"Bluebird," she murmured.

Then the frown lines softened and her body relaxed.

She looked at peace. Almost beautiful.

Jason stiffened. Where the hell had that thought come from? He narrowed his eyes, so much so that he thought his eyebrows would touch. She didn't look the type of person who would try to kill herself and a wave of heat washed over him. Sweat drenched his underarms. Excuses for this girl's behaviour filled his head. He rubbed his forehead and tried to clear the thoughts away.

Outside, a telephone rang. He heard a nurse's voice and went to the door. The sooner he woke this girl and got her prints, the quicker he could get the hell out of here.

CHAPTER SIX

The orderly's uniform felt coarse against his skin.

A stark contrast to the Egyptian cotton shirts Tav had become accustomed to wearing.

He scratched his thigh, which set in motion an array of itches across the nether regions of his body. He followed them, hunting down each one and growing short-tempered at his inability to stop them progressing. By the time he reached the hospital entrance, he wanted to rip the trousers off and do away with them altogether. Instead, he entered the foyer, tried as hard as he could to block the irritation from his mind, and looked around.

Just as he expected it to be. A short queue waited at reception while other visitors came and went. Some held gifts; others were empty-handed.

Tav walked to the lift and pressed to go up. In his hand, he clasped a plastic tray. Nothing unusual on it. Just a patient's lunch. The lift doors parted and he stepped aside while an elderly gentleman exited. Once inside, he waited until the doors closed and then checked his coat pocket. The syringe remained exactly where he'd put it.

The door opened on the fifth floor and Tav headed to room seven. He ignored the nurses at the station. He ignored the patients and their visitors. And, in return, everyone ignored him.

He didn't knock on the door before reaching for the handle. He didn't have time. The door flung open and a man with a similar build to his own headed out.

He stopped short of colliding with Tav. He didn't apologise, just looked down at the tray. "She's asleep."

Tav looked past him. The girl was indeed asleep in the bed. He turned back to the man but couldn't size him up. He didn't recognise him. And the bloke didn't seem like Old Bill. No uniform for a start. Definitely not a DC. But, something...

"You need to go in?"

Boyfriend maybe? Tav shook his head. Whoever he was, he shouldn't be in there. "I have her food."

The man made no further attempt to leave the room, despite having stormed through the doorway seconds before. Instead, he just stood there, eyeing him up – something Tav's dark brown eyes usually deterred people from doing. But not this guy.

The man took hold of the tray. "I'll take it."

Tav's shoulders stiffened. He glanced over the man's shoulder again at the sleeping girl. It couldn't have been more perfect. He just needed twenty seconds with her.

"Thank you, but I can manage." He tried to enter but the man blocked him. Tav stepped back and took a deep breath. "You are stopping me from doing my job."

"Bit of a stretch suggesting *tray deliverer* is a *job* when even the spotty oinks down at McDonalds can do it."

Tav felt his face redden. His fingers curled around the edges of the tray.

"Now, give me the tray or I'll make sure you pick up your P45 on the way out tonight."

Tav bit his lip and released the tray, begrudgingly. He'd see this little wanker again, that was for damn sure. "I'll come back later."

The man shrugged and took the tray. "Suit yourself." He stepped into the corridor.

Tav watched him walk to the nurse's station. Everything about him, his posture, his mannerisms…even his voice screamed trouble. Tav turned back to the room. The girl was just metres from him and the syringe felt as though it would burn a hole in his pocket. He was so close to completing his mission.

One quick injection and the girl would be gone.

But if experience had taught him anything, it was when to fight and when to save it for another day. Tav glanced back at the man. This was definitely not a time to fight – although Tav would sure as hell like to.

The man straightened and started back towards the room, a nurse beside him. He reached Tav and paused, allowing the nurse to enter the room first.

Tav forced a smile. "I'll see you later."

He hated to walk away from an unfinished job, but he backed away from the door and headed towards the lift.

CHAPTER SEVEN

Kate opened her eyes.

At first, the room was a blur. Voices spoke in low, mumbled tones somewhere in the distance, but their words made no sense. Kate turned her head, winced at the ache at the base of her neck, and waited for the man standing by the window to come into focus a little. He looked younger than his voice dictated, or maybe it seemed that way because she couldn't see him clearly. He stopped talking to the nurse and turned to look at her. His face hardened when he saw her awake.

A rather large woman leaned in front of him and blocked Kate's view. A watch swung from her navy uniform just above her right breast. "You have a visitor."

She said nothing else. Just puffed the pillow behind Kate's head and stepped away from the bed. Like a magic show, the man appeared again. Kate didn't know him – at least she didn't think she knew him. Maybe she did know him. Maybe she was married to him. Maybe…

The nurse walked to the door.

Was that it? She was just going to leave? No introduction? No nothing?

The door closed. Kate turned back to the man standing by the window. Dirty blond hair cut short. Beautiful, blue eyes highlighting an otherwise over-tired and impatient face.

"Do I know you?" If she did, would she have to apologise for asking the question?

"No. My name is Jason. I'm from the police forensics department."

"Forensics?"

"We're trying to find out who you are. To do that, I need to take your prints."

"Prints?"

"Fingerprints." Jason wiggled his fingers.

Kate sat up. She winced again and felt the back of her head.

"Head hurt?"

He asked the question but looked unbothered about hearing an answer.

"Apparently, I banged it." She got comfortable and reached for the beaker of water that sat on the bedside cabinet. "I've never had my fingerprints taken before – or I can't remember ever having my fingerprints taken before. Will they tell you who I am?"

"They may do." Jason reached for some papers and wheeled the mobile tray across her bed. "First, I need you to sign this."

Kate sipped at the water. "What is it?"

"Consent form." He leaned closer and pointed to the middle section of the page. "They'll only be used for the investigation of this case and then destroyed." He passed her a pen, exchanging it for her water. "Just sign where it says donor's signature."

Kate hovered, pen poised.

"Something wrong?"

Kate looked up at him. "I can't sign this."

Jason sighed. "I can't help you unless you do."

"Then what name do I put?"

"Sorry?"

"What name do I sign? I don't know who I am."

Jason's eyes locked onto hers. A blank expression fell across his face. He glanced at the form and blew out his cheeks. Stalled for a second, then reached for the band around her wrist. "Use the hospital's admission reference."

Kate duplicated the number onto the form. "And the signature?"

"Squiggle anything. No one can read those things anyway."

He refilled the water glass and passed it to her – a rather chivalrous action for such a gruff and to-the-point man.

Kate shook her head nonetheless and Jason sat the beaker on the tray.

She looked back at the form and squiggled a shape that resembled a couple of haphazard loops. "Like that?"

"That'll do." Jason laid some pre-inked strips beside the paper. He lifted her index finger. "Just lightly roll your finger across the ink."

"It's so weird," she said, rolling her finger as instructed. "I know how to eat, but I don't know *what* I like to eat. I know how to dress but have no idea if I prefer dark clothes to light."

A slight grin cocked one side of Jason's mouth. It was enough to soften his eyes a little. "That would be dark."

Kate stared at him.

"The clothes you were wearing last night – they were black."

"Oh."

"They're drying back at the lab." He reached for her middle finger and began to roll. "Clothes tend to get wet when you go swimming in them."

"Some party-goers said they saw me jump. On purpose."

Jason stopped rolling and looked at her. "Did you?"

"Did I try to kill myself? I have no idea."

His grip tightened and he finished rolling. "It's a miracle you survived. A drop from that height."

"So I've been told." She watched him reach for the next finger. "How high was it?"

"Hundred and thirty feet at least."

He reached for her next finger. But he didn't speak again.

"The people on the party boat pulled me out," Kate offered.

Jason remained quiet, his eyes focused on the paper. He took her left hand and began the printing process all over again.

"I've had doctors up here asking me all sorts of questions."

"Uh-huh." Jason moved onto her thumb.

"Wanting to know if I remember how to eat, how to dress, how to…" She stopped short of saying toilet. "It's embarrassing."

"So is jumping off a bridge."

Kate looked at him. His whole posture seemed rigid. "Have I said or done something to offend you?"

Jason shook his head, but he still refused to make eye contact. "I'm just here to fingerprint you."

He released her thumb and passed her a wipe.

"If it's any consolation, I don't think I did jump," Kate said, wiping the black from her fingertips.

Jason collected up the paper and the ink strips and walked to the window where a small folder lay on the sill. "Why's that?" He placed the paper inside the folder, then pulled a giant cotton bud from a clear tube. "I need a swab from inside your mouth."

Kate parted her lips and opened wide. Jason lightly rubbed the end of the stick against the inside of her cheek. When he finished, he popped the cotton bud back into the tube and sealed it.

"I don't feel like I'm the type of girl who would try to kill herself."

Jason paused. He turned to her. "Can you honestly not remember anything about what happened? Or are you faking it?"

Kate's eyes widened. "Why would I fake not knowing who I am?"

Jason shrugged. He turned back to the tube and began to write on the label.

"A shrug? That's your answer?"

"It was just a stupid thought. Forget it."

"Damn right it's stupid. Why would anyone want to fake amnesia?"

Jason stopped writing. He looked at her and his eyes narrowed. "Maybe you committed a crime. Or maybe…" He wavered, suddenly looking uncomfortable.

"Come on. Maybe what?"

"You're just a nut."

Kate grabbed the beaker from the tray and threw it at him. He ducked and the cup bounced off the wall behind him, spraying water everywhere.

She winced and slumped back against her pillow. The ache inside her head intensified and her arms dropped to her sides, dead weights. She glanced at the sandwich sitting on the tray.

"You want me to open that for you?" Jason said, the sharpness behind his previous words now gone.

Kate shook her head and exhaled. "I cannot imagine what could have been so bad that I thought killing myself would be the better option." She rubbed her eyes and yawned. "So, what happens now?"

"I'll take all this to the office and see if we can find out who you are."

"No. I mean what happens to *me* now?"

Jason shrugged. "You'll probably stay here for a night or two."

"And then what?"

"Not my problem." Jason froze. Just for a second. He closed the folder and turned to look at her. "Let's deal with this first."

He walked to the door and reached for the handle but didn't open it. Instead, he pulled out his mobile and turned back to face her. "Let me take your picture." He held the phone towards her and touched the screen. "And one of your head injury."

He approached her and Kate felt his fingers gently part her hair.

A moment later, he stepped back. "I suggest you get some rest. I'll send someone in to mop up the water."

CHAPTER EIGHT

Tav clenched his fingers around his ringing phone, ready to crush the thing in half.

He thought of Heather lying in the care home while those fuckers breezed in and out snapping pictures like they were on a fucking sightseeing holiday. The phone continued to ring and his body tightened, unable to relax no matter how much he tried to force it to.

He waited until a missed call notification replaced the caller's withheld number and threw the device onto the passenger seat. The bloody loan sharks would get their money when he was goddamn good and ready to pay it.

He opened his glove box and took out the pill bottle. Shit. Only two left. He swallowed both and continued to watch out of the window. Doctors and nurses came and went. Visitors and patients came and went. Ambulances and paramedics all came and went. Everybody in the world came and went. Everybody, that was, except the guy who'd been in the girl's room.

He saw the shadow at his window a split second before the face came into view.

Scarred knuckles rapped at the glass and, in the wing mirror, Tav saw another two goons standing at the back of the car. He swallowed the urge to get out of the car and send all three of them packing with their dicks up their arses, and instead wound down the window.

Goon One leaned down and glared. Relatively scary in that he had that debt-collector thug look down to a tee: fairly old; a worn, leathery face that had had its fair share of broken noses; acting like he was harder than shit. It'd definitely do the trick if you happened to be a scumbag off the street. But Tav wasn't. Tav was ex-British Army of the highest order. And dickheads like this did not frighten him one little bit.

"You've been ignoring our calls," Goon One growled.

"You have nothing new to say, and neither do I. You'll get your money when I have it."

The man's lips hardened. His fingers curled and his fist whipped through the window. Tav's fingers were already on the door release. He spun in his sports seat and kicked the door open. It knocked the goon back before his fist got anywhere near connecting with its target.

Tav pulled the door back then kicked it open again. It whacked the guy a second time and he stumbled backwards.

His colleagues raced forward. Tav was already out of the car, his stance urging them to come at him. They did. Tav side-stepped the first punch and grabbed the guy around the neck. He tightened his fingers around the guy's throat and kicked his legs out from underneath him. The second guy tried the same move. He got the same response with an added stamp to the gut for his lack of imagination. Tav straightened his jacket and looked around. He'd kept the assault contained and, thankfully, undetected by the hospital visitors across the street.

He looked at the three men groaning on the ground. Then he looked at the dent in his driver's door.

"Motherfucker."

He turned to Goon One, lifted his foot, and stamped down on the guy's prized jewels.

The guy cried out and clasped his hands between his legs.

Just as Tav thought. A fucking pussy. He sat back in the car and rewound the window to drown out the whimpers.

Again, he thought of Heather – in a coma because, so many years before, she'd thought he'd left her and taken a razor to her wrists. And now she lay alone again, vulnerable without him there to protect her. And these fuckers thought it was acceptable to just walk in and snap a few selfies with her. Anger bubbled up and Tav opened the car door again. He grabbed Goon One by the wrist and twisted his palm upwards. The guy cried out and writhed in pain.

Tav put his finger to his lips, demanding the goon to quieten, and knelt beside him, bending the man's wrist with him. Sweat covered the guy's forehead, and his steroid-enhanced chest rose with each erratic breath. But he heeded Tav's warning and quietened.

Tav heard the two men behind him get to their feet. "Think before you act, fellas."

No more sound or movement came from them.

Tav refocused on Goon One. "Now, if any of you cunts go near Heather again, I will kill each and every one of you. Slowly. Do you understand?"

The man's eyes widened and he nodded.

"Good boy." Tav snapped the wrist quick. He stood and turned to Goons Two and Three. "Well, don't just stand there, you fucking muppets. Get him to the hospital."

Tav got back into his car. This fucking off-the-books shit was causing him no end of aggravation.

He reached for his mobile again and punched in a number. Held the phone to his ear but didn't give the recipient time to speak. "Jimmy, your information was only half right. The girl's not alone."

"I was told the filth had finished with her."

"Well, clearly they haven't." Irritation threatened to overspill. He watched the three goons cross the road to the hospital. Fucking pussies.

"My info's always solid, man," Jimmy continued.

"And who gives you this information?"

Jimmy chuckled. "I can't reveal my sources, dude."

"Well, you'd better reveal something or I'm going to permanently retire you."

Jimmy started to protest but Tav silenced him. "Just get me her address."

"That's what I've been trying to do for the last couple of months. I'm telling you, there's nothing to get. The girl's a ghost."

"She was a ghost. Now she's back on the grid."

Jimmy sighed. "Okay, I'll get my people back on it but it's gonna cost you, man."

"I already paid you."

"Yeah, for the hospital info. Not none of this new shit."

Tav took a deep breath. He thought of Heather and tried to relax. He failed.

"Just find something." He hung up and, for the second time, threw his phone on the passenger seat.

He gripped the steering wheel and turned back to the hospital entrance. More of the same people came and went.

And then he saw him. The cop – or whoever the hell he was – exit the hospital. Tav watched him walk the edge of the pavement, a case in one hand and a folder clasped in the other – details of his visit with the girl no doubt. Had she told him something? Remembered something? Identified Tav maybe? Or had this tough-guy discovered her identity?

Either way, the clock was ticking. He'd dealt with those goons today but more would come for him…for Heather. Tav held up his mobile and snapped a picture of his mystery guy. Then he watched him jog across the road and disappear around the corner.

Tav glanced back at the hospital. With the guy gone, the girl was probably alone again. Tav could easily nip back inside and finish the job. But an annoying feeling gnawed at his gut. The same kind he felt when playing the cards at the casino. Call it intuition or some sixth-sense cobblers – Tav very rarely listened to it and that was probably the reason he was into the casino for sixty thou'.

But he was listening now.

He had another job for Jimmy. He typed the short message: *WHO THE FUCK IS THIS?* And attached the picture.

Tav started the engine. Whoever this guy was, he meant trouble.

CHAPTER NINE

It was early afternoon by the time Jason got back to the station.

He pushed open the door to his office and switched on the desk lamp.

The bulb blew.

He took a deep breath and tried to calm the building aggravation that cramped his neck. His jaw tightened further from the effort, only making it ache more. The lights in the panelled ceiling had never sufficed and he knew after thirty minutes of paperwork his eyes would begin to throb. He laid the folder of fingerprints on his desk, switched on his computer, and waited while the processor booted up. It took seconds for the station's intranet to light the screen.

Wheeling out his seat, he punched in his password then glanced at the fingerprints. It was a long shot – the girl seemed far from being a criminal – but maybe, just for once, he'd get lucky. He scoffed. Who was he kidding? Luck hadn't visited him in a long, long time.

He lifted the scanner lid and placed the consent form face down on the glass. Pressing a button, he waited for the prints to materialise on his screen. He didn't have time to deal with the girl's problems, but something about her didn't sit right with him. And when his intuition spoke, he always listened. He reached for the phone and punched in a number he'd dialled so many times he was surprised the keys weren't worn.

Karen answered on the second ring. "What do you want, Jason?"

"Straight to the point, I see."

"I'm busy."

"And I need a favour." The line went silent. "You still there?"

"Isn't it about time you did me a favour?"

"Like what?"

"Like…" A moment of silence. "My bathroom tap is leaking."

"You want me to fix it?"

"No."

"Then why mention it?"

Another silence.

Jason tightened his grip around the receiver. "How about I never ask for another favour after this one?"

Still silence.

"Ever?"

Karen laughed – an unconvinced, sarcastic laugh.

Jason laughed too, more at being called out. He let out a sigh. God, he hated the bods at Scotland Yard, even the ones he'd slept with.

"Okay, do this favour for me and I'll owe you one – and it can be for anything. Work, personal. There's no limit."

He heard victory in her tone when she said, "What do you want me to do?"

"I'm sending over some prints. I need you to run them."

"That's it?"

"Yes."

"If you're sending them over, they'll be run anyway."

"I need you to let me have a copy of the results."

"Unofficially?"

"Is there any other kind for me lately?"

"Still grounded, eh?"

"And it's driving me insane."

"Whose prints are they?"

"A young woman—"

Karen laughed. "I might have known."

"It's not like that. She has amnesia."

"Convenient."

"Hey, she's scared and just wants to go home. You think you can help me achieve that?"

"She a tourist?"

"Nope. Londoner by the sound of it." He paused. "Come on, where's that Christmas spirit?"

Now it was Karen's turn to sigh. "You do remember I'm only a detention officer, right?"

"I know that you and that sergeant of yours have a special friendship."

Karen sighed again. She muttered something under her breath, then said, "Fine. Give me the details."

Jason quickly reached for his keyboard. "Emailing them over now."

"Wait. This isn't the girl who was fished out of the Thames last night, is it?"

Jason remained quiet. Karen was a smart girl. He'd been a tad naïve thinking he'd get through this phone conversation without her making the connection.

"Jason. It's been eight months since Leah died. You need to move forward."

"This has nothing to do with Leah's death."

"Really? Two girls falling into the Thames…at night…not far from each other, and less than a year apart?"

"Careful. You're sounding like there's a connection."

"Jason—"

"I know." Jason's palm began to sweat and he swapped the receiver into his left hand. "Leah didn't fall in to the Thames and, from what witnesses say, the girl last night jumped. So, no connection."

"But you're going to obsess over her like you have—?"

"I feel sorry for her. That's all."

"Funny. I never had you tagged as a sucker for the damsel-in-distress type."

Jason ignored her jibe. He needed this information. "Will you just do it?"

"I'll get to it first thing tomorrow."

"I need it done now."

"Jason, I do have other work to do."

He paused then added, "I'll throw in Friday night at the Oyster Shed."

"Just like the old days, eh?"

"You say it like we didn't have fun." Jason's mobile buzzed with a text message.

"Oh, we had fun alright. Right up until you gate-crashed my work's summer party."

Jason sighed. She always reverted back to that. "So, Oyster Shed's out then?"

Silence. He knew she was still there though.

"Okay, leave it with me. No promises, mind you."

Jason hung up and opened the message. An address over in Peckham blinked up on the screen, but he didn't recognise it. He thought about phoning the sender of the message, a girl Leah used to work for, but the walls in this place had ears the size of an elephant's. Back at the computer, he opened the station's home page and entered the door number and postcode. Jimmy the Junkie's name immediately flashed up. As did a list of convictions – all drug related – and several complaints of noise, one of domestic abuse. Nothing that mentioned Leah though. Back on the home page, Jason typed in Leah's name. Several files were listed but when he clicked on them – like he had several times since her death – he was blocked from accessing them.

He leaned back in his chair and clasped his hands behind his head. Tension wound across his shoulders and frustration stiffened his neck. Carter sat in his office behind his desk, scribbling his pen across a pile of paperwork. Jason glanced at his phone – it was nearly three. Another couple of minutes and Carter would get up and go for his usual coffee break. He was nothing if not punctual.

Sure enough. Three came and Carter got up from his chair.

He walked to the door. Called to Jason over his shoulder. "You wanna coffee?"

Jason shook his head. What he wanted was the fat fuck to get out of the office so he could get to his computer.

As soon as the door closed, Jason hurried into Carter's office. He opened the computer's home screen and entered Leah's details. The same list of files appeared and he clicked the top one, this time gaining access. He glanced towards the door. No sign of Carter. Then back at the screen. Scanned the list of his sister's known hangouts, surprised to find the Peckham address was not one of them. Shit. He closed the application down, deleted his search from Carter's history – he knew his boss checked it – and headed out of the office.

Jogging up the four flights of stairs was little effort to him.

Jason headed along the corridor and knocked on flat thirty-two's paint-peeled door. Nobody answered, so he knocked again. Inside, a lavatory chain pulled – once, twice, three times – and the system flushed. A chain rattled into its catch and the door opened a slither. A female peered out at him, yesterday's eye make-up smeared around her eyes.

Slight tremors betrayed she was in need of her next fix. "Yeah?"

"I've got something for Jimmy," Jason said, shoving his hands in his pockets.

"Who are ya?"

"Santa's little 'elper."

The girl looked him up and down. "What ya got?"

"What he ordered."

Again, the girl eyed him. "Never had no home delivery service before."

"Then today's your lucky day."

The girl hovered. Her tongue flicked across her teeth, revealing a tarnished, gold-plated stud. "Hang on."

She closed the door.

Jason removed his hands from his pockets. He prepared his stance, ready to kick the door in if she re-bolted it.

The chain rattled and the door opened. "Come in."

Jason entered the hallway and the girl closed the door behind him. Her dreadlocked hair was tied with what looked to be another dreadlock. A red bandanna kept any other hair off her face.

"Follow me." She walked off down the hallway.

Jason followed. He passed a room and glanced inside. A bedroom – well, it had an old, stained mattress on the floor at least. Opposite was a bathroom he wouldn't let a dog piss in. Both rooms were void of people.

He followed the girl to the end of the hallway. Another room and a layer of smoky fog that made it almost impossible to see the string of festive paper-chains hanging across the closed curtains. Same went for the two men slouched on the sofa and the one slumped in the corner armchair – a baseball bat laid across his lap.

The place reeked of cannabis. The ashtray on the coffee table overflowed with what looked to be a mixture of joints, spliffs, and blunts. In the other corner, Teletubbies pranced around on the small TV screen, seeming to hold the attention of everyone in the room. Apart from Jason.

"I'm looking for Jimmy," Jason said.

The man sitting on the left-hand side of the sofa dragged on his spliff. "You got some drugs for me, man?"

"Depends. Where's Jimmy?"

"He'll be here." The man blew a long line of smoke into the air.

Jason wafted it away from his face. Now he saw the second guy at the other end of the sofa was sound-O. Back to the first guy. "You know a girl called Leah Wade?"

"Watch it," the man in the armchair muttered. "I smell bacon."

Jason stepped back. Now, he had all three of them in sight.

"Yo, bitch," armchair guy shouted at the girl. "What ya letting pigs in 'ere for?"

She tutted and headed to the kitchen.

"Need to get da fucking paedos off the streets instead of bov'ring us decent folk." He sucked on his joint, his eyes never leaving the TV. "Fucking cop pigs."

Jason glanced at him. "I'm a lot more than that, pal. Now one of you had better answer me."

"Yo, that Wade girl is gone," armchair guy said.

"That's not what I asked you."

"Man, if you ain't got no drugs on you then get da hell outta my house," Sofa guy piped in.

The man in the armchair stood up, his rollie gripped between his lips and the bat clasped in his hands. He was taller than Jason had first assumed. Much taller. A good few inches above Jason's six-two.

"Get him outta here, Hugo," the guy on the sofa egged.

Hugo? What a fucking stupid name.

But, He lifted the bat shoulder height, and swung. It was slow and sloppy. Jason raised his hand. Stopping the wood dead, he curled his fingers around it. Hugo tugged back. Jason's grip tightened.

Sofa guy stood up, tiny fists clenched at the ends of his scrawny arms. Jason pushed him back down.

"Hugo," Jason said. "You don't wanna have a problem with me, pal."

Hugo smiled, stained teeth barely visible behind his overgrown beard.

Jason shrugged and tugged the bat. Hugo pulled back. Jason tugged again. Hugo yanked the thing back. This time Jason released his hold. Hugo stumbled back into the chair.

He started to stand again, but Jason pounced and straddled him. He punched Hugo right in the middle of his face, crumpling what was left of his joint. Hugo grunted and clasped his nose. Blood trickled through his fingers and weaved through his beard until it found his lips. He licked it away and glared at Jason.

Jason knew that look all too well. It stared back at him every morning when he faced the bathroom mirror. "Think before you act, mate."

Hugo reached for the bat.

Jason punched again, this time connecting with the side of his adversary's face. Skin discoloured and split open. Hugo's head lolled to the side and blood gushed down his cheek.

Blood pumped through Jason's veins and he punched out again. His vision blurred. He punched again. And again. When he stopped, the fog cleared and he saw Hugo – eyes closed, his face covered in blood. Jason glanced down at his hand, still clenched tight, his knuckles red and swelling. Past images welled up – images of Jimmy the Junkie lying sprawled across the ground.

The girl walked back in from the kitchen.

Jason glanced her way. Her arms hung by her sides and her eyes were more glazed than before. The sight of Hugo certainly didn't seem to bother her. Jason inhaled and tried to calm. Remembered why he'd come here in the first place. "Put the kettle on, sweetheart."

She tutted but u-turned. A moment later, she swayed into view again, the beaded screen swinging down behind her, her unfocused eyes staring aimlessly at the sofa. She wobbled towards it, slumped beside the sleeping guy, and took the unsmoked joint from between his fingers.

Jason shook his mind clear and took the bat from Hugo's lap. He straightened and turned it towards the guy on the sofa.

He pressed the end against his cheek. "What's your name?"

The guy's eyes widened. "Paddy."

"Well, Paddy. You'd better start telling me what I want to hear or this bat's gonna make your balls pop."

"He's hiding in the kitchen," the girl slurred, mid-drag.

The beaded screen rattled and Jimmy rushed through it. He darted towards the hallway – as quickly as his limp would allow – but Jason blocked his path.

"'Ello, Jimmy, you piece of shit. Me and you are going back in the kitchen for a little chat."

"But I don't wanna go in the kitchen."

Jason shoved him across the room and back through the beads.

"I have witnesses this time if you hurt me."

Jason smiled. "I'm not gonna hurt you."

"Then why can't we talk out there?"

"You shouldn't be concerned about where we talk."

"No?"

"No." Jason gripped him around the back of the neck and pulled him close. "You should be more worried about what happens to your fingers if you don't tell me what I want to know."

Jimmy's eyes widened. "Don't bust me up again, man, please. I told you everything already."

Jason grimaced. "See, I think you may know more."

"I don't."

"Are you sure? A lot of time's passed since April. Maybe you remember something else."

"Okay, okay. What d'you want to know?"

"Leah Wade." Jason released his grip and Jimmy fell against the work surface. "Tell me everything."

Jimmy didn't straighten. Instead, he remained cowered against the counter. "Man, I don't want to be out here."

"This is your one chance to answer and leave with your body intact."

"But I don't know—"

Jason opened the fridge. He grabbed Jimmy's hand, trapped it against the side, and slammed the door shut.

Jimmy yelled out. "I sold to her. And I saw her a couple of times when I picked up my gear. That's all. I swear."

"You already told me that." Jason opened the door.

"No, I mean, I remembered seeing her somewhere else."

"Somewhere where?"

Jimmy slumped forward and tried to cradle his hand.

"Hey." Jason clicked his fingers. "Don't zone out on me, you little punk. Now where'd you see her?"

"End of Old Park Lane."

"Good. Now put your hand back in the fridge."

"Please, man…" Jimmy sobbed.

Jason raised a brow.

Jimmy swallowed. Short, sharp breaths blew from his mouth.

"I'm gonna count to three and then I'm gonna shove that noggin of yours in there instead."

Slowly, Jimmy raised his hand and placed it back against the side of the fridge.

"Now, what end of Park Lane?"

"Green Park." Sweat dripped down his face. "There's this burger stall…"

"The burger stall is old news to me, Jimmy. I want to know what happened to her."

"The road wrapping the park."

"I'm listening."

"Oh God, I don't remember, man."

Jason slammed the fridge door shut. Jimmy screamed and tried to yank his hand free.

Jason pressed against the door harder, firmly trapping it. "I suggest you start remembering."

"I don't know," Jimmy cried out.

Jason released the door. He kicked Jimmy's feet out from under him.

Jimmy fell to the floor, his hand cradled against his chest. "I'm gonna have the police on you, man. I won't be threatened into silence this time."

Jason took hold of the kettle. Steam floated from the spout. He held it above Jimmy's head. "Did I ever tell you about my RSI? Caused by my bloody phone and all this shitty texting I keep doing. It's made my hands weak and my grip very unpredictable."

Jimmy's eyes widened. He gave the side of the fridge a sideways glance before locking back on Jason again.

Jason turned to the fridge. Magnets held several papers to the side. He pulled them away. Two were shopping lists – drugs, not food. An address in Bethnal Green was inked on the third.

"What's this?"

Jimmy shrugged.

"You want your other leg crippled?"

"There's a guy."

"Who?"

"I don't know. Some Scottish dude. I seen him a couple of times going into the casino. Big guy, handy, y'know what I mean?"

"He work there?"

Jimmy shook his head."

"Then what? Security? On the doors?"

"Nah, man. He gambles."

"What's he or this address got to do with my sister?"

"Oh man. Shit. I don't know. I sold him stuff a couple of times."

"Drugs?"

Jimmy shook his head "Information."

"On what?"

"Names. Things like that."

"This address?"

Jimmy nodded. "Leah used to hang out there sometimes."

Jason's shoulders tightened. "Why'd he want it?"

"I just sell the info, man."

"He want it because of my sister?"

Jimmy shook his head. "Some other chick."

"Who?"

"I don't know, man."

Jason held the paper up. "So why look at it at the mention of Leah?"

Jimmy said nothing.

Jason tipped the kettle. "I can see the water, Jimmy."

Jimmy raised his arms above his head. "I seen him with her."

"When? The night she died?"

"No, no. Before."

"Where?"

"Down the road a bit. Near the burger van. I seen her get into his car."

"Make?"

"The car? I don't know. A light-coloured one. I'd just shot up, man. He could've been riding Big Bird for all I knew." Jimmy eyed the kettle. "Please, man. I told you everything."

Jason put the kettle down and pulled Jimmy up off the floor. "Tell me more about this man. How d'you make contact?"

"He calls me."

"He have a number?"

"It's always blocked."

"I need more, Jimmy."

"I told you. He's big."

"Muscle big or fat big?"

"Just big. Last I saw him, he wore a coat. Looks handy."

"He have a beard? Tattoos? Is he blond, dark, white, black? I need something more to go on, Jimmy." Jason reached for the kettle.

"No beard." Jimmy hurried. "Tattoo covers his hand, but I never seen it properly. Hardly any hair, but not bald. Tall, but shorter than you."

"How d'you give him information?"

"He gives me a time limit for the info then calls with a drop off point. A couple of times I hid to see who'd pick it up. Only got a glance but it's the same guy."

Jason released him. "And he was in the casino the night Leah went missing?"

"I don't know. Maybe. I wasn't paying no attention."

"Then when? I need a date. Time. Shit. Even a month."

"I don't know. Dates all blur into one, y'know?"

Jimmy sunk back down to the ground.

Jason sighed. It wasn't much to go on, but maybe CCTV would turn something up.

"You'd better not be bullshitting me, Jimmy."

"Man, I never would."

Jason squatted beside him. He clasped his jaw and lifted the junkie's chin until they locked eyes. "If you are, I will be back…and with more than just this baseball bat to keep me company."

Jason rested the bat on his shoulder and walked to the beaded screen. He stopped short of walking through it and turned. "This info he wants. Where d'you get it from?"

"My source." Jimmy started to back away from the fridge. "But I can't tell you who."

Jason raised the bat.

"Okay, okay." Jimmy backed up against the wall. "I don't know much about him. He's one of you lot."

"A CSI?"

"I don't know what he does. He works for you lot though."

"Police?" He certainly wouldn't be the first cop to sell info.

Jimmy shrugged. "I've never met him."

"Then how d'you know who or what he is?"

Jimmy shook.

Jason stepped towards him and squatted. "How d'you know he's Met?"

"I don't. I just know what he sounds like."

"And he sold you information to pass on to this guy?"

"Lots of times. On anything and everything."

"How d'you make contact with him?"

Jimmy looked at the floor, avoiding eye contact.

"If you keep something from me…"

"He was at the casino once."

"Doing what?"

Jimmy still wouldn't look at him.

Jason grabbed a tuft of Jimmy's hair and yanked his head up. Still Jimmy refused to meet his stare.

"He was in his car…I heard him – his voice I mean – talking to a girl. I know voices, man. It was him."

"And…"

"Hit her. Told her to get back inside and get him something to sell."

"Who's this girl? She work there or what?"

Jimmy began to sob. Jason yanked the junkie's hair again and whacked his head against the wall.

"Tell me who she is, Jimmy-boy."

Jimmy cried out. "Your sister." He crumbled. "It was your sister."

CHAPTER TEN

The door opened and Doctor Taylor entered the room.

Kate sat up. She'd been staring at the same four walls for the best part of three hours while waiting for him to hopefully bring her some good news.

"Miss…" He glanced up from his notes and smiled at her, age-old lines wrinkling his eyes. "We'll have to come up with a name for you, won't we?"

Kate smiled back, but she wasn't in the mood for jokes. "I'd rather have my real name."

The smile didn't wain. He closed the door. "So, how are you feeling today?"

"I still can't remember what happened."

"That's perfectly normal."

"But I can't remember anything. Not my name or who my friends are. My family. My childhood. Nothing."

The doctor perched on the edge of the bed. "You've been through a very traumatic experience. You've taken a knock to the head. You were submerged in freezing water. Personally, I'm surprised memory loss was the only ailment you walked away with."

"Am I going to stay like this?"

"Some people have been known never to regain their memories."

Kate glanced down at her hands. They gripped the blanket tight. The doctor must have noticed her dismay because he placed his hands on hers. She glanced up and found him still smiling at her, warm and relaxing.

"That doesn't necessarily apply to you, though." He patted her hands and pulled some glasses from his pocket. He sat them on the bridge of his nose and opened his file. "I have your test results. You have what is called Retrograde Amnesia."

"There are different types?"

"Uh-huh. Yours being that you cannot retrieve information acquired before a particular date or incident." He glanced up at her. "In your case, your fall."

"But I know how to do things like walk and talk, drink and eat. I look at the television and I know how to turn it on. How can that be if I have no memory?"

"RA can cause memory loss dating back decades. It negatively affects episodic, autobiographical, and declarative memories while, more often than not, keeping procedural memories intact."

Kate frowned.

The doctor grinned. "It means you'll remember how to brush your teeth and drive a car, but you won't remember what toothpaste you like or if you even own a car."

"But my memory will come back?"

"It's more than likely. The statistics certainly think so at least. Unfortunately, there's no instant cure and no telling how long it will take. When and how much you remember differs from patient to patient, you see. Some memories return spontaneously. Anything can trigger it – a familiar sound or touch, a voice, a sight, even a smell."

"So, you're saying it would help if I jumped in the Thames again?"

A light chuckle and the doctor smiled. "Not anything quite as dramatic as that."

There was a moment's silence and the smile faded. "There is one other option you need to think about."

Kate waited for him to elaborate.

He turned to face her full on. "There could be a reason why you don't want to remember your life. Or what happened to you."

"What do you mean?" Kate released the blanket and straightened.

"I mean that you may have experienced a traumatic episode or event –– something so bad or so wrong that your brain has chosen to completely block it out on purpose."

"Like what?"

"Ah, that, I'm afraid, I do not know the answer to."

"Could *I* be bad?"

The doctor shrugged. "There have been cases where amnesiacs have blocked their lives out due to their committing severe misdemeanours or wrong-doings." Again, he patted her hand. "Although, I hardly think that applies to you."

Kate wished she had his faith. Truth was, she had no idea who she was or why nobody had come forward and reported her missing.

"When can I leave the hospital?" Although, with nowhere to go, leaving didn't seem that great an idea.

"I'm not sure yet. A couple of days maybe."

"Where do people like me go?"

"There are halfway houses that would look after you."

Kate sat back. A halfway house? Weren't they for waifs and strays, and abused women? Was that what she was? "You said little things could jog my memory."

"Yes."

"Then could I trouble you for some paper and a pen – so I can note down anything I remember?"

That smile again and another pat of the hand. "I'll have the nurse bring some in for you."

CHAPTER ELEVEN

Jason dug his hands into his pockets.

Old Park Lane was situated between Hyde Park and Green Park. It was not a particularly long road. But it was a very affluent part of London where Arabs owned apartments, the wealthiest of businessmen wined and dined their mistresses and potential clients alike, and where CCTV cameras were pinned to every single building. Jason knew because he'd had Karen check them all at great restaurant expense to himself.

The rear of Hyde's Casino was less glamorous. Tucked away from the glitz, the alley stretched the rear of the casinos and hotels, servicing mainly day-to-day deliveries. Still a busy back street – with the snow part-swept, part-trodden down, and grit covering any pavement revealed to the elements.

When Jason glanced up at the buildings, he was dismayed to see only one CCTV camera – and not council owned by the look of it.

Money was, if nothing else, always serious about its security – unless it was around the back of a building where no important sod ventured.

Jason walked on, stealing an off-hand glance through the open door as he passed. Nothing much to see inside. A bland-looking corridor with several boxes of plonk waiting, he presumed, to be taken to the bar.

He paused outside the Rose and Crown – a pub that had occupied the end of the street for the best part of four hundred years – and wondered how to get his hands on this particular camera's CCTV footage.

The easiest way would be to tell Ed what he'd discovered and let the police handle it. Problem with that, though, was that Ed wanted him to move on from his sister's death just as much as Karen did. Plus, as far as the police were concerned, Leah's death was a closed case. An accident. They certainly weren't looking for a killer. And they certainly wouldn't make an exception – not for Jason at least. Just like they hadn't when he'd wanted to seize the footage from inside the casino.

There was only one person who could help him. Who would help him. He glanced at his watch. Late afternoon already and she'd probably be at home by now.

This time it was going to cost him more than a Friday night out.

He turned and looked across the main road where a burger van had pitched up near the park entrance. Its owner would not be pleased to see him. Regardless, Jason looked for a gap in the traffic and crossed the road.

A weedy-looking man glanced up from the grill and locked eyes long enough for worry to age his face ten years. Then he glanced down, quickly shovelled onions onto a hot dog, and passed it to the waiting customer.

He threw a napkin at the young man, hurriedly waved him away, then turned back to Jason. "Man, I told you months ago. I ain't never supplied your sister that shit she was on. That was Jimmy."

"That's not what I'm here about." Jason walked round the back of the van.

The weedy man raced to lock the door, but Jason yanked it open before he had time to secure it.

The man stepped back. "This is trespassing."

"Calm down. I'm not the hygiene police," Jason said, climbing inside.

"I meet all the health and safety shit."

Jason picked a spatula up off the floor. "I wouldn't let my dog eat out of this fucking shit sty."

The man swallowed but didn't argue the fact that the van was disgusting.

"It beggars belief how you're allowed to keep trading." Jason kicked an uncooked burger from his path. "I think it's my public duty to report this to the relevant authorities."

"Man, I told you. I meet all the—"

"Yeah, yeah." Jason held up his hand. "I'm not talking about those blue-collar knobs." He moved a plastic container of baps off the shelf and pulled out a bag of white pills. "Do these look like cheese-fucking-slices to you?"

A nervous chuckle died in the back of the van owner's throat. "I don't know how—"

Jason reached for the bloke around the back of his neck. He pulled him close. "I want to know about who my sister spoke to out there." He nodded towards the main road.

"What d'you mean?"

"Tell me about the driver Leah used to meet."

"What driver?"

Jason released the guy. Smiled. Took a patty of ground beef and slapped it onto the grill. It immediately sizzled.

The van man's eyes widened. "Oh, yeah. There was a car."

Jason took the spatula. He pressed down on the burger. Grease squeezed free and spat into the air.

"A silver one," the man hurried. "Sporty."

Jason flipped the burger. "Number plate?"

"Ended in SMV. I remember because I read it as smooth – as in smooth bastard for having a car like that. That's all I know. I never saw the driver. Your sister would buy some gear off me, then go off with him and not show her face again until the next night."

"What'd you sell her?" Jason held up the pills again. "These?"

The man shook his head. "Nah. She wanted painkillers."

Jason waited outside Karen's front door.

He knew she was in. Christmas lights twinkled around the window and Ed Sheeran blasted from her speakers. She pulled back the side curtain.

He smiled and held up a white, paper bag full of sweets. "I have flumps."

Her eyes narrowed. She did not look pleased to see him. The curtain dropped across the window and she opened the door. "I haven't got the results yet."

"That's not why I'm here."

Her shoulders sagged. "Shit. Is this going to get me the sack?"

"It's important."

"It always is with you."

She walked away from the door, leaving Jason to enter and close it behind him.

He didn't bother removing his coat and followed her through to the living area. He felt more at home here than in his own place. A large Christmas tree – real, not fake – sat in the corner of the room, a stack of presents beneath it. Jason thought of the present he had lying unwrapped on his bedroom dresser – still undecided if he was going to give it to her or not.

She snatched the bag of flumps from him. "So, what is it you need now?"

He walked through to the kitchen and opened the fridge. "Where the hell are the beers?"

"There aren't any."

"Unlike you."

"I do have guests other than you.

"I didn't mean—"

"The girls were over at the weekend, you know – a pre-festive drink. I haven't replaced anything yet. Besides, you drink too much." Karen reached past him and closed the door. "You can have tea."

Jason sighed. He opened the cupboard behind him and found tins of soup and boxes of cereal. No cups.

Karen switched on the kettle then pointed to the cupboard next to him. "Where they've been for the last six months."

Jason looked. Sure enough, mugs galore. "Has it really been that long?"

"Since you stopped being an overnight guest?" She put her bag of sweets on the counter, squeezed past him, and retrieved two mugs.

"You told me to go."

"I told you to get some help."

"Listen, Karen—"

She held up a hand. "Seriously, we don't need to talk about it. It was fun while it lasted and now it's done."

"I never apologised."

"No. You never did." She reached for the teabags, stopped, and turned to him. "Jason, you are a sweet guy. Honestly, you are. But you changed when Leah died – for the worse. And you're gonna remain like that unless you get some help."

Jason glanced at the floor. He hadn't meant to hurt her. Truth be told, she'd hurt him when she finished it.

"So, what is it you need?" She dropped a teabag in each cup.

Jason closed the cupboard door and perched on to the work surface. "I need some CCTV checked."

Karen glanced over her shoulder. "I've already checked enough CCTV. I'm not checking any more."

"This is round the back of the casino."

"And you can't request it through the appropriate channels?"

Jason raised a brow. She knew he couldn't – he wouldn't be standing here asking her if he could.

"Shit." The kettle boiled and Karen poured water into the mugs. "So, what is it you're looking for?"

"A man who was with Leah."

Karen glared at him. She didn't say anything. She didn't *need* to say anything. Fuck. He hated it when she stared at him like this.

He turned away and opened the fridge again. He wanted to stick his head inside and hide from her. Instead, he brought out the milk and handed it over as a peace offering. It was a poor apology, but he had little idea what else to do. To be honest, he thought the bag of flumps would have chipped away at least some of the hostility.

Karen snatched the milk. One last, hard glare and then she turned back to making the tea. "I see your knuckles have been hitting out again."

Jason glanced at his hand, still red and a little swollen. He shoved it into his coat pocket. "I was following a lead."

"About Leah?" Karen tutted. "And you had no other option but to punch the information out of him?"

"It wasn't like that."

"No?" Karen glanced at him. "So, it wasn't like the time you went schizo on my colleague? Or like the time you forced your way into the casino?"

"Karen—"

"I honestly thought you were trying to move on from this situation."

"Situation? This situation is my sister's murder."

"I refuse to discuss it." Karen turned. She thrust one of the mugs into his hand. "I am not getting pulled back into your bloody conspiracy theory again."

"It is not a theory."

"You're in denial, Jason. All this? It has nothing to do with Leah's death, but with your guilt at not being there for her after your mother died."

"For fuck's sake. I was eight years old then. How could I feel guilty for that?"

"You mean you don't feel guilty at not being able to protect her? At not stopping her from getting involved with drugs? For not keeping her away from the undesirables she was clearly mixing with?"

"No."

"Not even a little bit?" Karen tilted her head to one side. "Then, shit. You're in deeper denial than I thought, and I'm a stupid cow for believing that you ever wanted to change." She scoffed. "You know what else is stupid? I honestly thought that when you stormed my office party and punched out the D.S. for resting his hand on my shoulder that you realised you needed help."

"He shouldn't have touched you."

"You had no right projecting your possessive jealously onto me. It was an innocent gesture and not one that I needed saving from." She slammed her mug down on the counter. "Did you think that by saving someone else, no matter how imaginary their danger was, that you were going to cleanse yourself of the blame you feel for Leah?"

She paused and the anger faded from her eyes.

She reached for his hand and lightly clasped it. "You are not to blame for Leah. And you need to go to that doctor of yours. Let her help you."

"You have no idea what you're talking about." Jason pulled his hand free. "And, for your information, I did go see the fucking doctor."

"You went, like, once."

"Three times."

"You missed one and didn't stay for the other."

"Well, I went today."

"And?"

"And…we talked."

Karen's eyes narrowed.

"So, it was a short chat." Jason admitted. "More an argument really."

Karen smiled. "But you spoke?"

"It changed nothing." Jason looked at his tea but what he really wanted was a beer. He glanced up. Karen had her mug of tea back in her hands, but she still watched him.

"I did buy you flumps."

Karen's smiled died, but the warmth remained in her eyes. "Shit. That you did."

"So, will you check the camera?"

"This has to be the last time. If I don't find anything, which is highly likely, you have to accept this is a dead end. Let it drop and move on."

Jason put his tea on the side. "Promise."

He leaned forward, planted a peck on her cheek, and headed for the living room.

Karen followed. "Where're you going?"

"To check the footage. You said—"

"I'm not doing it now."

"Why not?"

"Because it's six thirty, nearly bloody Christmas, and I have the next couple of days off."

Jason took her by the shoulders, his grip deliberately light and gentle. "Please, Karen. I need answers – to put this to bed. It's not guilt that's eating at me; it's the not knowing."

Karen looked up at him. "You're wrong."

"Put it this way. You'll check, find nothing, and I'll have to move on. You're gonna be the only winner here."

Her eyes softened. "Christ, Jason. You owe me big time for this."

"How about we upgrade the Oyster Shack to something that involves silver cutlery?"

"That'll do for starters." She sat her mug down on the corner of the coffee table and walked into the hallway. Her Uggs waited by the door, ready for her to slip on. "If I don't find anything, you have to promise me this will be the end of it."

Jason took her coat off the peg and held it open.

Karen threaded her arms through. Then realisation hardened her eyes. "You're not coming with me."

"Two pairs of eyes are better than one."

"No. It's going to be hard enough explaining why *I* need access to the footage, let alone coming up with a plausible reason why I have you with me."

Jason went to argue, but Karen held up her hand and quietened him. "Just tell me where the camera is, who it is I'm looking for, and the dates. I'll let you know if I find anything."

Jason remained in front of the door. He pursed his lips and exhaled.

"You can stand there and puff your chest as much as you want. This is the deal. Take it or leave it."

"Fine. One private camera at the Rose and Crown. Back of Lee's Chinese. Around Valentine's. Leah's talking to someone in a car."

"I'll look and then we're finished."

"There is one other thing." He unfolded a piece of paper. "Run a check on this."

"Jesus Christ. What is it?"

"Partial plate. Sporty-looking car."

Karen snatched the paper. "Then we're finished."

"Yes."

"Swear it, Jason."

Jason forced a smiled and fingered an X across his heart. "I swear."

"You're a condescending prick…and that's gonna cost you the most expensive bottle of bubbly the restaurant has to offer."

She pushed past him, and left the house.

CHAPTER TWELVE

Tav glanced at his mobile.

His informant was late. By fifteen minutes.

He slipped the phone in his pocket and turned back to the booklet rolled tight in his hand. Shit, he was cold out here, but as he was avoiding the casino for a couple of days until he'd made good on his contract, the Romford dog track was the next best place to be.

He flicked to the middle of the book. Number eight in the nine-ten looked on good form and had won him a small fortune in the past. The board outside showed better odds than inside so Tav placed a nifty – one way – then glanced at his phone again. Twenty minutes late. He glanced over the sea of heads towards the bar or, more precisely, the rows of seating just in front of it. His agitation did not lessen when he saw Jimmy limp up and take an aisle seat.

Tav held back and watched for a while, but Jimmy made no attempt to leave a newspaper or anything that might hold the information he'd paid for. Tav cursed. He waited a further ten minutes. Watched the number eight dog come in second – losing the fifty Tav had bet on him. Then he broke his cardinal rule of staying in the shadows and walked over to where the junkie sat.

Tav took a seat a couple of rows behind. He stepped his foot on the chair in front and rested the booklet against his knee. Making out he was checking the next couple of races, he scoped out the people around him. None were police – that he was sure of. So, if Jimmy wasn't here trying to lure him out for the good old boys in blue, then what was he waiting for? Why not leave the information and limp off?

Another couple of races came and went. He'd picked winners for both of them but missed placing the bets. Fuck this. He got up and headed to the bar. Pushing his way through to the front, he threw a tenner at the barman and demanded a beer. The barman passed him an open Bud Light – a pussy's drink. Tav wanted to ram it up the youngster's arse.

But he didn't. Instead, he took the beer, waited for his change, and headed back outside to the seats. Jimmy still sat there. What the fuck? Tav gave the area another once-over. What was the junkie waiting for?

Another race. And another winner Tav hadn't placed a bet on. Shit. His night was going from bad to worse.

Another glance around. Another sip of beer.

Fuck it. He walked up to the seats and took the chair directly behind Jimmy. "Why the fuck are you still here?"

Jimmy started to turn.

Tav slapped him across the back of the head. "Eyes forward, dope-bag."

Jimmy turned back to face the track. "I have the address you wanted."

"Then you leave it and fuck off."

"I don't have it written down."

"Are you illiterate?"

Jimmy shook his head.

"Then you fucking write it down." Tav glugged on his beer. It was like drinking a watered down shandy.

"I did. It was taken from me."

Tav stopped drinking. He wiped his mouth. "By who?"

Again, Jimmy started to turn.

Tav slapped him back forward.

"A man. Came to the flat and beat me up." Jimmy raised his badly bandaged hand.

"What man?"

"Same guy who gave me this limp. And the same guy you took a picture of. Name's Wade. Jason Wade, I think. Was a boxer once. Now works for the police."

"What'd he want the address for?"

"He's trying to find out who killed his sister."

"Who's his sister?"

"Just a tart who drowned in the Thames." Jimmy turned again, Tav's slap not halting him this time. "Thing is, you knew her."

Tav frowned. He didn't know many people. Certainly didn't mix with them.

"Leah Wade. Used to get your painkillers from the burger man."

Tav sat back. He'd wondered what had happened to her. Gave a good Friday night blow job for a score and then, one night, she just disappeared. Tav had always thought she'd OD'd or something. "How d'you know about the pills?"

"I have my resources."

"Resources that will get you killed."

Jimmy said nothing.

Tav swallowed some more beer and made a mental note to end this Jimmy character as soon as he'd outlived his usefulness. "You know who killed her?"

Jimmy remained silent.

"Of course you do." Tav smiled. "You tell this cop?"

Jimmy shook his head.

"But he knows the address?"

Jimmy nodded slightly, certainly not wanting to admit it.

"And you're sure this address is the one I need?"

"It's the girl's last known residence over here."

This was going to be an interesting trip if Tav wasn't the only person checking the place out. Then again, he liked a challenge. "This Wade guy know about me and his sister?"

"No. I don't think so."

Tav sat back. This certainly spiced things up. "Give me the address."

CHAPTER THIRTEEN

Jason walked into the shrink's office.

The receptionist – her desk clear of paperwork and hidden in the shadows of the darkened foyer – looked to have long since left for the evening. The shrink, however, appeared to be working overtime. Light slithered out from beneath her door and Jason wasted no time in opening it.

"Mr Wade?" Doctor Tandy stood from her chair. "Our appointment isn't until tomorrow."

The guy sitting across from her desk turned and glared at Jason: Well-to-do. Jacket made to fit. Top button of his shirt undone. He screamed money.

Jason looked back at Tandy. "I need to talk now."

A forced smile found her lips and she glanced towards her client. "Can you excuse me for one moment?"

She rounded the desk, grabbed Jason's bicep, turned him towards the door, and forced him into the foyer. She followed, quietly pulling the door closed behind her.

"What on earth are you playing at?" Her voice was sharp but hushed.

"Hey, I came voluntarily. I'd call that progress."

"Not unannounced and not when I am with another client. Your appointment isn't until tomorrow."

"So, I'm early for a change."

She stepped back, held up her hands, and exhaled. "This conversation needs to wait until the morning."

Jason shoved his hands in his pockets. Images from the night of Leah's death filled his head and just wouldn't go away. He wanted to tell the doc. Hopefully receive some wordy miracle from her and move on with solving his sister's murder.

Instead, he said, "Suit yourself, doc. But if I do something reckless tonight, on your head be it."

He turned to leave.

She cursed beneath her breath. "Wait."

Jason stopped.

"What did you want to see me about? And give me the edited version."

Jason spun back to face her. The words stuck in his throat. "I'm surprised you're here so late."

"That's what you wanted? To discuss my working hours?"

Okay, so it was a bad time for pleasantries. "I asked someone to do something for me today…" He paused. "Even though I knew it could cost her her job."

Tandy remained quiet.

Her eyes narrowed. She was silently scrutinizing him. Dissecting his words, his body language, his…oh fuck. What the hell was he doing here?

"You know what, doc. I'll see you tomorrow when it's on the clock."

Still, Tandy watched him. "I bill every minute, including this one."

Jason eyed her. Had she just attempted a joke?

Her face remained set in stone. "I'll be finished in twenty minutes. We can talk then."

Jason looked at the seats in the waiting room. He no longer wanted to talk. He'd been stupid in coming here. Karen's words about his drinking and being obsessed had gotten under his skin. And, now, here he was – a moment of weakness. He turned away and shrugged.

"Good. Take a seat. I won't be long."

He felt her eyes boring into his back as he walked to the waiting room. He heard her walk back into her office and apologise again to her client.

As soon as her office door closed, Jason made for the exit.

The taxi pulled up at the entrance to the Gurton Estate in Bethnal Green.

Jason leaned forward and passed the driver some money through the window. "Wait here for me, mate. I won't be long."

He jumped out and headed towards Mayflower House. He hadn't been around this part of the world for the best part of a decade. By the looks of it, nothing much had changed. The place was still a shit-hole. Dull light flickered around some of the windows. Others had mini Santa's on the sills. The rest were dark and dull and lacking any Christmas spirit whatsoever.

He crossed the car park and entered the tiny stairwell through two swing doors – one of them boarded up. Jogging the three flights of stairs to the top, he strolled out onto the walkway, which ran the length of the building. Across the horizon, he saw Stratford's Olympic Stadium standing proud, but otherwise not much else had altered. Distant lights dotted the landscape, casting the romantic illusion that hope and aspiration were close enough to touch, while the darkness that the evening brought hid the true ugly mess that was the east end of London.

Jason continued along the walkway. Most doors and windows he passed were secured and protected with iron gates – one thing that *had* changed. When he'd been growing up here, the only bars residents ever saw were either inside the local boozer or inside the clink as the prison doors slammed shut behind them.

Halfway along was another iron gate – this one securing the walkway and blocking his path. Jason pulled on it, but the padlock held it shut. He hopped up onto the railing and swung out over the balcony, landing on the other side.

He continued onward, counting down the door numbers until he was outside number fifty-six. The door – dirty, paint-chipped wood that had been graffitied with a logo he couldn't read – was ajar. Jason shook his head. Had his own sister honestly been associated with this place?

Beside the door was a window. The room behind it sat in darkness. Jason turned back to the front door. No signs of forced entry. He slowly pushed it open. Inside, darkness shrouded the hallway. Only when he moved from the doorway did the light from outside move in. Paper and used cartons littered the piss-stained floorboards. Jason stepped inside, covering his nose to protect it from the stench of shit that smeared the walls.

Why had he not seen Leah's life spiralling so much out of control? All the signs had been there – her erratic behaviour, her distancing herself from him. If he'd just pulled his head out of his arse for two minutes, he would have seen.

Now, only junkies and squatters looked to live here. That much was clear. So, what? Everyone had been right? Leah really had been a junkie and a prostitute all along? He clenched his fists and inhaled. He couldn't believe that of his sister – even if the evidence pointed to it.

He walked through to the back room – the living room, he guessed – and pulled out his phone, activating the torch. The room was in a worse state than the hallway, although the reek of shit wasn't as bad in here. He shone the torch around the floor. Sleeping bags – he counted seven – lay scattered across the floorboards. Nobody slept in them. Used condoms, broken bongs, silver foil, needles – Jesus, just about everything he didn't want to come into contact with.

This search was ridiculous. If there had ever been a trace of his sister here, it was long gone now. That was if she'd ever been here in the first place. He turned back to the hallway. A quick check upstairs to see if anyone was home, otherwise he'd return tomorrow. He'd reached the living room door when he heard a floorboard creak above him. He froze and listened. Another creak, this time at the top of the landing. Then footsteps, quiet and careful, coming down the stairs. Not the sound of a squatter.

Jason hid his phone beneath his jacket and smothered the light. A figure, bulky, crept down the stairs and entered the hallway. Definitely not a squatter.

Jason held up his torch. "Hey."

The man whipped up a hand and blocked the light, whether to shield his eyes or to hide his face, Jason couldn't decide.

"Who are you?" Jason stepped forward.

The man tilted his head and lowered his hand, the brim of his baseball cap now hiding his face. He didn't appear startled. In fact, his stance remained strong.

"I asked you a question."

The man glanced over his shoulder. He turned back to face Jason, the majority of his face still obscured by the cap. A smug smile touched his lips. Then he spun and fled through the open door.

Jason sprinted out onto the walkway after him. The man had already put a fair distance between them. Jason started after him. The guy was fast; Jason would give him that.

The man reached the gate and swung around the outside of it, pretty much the same way Jason had when he'd arrived. This guy was way too athletic to be a junkie or a squatter. Regardless, the man's foot caught the edge of the railing and he tumbled to the ground on the other side. His arms flailed and his hat flew from his head, yet he dived into a forward roll, recovering his dignity – a little. He glanced back at Jason, his features hidden by the confines of the walkway, and got to his feet with no urgency to his actions. Then he brushed down his coat, casual as you like.

He was a cocky son of a bitch who then straightened, glanced Jason's way, and saluted.

Now Jason saw he was white, slightly balding, with smart clothing beneath his coat. Was this the man Jimmy had described earlier? Had he known Leah? The guy still watched him. No smile this time, though. Then turned and charged for the stairwell door.

Jason grabbed the gate and swung out over the railing. Unlike the man he chased, he landed two-footed on the other side. He raced for the stairwell door, making up valuable seconds, and burst through without checking if danger waited for him on the other side. Footsteps bounced off the walls and echoed around him. Jason leaned over the railing, saw the man pummelling the stairs below him, and started his own descent, taking the stairs two at a time. A woman screamed and Jason jumped the last five steps to the second floor. Grabbing the bannister, he swung around and started down the next flight.

Another jump and he came face to face with an elderly woman. She stood frozen against the far wall, her groceries running wild over the stairs. At the bottom, spread face-down across the first-floor landing, was the man – an overturned shopping basket on top of him.

The guy rolled over and kicked the basket away. He got to his feet, his shoulders rising with every heavy breath, and looked up at Jason. The bad lighting didn't fully reveal his features, but the glow was enough for Jason to see the cocky look had vanished. Instead, a feeling of familiarity spiked Jason's senses – he'd seen this guy somewhere before.

The man's shoulders curled forward, his stance set to flee – or fight. It was hard to tell.

The man didn't twitch. He stood firm and glared up at Jason.

Neither man moved. They both remained rooted to the concrete floor, each staring at the other – Jason at the top of the stairs, the man at the bottom. Where had he seen this guy before?

"Who are you?" Jason finally said, aware the old woman remained just to the left of him.

The man stayed silent.

Jason came down a step, his hand motioning for the woman to stay put. The man waited at the base of the stairwell for him.

Jason took another step, then another. Still the man waited.

A sixth stair. Then a seventh, until only three steps separated them.

"What were you doing inside that house?" Jason said.

The man moved quick. He jumped, twisting mid-air, and kicked Jason in the stomach. Jason fell back onto the stairs and the man pounced on him. Jason caught him with a right hook, grabbed his coat, and hit him again. The man fell to Jason's right and Jason lifted his arm, bringing his elbow down towards the guy's face. The man blocked it, trapped Jason's arm, and elbowed Jason in the ribs. Jason curled forward and another blow hit him across the side of the face. He rolled across the stairs and away from his attacker. Tried to lift himself – to get to his feet, but the man kicked his arms out from under him and Jason fell back against the stairs.

Jason landed with a grunt and spun onto his back in time to see the man's boot stamping down towards him. Jason flicked onto his side and the man's foot hammered onto the step. Jason rocked back. His arm hooked the man's calf and he lifted upwards, taking the guy's leg with him. The man wobbled and Jason slammed him backwards into the wall. He stared the man in the eyes. Was this the man he was looking for?

The guy swung a punch. Jason pulled back and felt a fist skim his jaw. A succession of punches followed. Jason ducked and weaved, avoiding every one of them. The final strike came and Jason caught it inches from his eye. He wrapped his fingers around the man's fist and slowly twisted it outwards.

The man snarled and pushed back. His hand shook. His whole arm shook. Jason gripped tighter. He glanced towards the fist and saw a tattoo – a blue swallow…a blue bird. Jason glanced up and for a second the two men locked eyes. Seconds felt like minutes before the man grabbed the back of Jason's head with his free hand. He yanked Jason forward and head-butted him just above the nose. Jason staggered back. His vision blurred and he raised his fists, ready to fight. The man's punch smashed straight through his defence. Jason lolled forward and the man's knee cracked him under the chin. Jason's head whipped back and he collapsed on the stairs.

The man came at him, planting his boot into Jason's stomach. Jason curled away, but a second kick came at him. Jason blocked it best he could. He tried to hold onto the man's foot, but the guy shook him free.

Jason remained curled up, waiting for the next attack. It never came. He heard footsteps on the stairs and tried to straighten. He coughed, but his body refused to move. The countdown clock screamed inside his head: ten…nine…eight…seven...six. Shit. He remembered where he'd seen this guy before – at the hospital. He remembered 'blue bird' murmuring past the sleeping girl's lips. Jason swallowed the pain away as best he could, rolled onto all fours, and reached for the railing.

He pulled himself onto his feet. Above him, the old woman stood and watched, looking too scared to move. He couldn't blame her.

Below, at the bottom of the stairwell, Jason heard the doors crash open. He glanced over the railings and caught the bottom of the doors swinging shut again. Staggered to the stairs. Every breath pierced his side. He stumbled down to the ground floor, amazed he managed to stay upright, and cursed. He'd taken beatings worse than this in his lifetime and not felt this inadequate afterwards.

He reached the two doors and pushed open the boarded one. Outside, the car park looked empty and still. In the distance, the hum of vehicles trickled along the main road, but here – no movement whatsoever. Jason scanned the area again, searching the light beneath the parked cars, the doorways, the shadows alongside the fences – anywhere a person might be inclined to hide on short notice.

Not a single sign of the man.

He felt the warmth of blood on his face and wrapped his arms tighter around his waist. Fuck it. He'd had this man within reach – and let him go. The taxi still waited by the car park entrance and Jason held up a hand, informing the driver he wouldn't be long. Then he turned back to the stairwell.

The old woman remained on the stairs. Her light-coloured overcoat was buttoned to the neck and a silk headscarf covered her hair.

Jason bent down, winced with pain, and stood her trolley upright. "Let me help you with all this."

He reached for a crushed box of tissues and dropped them into the basket.

Slowly, the woman edged towards him. "You need a hospital."

Jason grabbed a bag of apples. "Isn't it a little late for you to be out shopping?"

"I don't like crowds and the aisles are empty this time of night." She gathered up the loose oranges and a tin of soup.

"You do know it's dangerous for a woman to be out alone this time of night?"

The woman slid the groceries into the basket. "And yet you're the one standing there bloody and beaten."

Jason smiled. "I definitely got my arse kicked."

He carried her bag up the stairs, collected a packet of four toilet rolls as he passed, and walked her up to the second floor. He waited while she opened her door.

She entered and then turned to him. "Are you sure you don't want me to call someone for you?" She opened the tissues and handed some to him.

Jason shook his head. He nodded for her to go inside, then waited to hear the bolt slide across the door before he headed back to the stairwell. Blood still gushed from his brow and he used one of the tissues to stem its flow.

Then he remembered.

The baseball cap.

He hobbled up to the third floor and back to the gate. The hat was on the ground. Jason flapped open a tissue and picked the cap up. He cast a quick eye over it, but the poor lighting made it impossible to see anything. Shaking open another tissue, he covered as much of the hat as possible.

Excitement built inside and he couldn't help but smile. DNA was a wonderful thing. You could get a match from just about anything: sweat, spit, skin…hair.

"Got you, you wanker."

CHAPTER FOURTEEN

Tav checked over his shoulder.

The street was empty. The cop was nowhere in sight.

If he even was a cop. He certainly fought like the boxer the junkie had reported he'd once been. Tav slowed his pace and finally stopped beside his car. The doors automatically unlocked and he got in. For a moment he sat in silence, allowing his brain to process the events of the last half an hour. He gripped the steering wheel. Who the fuck was this Jason Wade? First at the hospital and now here at the squat.

He twisted the rear-view mirror and examined the bruising beneath his eye. The little prick sure had one hell of a right hook on him.

Shit. Tav slapped the mirror away. He'd known Wade had acquired the address but hadn't thought for a moment that he'd turn up nosing around tonight. He'd underestimated him. It was a mistake he wouldn't make again. This cop, or whoever the hell he was, was fast becoming a pain in the arse – a pain Tav didn't have time for.

He whacked the steering wheel. Wrapped his fingers around it and tried to simmer down his anger. His clasp tightened. Shit. He rubbed his head – and realised he no longer wore his cap.

Fucking shit.

His knuckles whitened and he closed his eyes. He inhaled deeply and held the breath. Anger still bubbled in the pit of his stomach. Fuck it. He opened his eyes and started the engine. He needed to get his bloody hat back.

Tav pulled the car away from the kerb and headed back towards the estate. There was no sign of the guy he'd fought and he ignored the nagging voice inside his head that told him to get the hell away before he did materialise.

Parking spaces were few and far between, but Tav found one along the far side of the car park and pulled in. He cut the lights and angled the wing-mirror so he could see the building's entrance. Maybe this Wade guy had already left. Maybe he lived in one of the flats there. Maybe he still lay crumpled on the stairs where Tav had kicked him down.

Tav crossed his arms and blew some warmth into his hands. Condensation already misted his view and he opened the driver's window a couple of inches. Cold air swept through and the car turned even colder.

The wing mirror caught movement exiting the building, but Tav couldn't make out if it was Wade or not. He twisted in his seat and glanced out of the back window. Yep. It was Wade alright, his arm wrapped around his waist and blood streaming from his eye. He carried something in his hand. Tav's baseball cap maybe?

Shit.

Tav reached for the door handle. He needed that cap.

An engine grumbled to life and a pair of headlights brightened, cutting a path through the gloomy car park. A taxi – parked just inside the entrance.

Tav closed the door and lowered himself away from the window. Jesus fucking crap. This night had gone tits up big time. But he needed that hat back. He watched Wade – clearly in pain – make his way to the taxi and thought about taking on both him and the driver. Wade got into the cab – hardly a police vehicle – and in less than a minute the taxi had turned around and driven out of the estate.

Tav remained crouched in his seat. It was time to rein this job back in before it got any more out of control. He pulled out his phone. Without bothering to block his number, he text: *This address was a bust. Get me another one.*

He wound up his window and started the engine. Then paused. Took out his phone again and, to the same number, sent a second text: *And get me everything you have on this Wade guy.*

He slipped the phone into his jacket pocket and reversed out of the parking space. Before he reached the entrance, his mobile buzzed with an incoming call – the junkie.

Tav hit the hands free.

Jimmy's voice filled the car. "I've texted you Wade's address."

"That was quick."

"Yeah, well, like I said, the guy fucked up my leg. I can find out the other information you want too, you know, but it'll take a little longer."

Tav's phone buzzed with the delivery of Jimmy's message. Maybe the junkie had some balls after all. "Is this him on an official investigation?"

"Nah. Just him on a crusade."

Tav smiled. "Anyone else know what he's up to?"

"He works alone."

"What about the girl. Anything on her?"

"She's leaving hospital tomorrow. Seems she'd been crashing with a friend."

"There'd better not be any surprises waiting for me." Tav pulled out onto the main road.

"My source wanted an extra grand to hold the info back for a bit. Thought you may need time to sort whatever shit you need to do."

Tav's phone vibrated with the arrival of a second text. He opened it and read the address – a pad in Shad Thames. Security would prove problematic, but then problem-solving seemed to be his thing of late. "One other thing. Who killed Wade's sister?"

The line went silent.

"This is me asking nicely, Jimmy."

He heard Jimmy's breathing quicken. Then, finally, the junkie said, "I'll see what I can find out."

CHAPTER FIFTEEN

The taxi pulled up outside the Playhouse Theatre.

Jason paid the driver, but this time didn't ask him to wait. He held his ribs as he stepped out onto the pavement and zipped his coat all the way up to his neck. It made little difference. The cold still found a way to freeze his bones.

He dug his hands deep into his pockets and thought about what Karen had said – that he had to put his obsession with Leah's death to rest. And she was right. He wasn't an idiot. He could see his life spiralling out of control. Truth be told, he'd like nothing more than to move on from that night before it completely destroyed him. But there were now a couple of things stopping him from doing that: this dude from the squat and the amnesiac girl in the hospital.

Jason walked, dragging his feet from his earlier beating and kicking snow from his path. He knew exactly where he was going. It was the only distraction he could think of. He climbed the steps to the Golden Jubilee Footbridge and paused for breath, pleased that, finally, it wasn't thoughts of his sister that dominated his mind – but of the girl in the hospital.

Karen's warning to let Leah's death rest echoed in his ear. He ran his fingers through his hair and clasped his hands around the back of his head – even though it hurt like hell. She was right, of course. She was always right. He just never listened.

He turned and scanned the bridge ahead. Glanced at the railing – not tall but well over waist height – and thought about the girl's clothes he'd dried. All pretty standard. But the boots or boot she'd been wearing was not an easy pair of heels for climbing railings on the best of days, let alone in weather like this.

He started to walk forward, unsure where the girl had jumped from. He wasn't even sure what he was looking for. Witnesses reported seeing the girl jump. The best Jason could do was try and find out who she was and maybe get a lead on a name.

The walkway was a mutilation of slush. Jason followed it and, when the river began to pass beneath the bridge, he began his search. Snow piled high at the sides of the pavement, burying the base of the railing. Everything looked pretty normal. Every so often, a few footprints strayed from the slushy path to the edge of the bridge and the top of the railings became visible.

Still, this nagging doubt, which had been floating quietly around at the back of his mind since his visit to the hospital, started to push forward. A nagging doubt that, based on his years of honed experience, screamed this whole scenario wasn't quite right. That this girl had not, in fact, gone off this bridge of her own free will.

Jason continued to walk. Continued to search the ground for clues. Not that he expected to find anything. Plod, along with their size twelves, had annihilated any hope of finding evidence to contradict the witness statements.

Jason stood and scanned the railing. White support pylons extended down from high above, designed like a pyramid that leaned outward and stretched the entire length of the bridge. If somebody wanted to jump, they'd have to use one of these poles to haul themselves up onto the railing. Even if just to keep their balance steady while mustering up the courage to actually leap off.

He leaned over the railing. Shit, his fucking side hurt and he took a breath. It was a hell of a long drop. How the girl had survived a fall like that…she was lucky to be alive.

He hugged his waist tighter and leaned over until he balanced on tiptoe. He needed evidence. Any bloody evidence. It didn't matter how small. Just something to satisfy this irritating niggle he felt. Below him, on the underside of the railing – lower than the pavement he stood on and covered in snow – he saw a narrow ledge. He started walking, still bent over the railing and still holding his side, but his eye never losing sight of the ledge. Two-thirds of the way across, he saw it. Eight perfect indentations. Or, to be more precise, eight perfect finger impressions.

Jason had what he'd been searching for. His gut screamed that this girl hadn't jumped of her own free will. And now he was certain of it. Because if she had jumped, her back would have been facing the bridge – and she would never have been able to grab hold of that ledge.

So, going on the assumption that he wasn't crazy and she hadn't jumped – or accidentally slipped over the railing – it left only one other explanation. She'd been pushed. By this guy from the squat perhaps? Clearly, he wasn't a hospital orderly. So, what did he want with this girl?

Of course, the squat raised another question. Jason had gone there looking for answers about his sister's death. Was this guy linked to her, too? Was he the man Jimmy the Junkie spoke of? The tattooed hand would suggest he was.

But all this conjecture, with its flimsy evidence at best, would never be enough to convince Carter.

Jason straightened. His body tightened and he drew another breath. He gripped the railing and shook his head clear. The pain calmed and he pulled his mobile from his back pocket and dialled.

As he expected, Karen's tone indicated she was less than pleased to hear from him again so soon.

"I've only just got into work," she said, bypassing the pleasantries and not waiting to hear what he wanted.

"This isn't about the CCTV."

"Then what? I am not doing any more favours for you."

"The fingerprints. They turned up a name yet?" He tried to keep his voice even, but it was a strain.

There was a silence before he heard Karen's keyboard click to life.

"Oh hell," she mumbled softly to herself.

"What?"

"Even in her mugshot this girl is pretty. Now I know why you want to help her."

"I honestly hadn't noticed."

"Jason, she looks like Snow White."

"Do you have a name or not?"

More mumbling, then Karen said, "Okay. There is a name. Kate Caldwell; D.O.B. eighth August ninety-one."

Jason had been sure her prints were going to be a dead end. His surprise broke through the pain. "What's she in the system for?"

"Being an airhead."

"Karen. C'mon."

More tapping on the keyboard. "Er. Looks like our princess got herself a drunk and disorderly charge some eight years back."

Surely it couldn't be this easy? "Is there an address with that?"

"You have a pen?"

"Yeah," he lied.

"Fifty-six Mayflower House, Gurton Estate—"

"In Bethnal Green?"

"Yeah. You know it?"

He rubbed his side, the ache around his ribs burning up. "I know it."

"Why do I feel you're about to do something stupid?"

"I'm not." It wasn't a lie. He'd already done the stupid thing by going there. "I'm heading home."

"I'm glad someone can."

He wanted to apologise. To tell her to forget the CCTV and go home to the bottle of wine he'd purchased from the corner shop and left on her doorstep before he'd headed off. "Want me to come and keep you company?"

"No, go home. I'll call you when I've found something."

She said *when*. Did that mean she'd started to believe him, or was she now just humouring him?

"Oh, Karen?"

"Yes?"

"Just for the record…her hair's brown, not black."

Karen hung up.

Jason headed back to the main road. He hailed the first taxi that came along.

"Havana Road in Peckham, mate." He struggled into the back and collapsed onto the seat. "Actually, go via a hospital."

CHAPTER SIXTEEN

Kate plumped her pillow and tried again to get comfortable.

Ceaseless questions clouded her mind: Who was she? Why had nobody reported her missing? What had she been doing on the bridge? But, hard as she tried, no answers came forth. She glanced at the pad beside her bed – still just a collection of blank pages. The doctor had promised she'd remember something, so why hadn't she?

She sat up, stretched the ache from her spine, and swung her legs out of bed. Sleep wasn't finding her, at least not in the foreseeable future, and certainly not while the rattle of trolleys in the corridor shuttled past on the hour, every hour.

She stood, the floor cold beneath her bare feet, and walked to the door. Two nurses sat at their station a little way down the corridor, chatting about something. Kate couldn't quite hear what. A vending machine stood at the other end of the corridor, a coffee machine next to that. Hopefully the thing dished out free hot drinks – although what she liked was anyone's guess. Maybe it would trigger a memory and she'd finally have something to write in that damn pad.

To her surprise, the drinks machine *was* free – at least, the hot water was. The tea bags, coffee and hot chocolate sachets came with a price. Kate pressed a few buttons and hoped something would drop from one of the spouts. Who was she kidding? Luck had run out on her the night she fell from the bridge.

She caught her reflection in the glass door of the vending machine. Dark hair, blue eyes, porcelain skin – the girl in the glass was a total stranger. Who the hell was she? She lowered her gaze and exhaled, not liking this unknown person who watched her. When she turned towards her room she collided straight into someone's chest. She glanced up, an apology mumbling past her lips, and recognised the forensics man, although his name escaped her.

He winced and stepped back. One arm was wrapped around his side; the other reached out as if ready to steady her. Jason – that was his name.

Kate felt her face warm. She straightened. She wanted to chastise him for sneaking up on her and standing so close, but he looked rough – as though he'd been through a war. The neck of his T-shirt was ripped. Light bruising shaded his cheek, dried blood trailed from the brow above his left eye, and scuffs grazed his jawline. As if he knew what she was thinking, he lowered his hand from his ribs.

"Are you okay? Shall I call a doctor?" she said.

"I'm fine."

"What happened to you?"

"Oh, this?" He glanced down at his shirt. "It's nothing."

His sudden show of strength didn't fool her. Regardless, she decided to leave it be. "So, what brings you here this time of night?"

"I came to see you." He leaned past her and slipped a coin into the drink machine. "What did you want?"

He motioned to the machine.

Kate shrugged. "Your guess is as good as mine."

Jason pressed a button and water spurted from the spout, filling the plastic cup with a brown liquid that finished with a layer of froth.

He removed the cup and handed it to her. "Every girl I know likes hot chocolate."

Kate took the cup but didn't drink.

"Your prints came back with a name: Kate Caldwell."

"Really? My name is Kate?"

"Has nobody been by to tell you yet?"

Kate shook her head. "Does that mean you know where I live? That I can go home?"

Jason's gaze hardened. "The address we have on file is derelict."

"Derelict? You mean empty?"

"I mean it's a squat in Bethnal Green."

"So I'm a squatter? I don't feel like I'm a squatter."

"Your designer clothes would agree with you."

"So, what then?"

"Does Bethnal Green ring any bells?"

Kate thought. She knew Bethnal Green was in the East End but, other than that, it meant nothing to her.

She shook her head. "What else did you find?"

"Your arrest record."

"Arrest record? What was I arrested for?"

"D and D."

Kate frowned.

"Drunk and disorderly." He gave her a moment to let that sink in, then said, "It was a while ago and juvenile stuff."

Kate sighed. "How long ago?"

Jason shrugged. "Uni age. Can you remember being at university?"

Kate stared at him. Was he trying to be funny? He knew damn full well she couldn't answer that. She glanced down at the drink – steam floating from the cup. "So, this squat. Is it my address or not?"

"I would say it used to be – but not anymore."

"So where did I move to?"

"I don't know yet."

He shifted his feet. It caused him to wince and his shoulders tensed. His face hardened and he took a measured breath. When he exhaled, it was very slowly.

It was a moment before he looked at her again. "There was a man at the squat."

Kate didn't wait for him to elaborate. "Did he do that to your face?"

Jason eyed her, but it was clear he wasn't going to give anything away. "He had a tattoo of a bird on his hand."

"Bird?"

"A blue swallow." Still he watched her. "The other morning you murmured the words 'blue bird' in your sleep."

"I don't remember." Why couldn't she remember? "Do you think I know him?"

Again, Jason shrugged. "It could just be a coincidence."

Kate didn't believe him for a second. His whole body seemed closed off to her. What was he hiding?

"Is this man dangerous?"

"No."

"And yet you look like you've gone ten rounds with Tyson." She sipped her drink. Jason was right. Hot chocolate was nice.

She stepped past him and headed back towards her room. Why couldn't she remember the tattoo if she was talking about it in her sleep? Surely something like that should trigger a memory – like the doctor said. Or maybe she didn't know this man and that's why the tattoo wasn't familiar to her.

She pushed open her door and entered. The mattress wasn't comfortable. Hard as nails, in fact, but she perched on the bed and crossed her legs. Jason remained in the doorway.

"You know," she said, "blue bird could mean anything."

"You're right. It could."

"You don't look convinced."

"I don't do coincidences." Jason crossed his arms. "Are you sure you don't remember a tattoo? Think hard."

"I am." Kate sat the chocolate down on the side table. "Don't you think I want to remember something? This whole thing is driving me insane. I can't go home because I don't know where home is. I can't stay here because I'm not technically ill." She put her head in her hands and mumbled through her fingers. "I just can't remember."

"I don't mean to push you—"

Kate whipped her head up. "Why have the police not brought this information to me?"

Jason uncrossed his arms. His face had softened a little but now he looked uncomfortable.

"I mean, it's almost midnight," Kate continued. "And I thought your job was to gather information…not dispense it."

"They'll probably be here first thing. I just thought you had a right to know, is all." He turned for the corridor. "I'll let you get some rest."

Something wasn't right. Kate jumped off the bed and rushed after him. "You being here – it's not even official, is it?"

Jason stopped and faced her. "You'd better get some sleep."

"What are you not telling me?"

Jason turned away.

"How do you expect me to trust you if you keep the truth from me?"

Jason headed towards the lift and pressed the button. The doors made him wait no more than a couple of seconds before they slid apart. "Get some sleep, Kate," he said, and stepped inside.

She watched the doors close behind him. So that was it? He turned up out of the blue and at this late hour, asked some questions, and then disappeared again? She glanced at the fire exit and wondered if she'd beat him to the ground floor. The two nurses at the station looked her way but seemed unbothered that she was out of bed. Kate ignored them and turned back for her room.

She paused. Something familiar…

The painting hanging on the wall outside her room – a wooden cabin set on what looked to be a Swiss mountaintop. She glanced at the signature – Alexandre Calame.

The corridor darkened and images gushed forth, flashing across her mind like a flick book: an empty gallery, a bench, a man in a blue uniform, stairs, large doors, snow.

Then the corridor lightened again.

Kate reached for the wall to steady herself. Had she just remembered something? It didn't seem over familiar now.

She hurried back to her room and grabbed the pad beside her bed.

Finally, she had something to write in it.

CHAPTER SEVENTEEN

Jason sat on a hospital bed a couple of floors below Kate's room.

The hospital's fucking Christmas tunes seemed to follow him wherever he went in this bloody place. He at least thought A&E would acknowledge the late hour. He hadn't even wanted to come here, but he'd had enough cuts in his time to know his eye needed stitches. During the initial examination, the doctor reckoned five would suffice. By Jason's count, the doctor was about to staple the sixth.

The curtain whipped back and Karen hurried inside. A scarf wrapped her neck and blotches reddened her cheeks. She froze when she saw Jason, her eyes fixed not on his face but on his bare torso.

Jason shifted and felt his chest, remembering he was shirtless, and rubbed the bandage that secured his two broken ribs.

The doctor tutted. "I cannot stitch if you move."

Karen reached for her hair, her cheeks colouring further.

"What took you so long?" Jason said.

Now she looked him in the eye. "You're kidding, right?"

Jason didn't respond. He just wanted to put on his damn top again.

Karen slid the curtain along its runner and closed it–much less erratically than when she'd entered. When she turned to him again she had the look of a headmistress hardening her eyes.

"You told me you were going straight home," she said, the sudden burst of attraction she'd shown him moments earlier now completely gone.

"Remember that thing about my sister that everyone thinks isn't a thing? Well, I think I ran into it tonight." Jason reached behind him and passed her the tissue-wrapped cap.

"Keep still," the doctor ordered.

Karen frowned but took the bundle of hankies. "What is it?"

"It's a hat."

Karen tilted her head. "I mean, what am I supposed to do with it?"

"Run a DNA test on it."

"Isn't DNA supposed to be your job?"

"I can't do it. You know that."

"And how the hell am I supposed to do it?"

"Put a false job number on it and give it to one of the other techs to deal with."

The doctor clicked the last staple and stood back. "You're all good to go." He pushed the small trolley back against the wall and headed towards the curtain. "Those ribs need rest," he called over his shoulder, as though he knew his words fell on deaf ears.

Karen waited for him to disappear around the curtain. Then, back at Jason, "I said the CCTV was the last time I'd help you."

Jason hopped off the bed. "It's all linked. I promise you." He grabbed his top from the back of the chair.

Karen's lips hardened. "This debt you owe me is racking up."

Jason smiled, but Karen tutted and turned away. Still, he knew she wouldn't let him down.

"It's also urgent," he said. He was pushing his luck big time.

"It's going to be two weeks before FSP come back with a result, you know that better than anyone."

"I know." He stretched his top over his head and winced. He half hoped she'd offer to help. Instead, she waited until he'd pulled the top down over the bandage.

"You need a lift home?"

Jason shook his head. He reached for his jacket and winked. "Just keep at it with the CCTV."

"Yeah, about that…I found something on the camera in the alley."

"What?"

"A car. Couldn't see the occupant and there was no violence involved – at least, not that I saw." She bit her lip. "Leah got in the car."

"You run the plate?"

Karen slipped a piece of paper from her pocket, an uncertain look in her eyes as she handed it to him. "Please tell me you're not going to do something stupid."

Jason looked at the paper. "This all you found?"

"So far."

"Good." He leaned forward and kissed her cheek, a normal gesture between them eight months earlier. Now, though, it felt misplaced. "Keep with it."

Jason wanted to check out the address Karen had given him.

Instead, he kicked shut his front door and headed straight for the kitchen. Opened the fridge, grabbed a beer, and took it to the living room. He didn't bother removing his jacket. Couldn't face the agony of it if he was totally honest with himself. His whole body ached from head to foot. But not as much as his pride for copping that beating.

He settled on the sofa as best he could. No position was comfortable – or none that he could find. So, he sipped his beer, pretended it numbed the pain, and glanced around the room. Boxing trophies crowded the glass cabinet. Photographs of himself and Leah lined the mantle. Framed advertising posters for his fights hung on the walls. He'd been good in his day. Unbeatable.

He swigged his beer. Tonight, though, he'd fought like a fucking pussy.

His ribs ached like shit, but he sat forward, planting his feet wide apart. Newspaper clippings covering Leah's death, and paperwork he'd swiped from the office covered the coffee table. He'd been so close to the man Jimmy the Junkie had talked about. The tattoo wasn't a coincidence. And neither was the fact he was at the same address Leah was supposed to have frequented. Shit. How could he have been so fucking careless? His hands started to shake and his vision honed in on a particular press clipping – the headline calling out his sister's death as nothing but a drunken addict's accident.

He threw the beer bottle across the room.

Immediately, he grabbed his side and pressed his hand against his ribs. Tried to calm his breathing. Swallowed.

Tried to wash the dryness from his throat. The beer ran down the magnolia-painted wall and he cursed. Now he had to clean that shit up. Fuck. He ruffled his hair, his short fingernails scratching the stress from his scalp. If ever he'd wanted to disappear into his garage and go a few rounds on his punch bag, it was now.

His side hurt like hell – more tender now than when he'd first arrived at the hospital. For fuck's sake. He wasn't even up to working on his motorcycle.

He looked back at the beer. Then towards the kitchen. Hell, he needed to take a leak anyway. He got up from the sofa, winced, cursed, and hobbled to the kitchen. Grabbing the remaining beers, he took them into the bathroom with him. Put them down on the washing basket and lifted the toilet seat – another movement he wasn't expecting to hurt as much as it did. He peed, he flushed, and he turned on the shower – he might as well go all out. He wriggled out of his clothes, removed the bandage, grabbed a beer, and stepped beneath the water.

And that's where he remained. Just letting the hot water cascade down his body. It seemed to be the only thing he'd found that didn't hurt. He swigged the beer and rocked forward until his forehead rested on the tiles. He'd recover from this. He needed to recover from this.

His mind drifted. For months he'd searched for clues about his sister's death. Then this Kate woman falls in the Thames and a busload of them come along all at once. She had to be involved in Leah's death somehow. There were too many connections. The elusive Bethnal Green flat for starters. What was the link between them?

Thoughts of the casino broke through the haze of theories. It had been Leah's place of work for many years, yet they claimed she'd been sacked a fortnight before her death – even though she'd asked him to pick her up there that night. The casino was hiding something – and it was more than just not wanting to be associated with any drug-using staff.

He turned off the shower and grabbed a towel from the rail. Gave up trying to dry himself after only fifteen seconds, and swapped the towel for his dressing gown. With the rest of the beers in hand, he trudged back into the living room. Finished his bottle, opted for a late-night Stallone movie, and settled on the sofa as best he could.

He cracked opened another beer.

The doorbell rang – followed by a rhythmic tapping on the door.

Only one person knocked like that.

"You know where the key is," Jason shouted out. That hurt as well.

He heard the key in the lock and then the door opened and closed again. Ed walked into the room, muttered something about beer, and headed straight to the kitchen.

"They're here." Jason held up an unopened bottle and waited for his friend to return. "Don't you ever sleep?"

"Karen called me." Ed took the bottle and fell into the chair opposite. "She's worried, you know."

"She needn't be."

"No?" Ed twisted the cap and swigged from the neck. "How'd you do the eye?"

"Fell."

"Fuck. On what?"

Jason drank. He kept drinking until the bottle ran dry.

"What are you doing?" Ed passed him another. "You may as well talk to me, mate."

"You don't wanna hear it."

"Try me." Ed settled back in the chair.

Jason eyed him. Ed had loved Leah, Jason knew that, but how Ed had so easily accepted her death as an accident – just like everybody else – was something Jason couldn't understand.

He swigged another mouthful of beer. "You gonna sit there all night?"

"Depends. You gonna tell me what's going on?"

Another swig of beer. "I gotta go see a guy about a car in the morning."

"Buying or selling?"

"Just enquiring."

"You want company?"

"You driving?"

"I am now."

CHAPTER EIGHTEEN

Tower Bridge was within touching distance.

A regal magnificence outshining every stunning skyscraper behind it. Just as glistening Canary Wharf stood proud way off in the distance and dwarfed a much closer Wapping. It was the kind of view Tav had imagined having upon his retirement – if the casinos didn't keep robbing him of his hard-earned money.

He pulled himself away from the view and looked at the passport he held. In the thirty minutes he'd spent exploring all four luxurious floors in the Shad Thames apartment, this was the only evidence he'd found that Kate had indeed been staying here. He threw the passport into the bowl on the side table and walked through to the kitchen. Held on the fridge by a magnet was a note – someone called Charlotte along with a number and a return date, which was two days from now.

He placed his bag on the floor, unzipped it, and took out a small, black box, two wires extending from one end of it. He sat it on the middle shelf of the fridge, pressed the small switch, and slowly trapped the wires against the door jamb as he closed it.

Back in the main room, he glanced around and sighed. It was a gorgeous place whose price tag came with seven zeros, and the prospect of destroying it saddened him. Nevertheless, shit happened. He slung his bag over his shoulder and walked across the room to the private lift, still a little miserable that he had to leave.

The door opened and he pulled the brim of his new cap down low before stepping inside. He knew the security camera in the corner of the elevator would be recording his every move.

The doors closed and the elevator descended towards the ground floor. When the doors pulled back, it was the garage parking lot that greeted him. He exited, eyeing the fine collection of Ferraris, Astons, and Maseratis. Then, casual as you like, he whistled his way between the cars and left the building.

Yes, he could definitely see himself living somewhere like this.

His mobile started to vibrate and, seeing it was Jimmy, he answered. "What you got for me?"

"Notta lot. My source said Wade's sister's file is off limits."

"Officially?"

"I dunno, man. That's all he'd say."

"Anyone else you can ask?"

"None with those kinda connections."

"I want you to dig up everything you can on this Wade guy. That includes his sister." Tav hung up.

No sooner had he slipped his phone into his pocket than it vibrated again. This time it was a withheld number. He answered, knowing all too well who would reply.

"You owe me money, Finley," the voice said.

"And you'll get it as soon as I finish this job."

"I don't like waiting."

"And I don't like people snapping pictures of my comatose girlfriend. You pull a stunt like that again and I'll come find you sooner than you'd like. You hear me?"

The caller laughed. "Then pay me so our business can be put to bed."

"Seven days. But if you go near her again…"

"You have until Wednesday. Then it's open season on the care home."

Tav waited for the line to go dead before swapping the phone for the newly acquired bottle of pills he'd scored. He tipped one into his palm, stared at it, then tipped out another two. He flung them into his mouth, swallowed two and chewed the other until he'd consumed it.

The buzz was instant. Not too much of a distraction but enough to feel the agitation simmer down. Slightly.

CHAPTER NINETEEN

Jason opened his eyes.

He immediately wished he hadn't.

He lay still for a moment, letting the ache behind his eyes settle, then opened them again. He turned his head. The sofa had been his bed for the night. Empty beer bottles covered the coffee table and leftover kebabs stank the whole place out.

"What time is it?" he mumbled to Ed.

Ed stirred. He remained in the armchair, still wearing his jacket, his half-eaten kebab on his lap. "Too early to be awake."

Jason reached for his phone. Ten past six. Shit. They'd only just gone to sleep. He tried to rub some life into his eyes. Failed. And sat up. Pain cramped his stomach, a reminder of the arse-whooping he'd taken at the squat, and clasped his ribs.

"I need to go out," he said to Ed.

Ed moved the kebab to the table and straightened. He stretched, something Jason wished he could do, and yawned – loudly. "The bogus car enquiry, right?"

Jason ignored the jibe. "You still driving?"

"Like I have a bloody choice."

Jason pushed himself up and stood. He tried to stretch. Raised his arm to his shoulder before his ribs called time.

"First, I need a shower," he said, heading for the bathroom.

It didn't seem to bother Ed that the six bottles of beer he'd consumed hours earlier probably still had him over the drink-drive limit.

Then again, not much ever bothered Ed.

Jason glanced at the paper Karen had given him. *Jean Smith. 63 Victoria Road.* Ed passed number fifty-seven. Three houses on and Jason called for him to stop the car.

Ed did. "You want me to pull in?"

A red Volvo sat on the driveway in front of the house, its number plate a match. "Nah, just pull across the entrance." Jason opened the car door.

"Want me with you?"

Jason shook his head. "This won't take long." He climbed out, biting back the discomfort, and shut the door.

The driveway wasn't too long considering the house was enormous. A typical design for this affluent part of the neighbourhood. Jason reached the front door and pressed the bell. Inside, he heard a female shouting that her kids were going to be late for school.

Opening the door, she paused as though she'd expected to see someone other than Jason standing there.

She pushed her fringe behind her ear. "Yes?"

"Morning, my name is Jason Wade, with the Metropolitan Police. I am making enquiries regarding this vehicle." He pointed at the Volvo. "Are you Jean Smith?"

"Yes."

"Does anybody else have access to this vehicle?"

"No. I mean, only my husband does."

"And your husband's name?"

The woman's eyes narrowed. "Can I see some identification first?"

Jason reached for his wallet and pulled out his card.

The woman looked at it. "Says you're a scenes of crime officer."

"Yes, with the Metropolitan Police. This vehicle may be linked to a case I am currently investigating."

"Then why are the police not questioning me?"

"Because I am."

She glanced at the card again. "You could have had that card printed at Snappy Snaps."

"But I didn't."

"How do I know that, though?"

Jason sighed. Usually, he'd tell whomever to check his credentials by phoning the police. However, this occasion did not offer that option. He turned to Ed, still sitting in the car, the window wound all the way down. Jason really didn't want to drag him into this any more than he had already, but he waved him over.

"Ma'am, this is Detective Sergeant Price."

Ed nodded and smiled.

Jason turned to Ed. "Mrs. Smith would like to see some official I.D. before she answers my questions."

Ed pulled a black wallet from his trouser pocket. Flipping it open, he flashed his warrant card. Mrs. Smith glanced at it, then up at Ed.

She turned back to Jason. "I'm sorry, but you cannot be too careful these days."

"I understand. Now, can you confirm your husband's name?"

She briefly glanced Ed's way. "Kevin Smith."

"And he has use of your car?" Jason said.

Mrs. Smith nodded. "Sure, sometimes. But he has his own car. Look, what is this about?"

"Is your husband home?"

"He's asleep. He works nights."

"Ma'am, can you tell me who was driving this vehicle on April sixth?"

"Well, probably me. My husband has his own car, like I said."

"Ma'am, I need you to be sure."

"I can check the calendar." She hovered. "Would you like to wait inside?"

"Thank you." Jason stepped over the threshold.

Ed followed, pushing the door to behind him. Both men waited in the hallway – a wide corridor with all the trimmings of a family that hadn't held back on the expense when decorating it.

Mrs. Smith hurried to the kitchen.

"What is it you're looking for?" Ed quietly asked.

"You're not going to like it."

"Well, that's a given."

Jason exhaled. "Leah was seen getting in to that Volvo."

Ed looked at him. "That's it?"

Mrs. Smith returned. In her hand she held an A5 diary. She began to flick through the pages and stopped on April sixth. "Okay, I used it during the day." She looked up. "Running the usual errands."

"What about the evening?" Jason asked.

She looked back at the book. "I didn't drive it."

"Are you sure?"

"I was out with friends. I took a cab."

"How about your husband? Did he drive it?"

"He has his own car."

Jason glanced towards the stairs. "Ma'am, can you go and get your husband for me, please?"

"He's asleep. I told you, he works nights."

"I know, and I appreciate that this is not ideal, but I do need to talk to him."

Mrs. Smith glanced at Ed, who offered nothing in return. She turned back to Jason. "Can you tell me what this is about?"

"I'm sorry. I cannot discuss information pertaining to an ongoing investigation."

She held his stare for a couple of seconds, her eyes wide. The not knowing looked to be eating her up. "I'll go and wake him."

She disappeared up the circular staircase.

Ed leaned in. "Jason, please don't tell me I'm here to assist in another of your fuck-ups."

"Okay, I won't."

Footsteps sounded on the stairs and a man, bare-foot and half asleep, plodded down. He pulled a T-shirt over his head and ruffled his hair.

Reaching the bottom, he held out his hand. "Hi, I'm Kevin Smith."

Halfway up the stairs, the wife hung back, almost out of sight, ear-wigging.

Jason shook Mr. Smith's hand. "I'm Jason Wade and this is Detective Sergeant Price. Your wife's Volvo flagged up as a car of interest on the evening sixth April and I am trying to trace the driver. Would that be you?"

"I don't drive the Volvo. I have my own car."

"Which is?"

"An Audi."

"And where is it right now? It isn't parked outside."

"It's in the garage for a service. Look, what is all this about?"

Jason glanced towards the stairs. "Can you tell me where you were on the evening of April sixth?"

Mr. Smith laughed. It didn't cover his nervousness. "Look, do I need to call my solicitor?"

"You are always free to call a solicitor, Mr. Smith," Ed chimed in. "But that would involve us all going down to the station. At the moment, we are only here to eliminate the Volvo from our enquiries."

Smith turned back to face Jason. "I have no idea where I was. It was months ago."

"Your wife says she was out with friends and did not drive the car that night." Jason let that sink in. "And yet the Volvo was spotted at a Mayfair Casino."

"Ah, well then, there definitely has to be a mistake. I don't gamble. Have never even been to a casino, let alone one in Mayfair. Maybe it's a different car."

"The CCTV footage we have says different."

The colour drained from Mr. Smith's cheeks. Now he glanced towards the stairs. His wife remained there, listening.

He leaned closer to Jason. "Can we speak outside?"

Jason shrugged and turned for the door.

Ed stood to one side, allowed Mr. Smith to lead, then followed him outside.

Mr. Smith reached past him and pulled the door to. He spoke in a hushed tone. "Okay, yes, I was probably there."

"Probably?"

"I sometimes go there."

"To gamble?"

Mr. Smith shook his head. He swallowed. Exhaled. "I go there for women."

"Women?"

"Look, if my wife ever found out, it would be the end of my marriage. I am not prepared to lose everything over a hooker."

Jason's shoulders tensed. He stepped forward, but Ed pushed him back.

"Mr. Smith," Ed said, "are you saying you were obtaining the services of a prostitute at the casino?"

Mr. Smith glanced at the ground. "I know it's wrong, but my wife, she's always so tired…"

"Mr. Smith, do you know the name of this prostitute?"

"Yes, well, they give me names, but I always assumed they were aliases."

"So, there was more than one girl?" Ed flicked a glance towards Jason. "How did you book these girls?"

"Through the casino."

"The casino supplies them?"

Mr. Smith nodded. "My friend told me about them. It's all very discreet and only for a select clientele. The girls are upmarket but not afraid to try out new things, if you know what I mean."

Jason pulled Leah's picture from his pocket. It was from a couple of years back, when her hair was glossy and her eyes still had that sparkle.

He held it inches from Mr. Smith's face. "Is this one of them?"

Mr. Smith nodded. "Leila. Yes. Nice girl. I often asked for her…"

Again, Jason's arms tensed. He clenched his jaw and started to rock lightly on the balls of his feet – anything to stop him from knocking this jerk on his arse.

"She became unavailable though."

"Oh?" Ed interjected. "Why?"

"When?" Jason added.

Mr. Smith shrugged. "I saw her on the sixth. My wife had gone out and the kids were with her parents. I was lonely and the back seat in my car…well, it just isn't big enough—"

"You had sex with her?" Jason said.

Smith shook his head. "She wanted money. I was there to meet another girl, but Leila showed up at my window. I was pleased at first. I mean, I thought she was back to working, you know."

"So, what happened?" Ed said.

"She got in my car and I began driving. Turns out she just wanted money from me – to get out of town. Was desperate, in fact. I always liked her, but I'm a businessman. I don't hand out cash for free, if you know what I mean?"

Jason punched him.

Ed pulled him back. Jason went for a second punch, catching Smith across the side of the head.

Smith went down. He clasped his head. A little blood trickled from his nose.

Ed pushed Jason back and glared at him. "Get in the car now."

Jason remained where he was. Rage hardened his body. He wanted to haul this twat off the floor just so he could knock him straight back down again.

"I said get in the car." Ed nudged him back. Forceable this time.

Slowly, Jason turned. He still had questions, but Ed had that look that Jason didn't want to fuck with. He stormed off towards the car. Got in and slammed the door shut. He clasped his ribs. Punching that little wanker had hurt like hell but was worth every ounce of pain. Through the open window, he watched Ed help Mr. Smith to his feet.

"I'm going to complain," Smith cried.

Ed leaned in, muttered something, and Smith's face whitened. Ed tossed him a tissue. Muttered something else, then headed back towards the car.

He yanked the driver's door open and got in. Grabbed the steering wheel. Inhaled. Held it. Exhaled. Started the engine. But didn't move.

Then he exploded. "What the fuck was all that about?"

"You heard how he spoke about Leah. The prick deserved it."

"Shit, Jason." Ed shook his head, exasperation reddening his cheeks.

"What did you say to him, anyway?"

"If he complains I'll charge him with kerb crawling and his wife will find out her car's been used as a knocking-shop-on-wheels." Ed closed his eyes. "God help us if he ignores my threat and grows a pair, because then we've both had it."

"He doesn't have the balls."

"Fuck, you have to get your shit together." Ed pulled the rear-view mirror to face him. Wiped his forehead, then checked his watch. "I've got a couple of things to do at the nick, then I need to get to the hospital – the amnesiac girl's bag was found yesterday. Had her address inside."

"Oh? Where she live?"

"Fuck knows. South side of the river somewhere. Her prints also came back with a name, so I'll kill two birds with one stone."

"I'll do it. I've nothing on at work."

Ed seemed to contemplate it. "Nah, you got a date with the shrink, remember?"

Jason closed his eyes. That was the last place he wanted to be.

Ed pulled away from the kerb. At the end of the road he turned right – towards the doc's place.

Jason sunk into the chair and rested his head against the window. Ed telling Kate her name when Kate already knew it was another headache he now had to deal with.

CHAPTER TWENTY

Jason walked into Doctor Tandy's office.

After barging in the night before, it was the last place on earth he wanted to be, and he certainly didn't intend on staying for the full hour she'd no doubt demand. Maybe ten minutes – if she was lucky. Besides, his head was at the hospital. He needed to get to Kate before Ed and ask her – no, tell her…shit, beg her – not to let on he'd already told her her name. After this morning, he didn't need Ed on his case any more than he was already.

Tandy's assistant answered her phone then glanced up. "Doctor Tandy will see you now."

Jason stood, thought about making a run for the exit, and entered her office. Tandy sat behind her desk. She looked good – well turned out and groomed considering the late hours she'd been working the night before.

She didn't glance up, so Jason closed the door and took the seat opposite her. She continued to jot on her pad and Jason couldn't help but wonder if this was his punishment for barging into her office only hours before and then running out on her.

He waited. Patiently. The minutes ticked by inside his head.

When Tandy finally looked up, she wore a light scowl. "Did you get much sleep?"

"Sorry?"

"I assume you didn't. Especially after rushing out of here last night to deal with what could only have been a life or death emergency."

Jason smiled. "I apologise for last night."

"I would rather have an explanation."

"I don't have one. But, I shouldn't have come here. I'm sorry."

"And yet you did."

"I got lost." Jason shifted in his seat. "Listen, doc, can we get down to business so you can stamp my time card and I can get out of here?"

The doc eyed him. She tapped her pen on the pad, forced a smile, and sat back in her chair. "Please, talk away."

Jason grinned. "What? No probing?"

"Would you respect my questions by answering them?"

"Depends."

"On?"

"The calibre of the question."

Tandy lay her pen on the desk and crossed her arms. "What have you done since you woke up this morning?"

Jason frowned. "I thought you needed to assess my behaviour in regard to my sister's death."

"I am."

"By asking about this morning?"

"If it's insignificant then you won't have a problem answering."

Jason cocked a smile. The woman was clever, he'd give her that. "I was working."

"And the case? Would that be related to Leah?"

"If I said it was, what then?"

"I would ask that you share your thoughts on it."

Jason looked at her. His earlier anger had evaporated. "It appears that Leah really did have more than one job title."

"And how does that make you feel?"

"Angry. Frustrated." Jason stretched his hands and flexed his fingers. Tandy hadn't asked what the job was. Leah's extra-curricular activities were obvious to everyone but him. He exhaled. "I should have picked her up that night."

"The night of her death?"

Jason nodded. "She asked me for help and I fell short."

"Trying to make up for it now is not going to help her."

"Maybe not." He thought of Kate in the hospital. "But it may help someone else."

CHAPTER TWENTY-ONE

The food sat on the tray in front of her.

Kate turned her head, the nauseating scent of the eggs making her wish she'd lost her sense of smell as well as her memory. She pushed the tray away and looked around the small hospital room. No television. Nothing to read. Nobody to talk to. And she still couldn't remember who she was.

The crooked, polystyrene ceiling tile caught her attention. It didn't sit right in the metal bracket like the other ones did. It had bothered her for the best part of yesterday – so much so that she'd stood on the bed and tried to realign it. She'd not been able to and had stared at it last night until she'd fallen asleep. And now, there it was again, taunting her.

She forced herself to look away. Drawn curtains brought gloom into the room. It matched her mood, and she pushed back the covers and slipped her legs out of bed. Her bare feet quickly withdrew from the cold floor – Not even a pair of slippers or socks to wear. She shook her head and stood. Two steps to the window and, behind the curtains, the same snow-covered view she'd scrutinised the day before.

A yawn found her, and she stretched it away, hoping it would energise her tired body. It didn't. She rubbed her eyes. Still felt tired and pushed her hair off her face. It felt matted and her fingers struggled to comb through it. Finally, she gave up, and turned back to the room.

The wonky tile called for her attention again.

She glared at it.

Fine. It wanted a war? She'd give it a war.

She climbed onto the bed and stretched for the ceiling. As was the case yesterday, her fingertips barely touched the polystyrene.

A light tap at the door and she turned to see Jason peering in at her.

Concern quickly darkened his features. "Nice to see you're up and about."

Kate stopped stretching. She clasped the back of her gown together and quickly sat on the bed. God, she hoped he hadn't seen anything.

Jason entered the room, armed with several magazines. "How are you feeling?" He winced when he turned to close the door behind him.

Kate glanced at the magazines. "Are they some sort of apology?"

"Yes."

Kate pulled the blankets over her legs. She hadn't expected complete honesty from him, so decided to let last night go. "You going to tell me how you really got the black eye?"

"I got punched."

More honesty. Would the surprises never end? "On purpose?"

"Is there any other kind?" He stepped forward and laid the variety of reading material on the bed. "Wasn't sure what you liked."

"That makes two of us." Kate gave them a quick once over. Some women's magazines, one on gardening and home decorating. Two daily newspapers: *The Guardian* and *The Sun*. Nothing that perked her interest to look inside. "Thank you, anyway."

Jason waited, his hand tapping impatiently against his leg.

"Do you need to take more fingerprints?"

He stopped tapping. "There's going to be a police officer – a DS Ed Price – come see you today. He's going to tell you your name."

Kate frowned. "But you told me that last night."

"Yes. But I need you to forget it again until he tells you himself."

"Why?"

"Can you just forget I told you?"

"If you tell me what's going on. I may not be able to remember anything, but I'm not stupid. What was with you – turning up here in the middle of the night talking about Bethnal Green and blue birds?"

"It's just another case I am working on."

"Then why ask me about it?"

Jason half laughed. "It's nothing. Just two cases linked to the same address. That's all. It happens. A lot."

"And you expect me to believe that?"

"This officer is also going to take you home."

"I thought you said my place in Bethnal Green was a squat."

"The police now have another address – south side of the river."

Kate crossed her legs and rested her elbows on her knees.

Jason watched her. Again, he started to tap his leg. It was more annoying than the wonky ceiling tile.

"I went to the Golden Jubilee Bridge last night." Jason pushed the magazines to one side and perched on the end of the bed. His face tightened and he reached for his ribs while he repositioned himself.

He'd taken more than a punch to the eye yesterday, that was for sure.

Jason saw her watching and his hand dropped away. "I found evidence which leads me to believe you did not jump."

"Then how did I end up in the water? Was I deliberately thrown over?"

Again, Jason winced. This time he tried to disguise it with a smile. "Nothing that dramatic."

Kate liked it when he smiled. He didn't look like such an arsehole.

"It was probably a mugging gone wrong. Have any of Thursday night's events come back to you yet?"

"Actually, last night after you left." Kate reached for the pad and handed it to him. "The painting on the wall outside. I remembered it, or just quick flashes of it."

Jason glanced at the pad – at her scribblings. "I think you were at the National Gallery. Do you remember going there on Thursday?"

Kate shook her head.

"One of their postcards – a print of a painting – was in your coat pocket."

"Sorry. I only remembered these flashes." She sat up straight and ran her fingers through her hair. It still felt tangled. "I'm not much help, am I?"

When Jason smiled this time, it looked genuinely warm and inviting.

"Do you really think I was there?"

"Maybe."

The smile slowly faded from his lips but he remained watching her, his gaze lingering for longer than she thought necessary. He cleared his throat and turned from her. Got off the bed, and walked to the window.

"I get the feeling there's something else you want to say," she said.

Jason turned to her. He pursed his lips and began the leg tapping again. Only, this time, it was short-lived.

He moved towards the door. "I'll submit what I've found. The police will investigate it."

"Are you coming back?"

Jason shook his head. "I just wanted you to know you're probably not a suicide threat."

"What if I remember something?"

Jason paused. He reached inside his jacket and pulled out a pen and a business card. He scribbled on the back of it and laid it on the tray. "You can get me on that number."

He turned back to the door and opened it.

She clasped the card in her hand. "I don't know what's going on with you, but I won't let the officer know you've been here."

Jason looked at her and rubbed his chin. He hesitated and glanced back out into the corridor. When he faced her again, he looked uncertain whether to leave or not. Kate waited for him to elaborate – to answer her even – but he didn't. Whatever it was that bothered him, he was nowhere near ready to confide in her. Instead, he turned and left.

Kate stared at the back of the door, half expecting him to reopen it and walk back in.

She waited. And waited. But Jason never returned.

CHAPTER TWENTY-TWO

In Jason's mind, his body was capable of hurrying up the steps.

In reality, his two broken ribs made him pay dearly for it. He gripped his side and slowed his pace. He bloody hated feeling like this – like an incapacitated cripple unable to do his job properly. He reached the top and headed through the entrance. A security guard glanced at him then waved him through.

"Surprised you're open today. You have a shop here?" Jason asked as he passed.

The guard pointed behind him. "Follow the walkway to the right there. You'll see a cafeteria and the shop is just after that."

"Is it the only shop in here?"

"Yes, sir."

The guard moved on to the next visitor and started to check the contents of her handbag.

Jason left them to it. He followed the corridor as instructed and it wasn't long before he reached the café. Sure enough, the shop was a little way after it. He expected it to be reasonably quiet. After all, it was only eleven in the morning.

But it wasn't quiet. It was like sale day at Harrods. Shoppers stood around, some reading books, others poring over prints of paintings and parchments. Jason searched past them until he found the carousel rack. He squeezed through the crowds, holding the customers away from his ribs, and rotated the stand until he found a batch of postcards identical to the one in Kate's coat pocket.

He took one and headed over to the cashier. "Excuse me—"

"Sir, I need you to go to the back of the queue."

Jason turned to the customer currently being served. "I'm sorry. This'll only take a second."

Back to the cashier. He held up the postcard. "I just need to know—"

"Sir, this customer was here before you. You have to go to the back of the queue and wait your turn."

"But—"

The cashier glanced towards the door. Jason turned and saw a security guard standing by the shop's entrance. He hooked his thumbs into his belt and glared at Jason.

Bloody prick. But now he was paying close attention to Jason's every move.

Jason looked at the queue behind him. Four people waiting. He glanced at the cashier and wanted to scream at her. Bloody jobsworth. Instead, he spun on his heel, gritted his teeth at the pain it caused his ribs, and headed to the back of the line.

The wait was agonising. Not only because of the rush he was in, but because his ribs ached like fucking mad. The cashier continued to serve the next customer – rolling two prints, securing them with a band, and then sliding them into a carrier bag. It was too small, and she ducked behind the counter.

Jason sighed. He glanced at his watch. Ten past eleven. It felt later – like his life was slowly slipping the fuck away. The cashier reappeared with a bigger bag. Hoo-fucking-ray!

The line moved forward and Jason stepped with it.

The next customer's credit card was declined. For the love of God. They were only purchasing a three-pound notepad.

The third person moved quick. Jason liked that lad.

The next person – the one before Jason – was a foreigner who couldn't understand a word of English. After listening to the cashier trying to explain the print he wanted would cost him five ninety-nine, Jason leaned forward and threw a tenner at her.

She rung the charge through the till, passed Jason his change, and bagged the print.

Jason didn't wait for the customer to move. He side-stepped him and leaned on the counter, the postcard held up in front of him.

The cashier glanced at it, then at Jason. She was clearly less than amused. "How may I help you, sir?"

"Were you working on Thursday?"

"Are you a police officer?"

"No. But I do work with the police. A woman fell from the Golden Jubilee Footbridge and I am investigating it."

The woman narrowed her eyes. "I need to see your identification."

Jason pulled his wallet from inside his jacket. He held up one of his cards and fought back the urge to shove it down her throat.

The cashier glanced at it. Then at him.

Jason slid the card back in the wallet and flipped it shut. "Now. Can you answer the question?"

Her lips pursed and her face tightened. "I was working, yes."

"Excellent." He held the postcard out again. "Do you remember a girl – mid-twenties – purchasing one of these?"

The cashier laughed. When Jason didn't respond, her cackle came to an abrupt stop. "Do you know how many of those we sell? I can't remember the last person this morning who bought one, let alone a couple of days ago."

Jason slid his phone from his back pocket. He scrolled through some pictures and stopped on the one he'd taken of Kate at the hospital. "This girl."

The cashier looked at it and shook her head. "She looks like a million others who pass through here."

She glanced at the postcard Jason still held. "You going to buy that?"

Jason took the change she'd previously given him and fanned it out on the counter. He slid a pound coin towards her.

"It's two-fifty."

"For a piece of bloody card?"

The cashier shrugged. "It's the price you have to pay."

"It's daylight robbery." Jason slid some more coins across the counter. "And I'll have a bag."

The cashier took the cash and slapped a paper bag – a very large one – down on the counter. She smiled, a gleam of satisfaction in her eyes.

Jason took the bag and turned for the exit before his mouth could say something the lady would regret.

He paused by the security guard and held up his phone. "Do you recognise this girl?"

The guard hardly gave the picture a glance. Then shook his head.

Jason's shoulders tensed. He inhaled – too deep – and a fire exploded around his ribs. He took a second to calm down, then swapped his phone for the postcard. "Can you tell me where this painting is?"

"Level two. Room forty-six. Next to the Wohl Galleries."

"And the quickest way would be?"

"Go back to the main foyer and follow the signs."

Jason tipped his head and left the shop. In the main hall, he found signs to the Wohl Galleries and followed them up to the second floor. In room forty-six, he found the original *Chalets at Rigi* painting. The postcard did not do it justice.

This room was marginally quieter than some of the others he'd walked through. He counted five other people in here with him: two couples and a lone man. Jason perched on a nearby seat and wondered what to do next. So, Kate *might* have been here. Now what?

He glanced up at the painting. The same picture sat outside Kate's hospital room. It looked okay. Nothing special. No anomalies stood out that would explain why Kate ended up in the River Thames. It was just a painting sitting in a line of other paintings.

His hand started to shake and he ground his teeth. What was he hoping to find here –sitting on his arse, staring at a bunch of fucking paintings, not knowing what to do next?

He turned on his phone. Kate's photo remained on the screen, her brunette locks a little frazzled and her deep brown eyes overtired. Had someone tried to hurt her…tried to kill her? Or was her fall the result of something less dramatic? He thought about going to Ed and telling him about the finger marks on the bridge. He could explain his theory about her not jumping. Let Ed look into it and open an investigation – officially.

But he'd tried that with his sister – when both he and his credibility had been at the top of their game. Nobody had listened to him then and there wasn't a chance in hell anyone would listen to him now.

He glanced back at his phone. The pale-coloured hospital gown soaked up what little blush coloured her face. She'd been to hell and back.

He looked up, that damn painting still staring back at him, and stood. A guard strolled through from the other room, friendlier looking than the guard downstairs in the shop.

"Excuse me, mate." Jason gripped the phone. "Were you working on Thursday just gone?"

The guard nodded and smiled.

Jason held out his phone. "Do you recognise this girl?"

The guard pulled a pair of reading glasses from his shirt pocket and put them on. He took the phone and looked at Kate's picture for a second then handed it back and removed his glasses. "Are you a policeman?"

"No. Crime scene investigator. Do you recognise her? It's very important."

The guard nodded. "She was here. Sat looking at that painting until we closed."

"She was here all day?"

"Only left to get something to eat."

"Was she alone?"

The guard nodded.

"She didn't meet with anybody? Talk to anybody?"

"Nope. Sat alone the whole time. Nice girl. American."

"American?"

"Yes. We chatted while I walked her to the exit. Seemed a little nervous but I put that down to shyness."

"What did you talk about?"

"Oh boy. Memory ain't what it used to be. I talk to a lot of people. Now. Let me think. Um… she introduced herself as…Kim, Kelly…no, Kate. Then it was the normal chit-chat. Told me the painting was her nan's favourite. Mainly, though, we chatted about the weather. Clouds in particular."

"Clouds?"

"Yes. Was a bit strange. I mentioned the clouds were blocking out the stars and would bring more snow, and her eyes widened like they were ready to pop from her head. Then she hurried off."

"Where did she go?"

"Have no idea. I didn't watch either. We were closing up, you see."

"What time did you close?"

"On Thursday? Nine P.M."

Excitement fluttered in the pit of Jason's stomach, the same way it used to moments before he stepped into the boxing ring. A timeline was slowly beginning to knot together. Kate went over the bridge at half nine – or thereabouts. That was more than enough time to walk there from the art gallery. He'd cop a lifetime of misery, but maybe he could sweet-talk Karen into checking out her route on the CCTV cameras.

Jason's phone vibrated. He glanced down and saw he had a text from his boss telling him to get to the office ASAP. Oh, this couldn't be good.

"She is okay, isn't she?"

Jason slipped the phone into his pocket and smiled. "Yes, she's fine. Thank you for all your help."

CHAPTER TWENTY-THREE

Tavish Finley had had a gutful of this English weather.

He wanted a scorching sun beating down on his back. He wanted burning hot air warming his skin. But, most of all, he wanted to get out of London and away from its miserable winter. He missed the excitement of war purely for the hot weather the Middle East had provided.

Glasgow, where he'd grown up, had been even colder than the south of England. A hell of a lot more poverty stricken, too, with endless foster homes all carrying the same violence and abuse. Sarah had been his only salvation back then. Unfortunately, he had fallen short of being hers and the Glaswegian squalor had taken its revenge.

Tav popped a couple of pills, zipped his jacket up to his neck, and clapped his hands together. If Jimmy didn't turn up soon, Tav would go looking for him – and it would be the last encounter the little junkie would ever have.

No sooner had the thought warmed his heart than Jimmy turned the corner.

He caught sight of Tav and slowed his pace, eying him head to foot. "Whoa, someone sure did a job on you, man."

Tav seized Jimmy by the throat and pulled him close. "Do you think I lost?"

"No. No…I…"

Tav tightened his fingers around the larynx, cutting Jimmy's voice to a hoarse whisper. "Do you have what I asked for?"

Jimmy nodded. He held up a folder.

Tav released his hold. He opened the file. Inside, various reports on Leah Wade – her autopsy, witness statements, a toxicology report.

"Your contact came through?"

Jimmy clasped his throat. "For that one, yes." He coughed and rubbed his neck.

Tav continued to read the papers. All very black and white. The girl was tanked up and drowned.

"Why is Wade hung up on disbelieving this was an accident?"

Jimmy pulled a second file from inside his coat. He handed it to Tav. "This is the original report," he croaked.

Tav searched through the content. The same papers as in the first file. The tox report was the same. Witness statements – the same. But the autopsy. Now that made for interesting reading.

Tav glanced up at Jimmy. "This is definitely the original?"

Jimmy nodded.

Tav glanced at the pathologist's signatures. Identical. The time stamps – identical.

"Where did the second one come from?"

Jimmy shrugged.

"Your contact know anything more?"

Jimmy shook his head.

Tav glanced at the signatures again. "This guy here – Carter. Looks like he signed off on both of these. He your contact?"

"Look, man, I've done what you asked, and paid handsomely for it, too."

"And you'll be reimbursed."

Jimmy rubbed his throat. If he'd been thinking of asking for payment now, he quickly changed his mind. "Can I go now?"

Tav looked up from the file and nodded. "Don't disappear on me, though, Jimmy. I'd hate to have to come looking for you."

Jimmy scurried away.

Tav closed the folders and rolled them into a cylinder. He had to get Wade away from the girl and off the scene if he was to finish this job. And now, finally, he knew how to do it. But, first, he had to pay this Carter guy a little visit.

CHAPTER TWENTY-FOUR

David Carter did not look happy.

Jason walked through the office and headed to his desk. He was just about to sit when his boss opened the door to his office.

"Jason, get in here."

Jason headed into the office. His boss looked pissed.

"Close the door." Carter slumped back behind his desk.

Jason closed the door. He had no idea what was going on or what he'd done, but knowing his boss the way he did, he wouldn't have to wait long to find out.

"Did you scald a guy with a kettle?" Carter said.

Yep. Straight to the point. Carter was nothing if not predictable.

"Do I look like I'd scald a guy with a kettle?" Jason stepped up to the desk. That fucking little junkie grass – couldn't even tell a lie properly. "I threatened him a little, 'tis all."

"Jesus Christ."

"The guy's a junkie and I needed information."

"This junkie is the same guy you beat to a pulp six months back."

"I didn't beat him up…this time, at least."

"You crushed his fucking hand in the fridge door."

"So, what? His career as a brain surgeon is over? He's a fucking junkie. "

Carter threw his pen onto the desk. "What's going on inside that noggin' of yours, boy?"

"I had a lead…"

"Yeah. Into your sister's death. I've heard it all before. You should have let it drop eight goddamn months ago and seen that bloody doctor."

"What is it with everyone and this fucking doctor?"

Carter held up a file. "I have her report. All one page of it. You're not there long enough for her to write anything else." He threw the file at Jason.

Jason let it fall on the floor. He leaned on the desk. "My sister was murdered."

"So you say." Carter stood. He matched Jason's stance. "Unfortunately, your disregard for authority saw to it that we'd never find out."

Jason's arms trembled. He clenched his fists and bit down on his lip. His shoulders tightened. "Nobody even tried for DNA."

"You contaminated her shitting crime scene. Quincy himself wouldn't have found any DNA."

"It was there. I would have found it."

"CPS wouldn't have touched it with a barge pole."

"I—"

"Save it." Carter straightened. He shook his head. "You're too messed up and I can't cover for you anymore."

Jason remained quiet, frightened that if he spoke he'd also attack.

"You've left me with no choice. I have to suspend you." Carter stepped out from behind the desk. "You know the drill. You get full pay until the allegation is investigated."

"Then what?"

"Depends on the outcome. I hope to god you're squeaky-clean and there's nothing else you're hiding in that closet of yours."

"You mean apart from what you covered up."

"And it had better not become uncovered." Carter sighed. "With this alone, you're waist deep in shit."

"Is that it?"

"That's it. They'll want to talk to you so don't go booking any holidays."

Jason pushed himself away from the desk. He wanted to flip it over. He wanted to run his hands across the surface and sweep everything – including the shitty pen holder that resembled a deflated cock – to the floor.

He glared at his boss, almost daring him to say one more word against his sister.

Instead, Carter pointed towards the door. "Go home. Get some rest. If you want to help yourself, you will go and cry on that fucking doctor's shoulder."

Jason scoffed, and turned to the door and left.

CHAPTER TWENTY-FIVE

Kate looked into the bright light.

The doctor held it there for a second and then moved it across to her other eye.

Satisfied, he switched it off and straightened. "Everything looks fine. You still have a slight concussion, but you're on the road to recovery."

The door opened. Both Kate and the doctor turned to see who it was.

A large man stepped inside and Kate's heart sank a little. She'd been hoping to see Jason more than she wanted to admit to herself.

The man produced a black wallet. Flipped it open and showed her the badge and identification inside – DS Price.

"I also go by Ed," the officer offered.

Kate glanced up at him. This must be the officer Jason had warned her was coming. He didn't look like a police officer.

He turned the identification towards the doctor. "Is it okay if I have a quick word?"

The doctor popped his torch into the top pocket of his coat. "Absolutely." He smiled at Kate. "I'll see you tomorrow. Get some rest."

Rest? The man was a comedian. The continuous clattering of voices outside in the corridor throughout the night stopped her sleeping and the monotonous tone of the room bored her half to death.

DS Ed Price waited for the doctor to leave before he addressed her again. "I have some good news for you, Miss Caldwell."

Kate played along. "Caldwell?"

Ed nodded. "Kate Caldwell." He moved to the side of the bed. "Is it okay if I call you Kate?"

Kate nodded. "Feels funny being called a name I don't remember."

"You'll get used to it." He smiled. "Hospital said you are free to leave."

"But the doctor just said he'll be back to see me tomorrow."

Ed shrugged. "What can I say? You're a free woman."

"But I have nowhere to go."

"Maybe I can help with that as well. We have an address for you."

Wouldn't happen to be south of the river, by any chance?

Ed smiled. "You've been staying with a friend in Shad Thames. A nice little pad by all accounts."

"So, it's not mine?"

"No. Belongs to your friend. We've spoken with her. She's on her way back from Paris."

"And she is definitely my friend?"

"We have checked her out, Kate."

"Has she told you anything about me? Or how I ended up in the river?"

"No. Says she has no idea what you were doing near the river, so that remains a mystery for now. She's just glad you're safe."

"So, I can really leave here?" The notion came as a relief. After all, this so-called friend of hers could shed a little light on who she was and where she came from.

"As soon as you like." Ed pulled out a key ring with two keys on it. "And I will take you, so you will be perfectly safe."

Nerves knotted her stomach and Kate linked her fingers together. Leaving the sanctuary of the monotonous hospital room had been what she wanted, but now it worried her. Could this friend of hers be trusted?

"Can I leave now?"

Ed smiled again and nodded. "Just a little paperwork to sign."

She pushed the blankets back and looked at her hospital gown. "What am I supposed to wear?"

CHAPTER TWENTY-SIX

Jason stood outside the gym.

Nothing much had changed during the last twenty years. The same wooden sign swung above the door and the same old lamps – the ones that had needed updating a decade ago – were still fixed to the wall above it.

A mixture of emotions arose within him. He wanted to go inside but his obstinate feet refused to leave the gritted pavement.

A couple of lads entered – one carrying a sports bag, the other with his kit slung over his shoulder. Both of them were boxers. You could just tell. The way they carried themselves. The definition in their arms, their shoulders.

Jason glanced up at the sign again. Phoenix Boxing Club. A simple name meaning to rise from the ashes and be born again.

He smiled. He'd put on his first pair of boxing gloves inside that gym. Ten minutes later, he'd gotten his first tooth knocked out. It was within those four walls that he'd been taught how to be a fighter.

Life had been pretty okay back then. Then Leah, his once beautiful sister, smoked her first spliff, and his perfect life turned to shit. Jason reckoned he totted up more fights outside the ring than in it while going after the scum that she knocked about with.

He took out his phone and scrolled through a list of names. He stopped at Leah's number, something he'd been so far unable to delete from his contacts. His finger hovered millimetres from the screen. He wanted to call her. To bring her up to date on what had been happening. To tell her what he'd uncovered.

But he couldn't. Leah was dead and everything had changed. He knew he had to move on, but how could he when her death still cut so deep?

Jason pressed his finger against the call icon and waited for the connection.

"Hi, this is Leah—"

He ended the call. It was good to hear her voice but tormenting himself was not helping. Keeping her phone charged, kidding himself that it was in search of a lead…

He closed his eyes and let the winter cool his face. What would she have made of the irrational mess he'd become? Would she have begged him to let her rest in peace – to go seek the help of the doctor – or would she have urged him to continue with this crazy crusade?

A flush of warmth crept across Jason's face and he rubbed the back of his neck.

Vengeance was all he could offer her now.

Jason drained the glass dry. He held up the empty, caught the barman's attention, and signalled for another.

"One for me too, mate," Ed called to the barman.

He pulled out the stool beside Jason, nudged his shoulder and pointed to the four empty glasses already on the counter. "I see you've been here for a while."

"Your point being?"

Ed shook his head. "You should've gone and talked to that doctor."

"Fucking tossers, the lot of them."

"Jesus Christ." Ed rubbed his temple.

The barman put two pints down on the bar and slid them forward. Ed handed over a twenty but didn't reach for the drink.

"Can you get rid of those as well?" Ed said, pointing to the empty glasses in front of Jason.

The barman grimaced and gave a slight shake of the head.

"Why the hell not?"

"Because I want them there," Jason said.

"Fuck me." Ed turned to Jason. His eyes narrowed slightly. It was the first time he'd properly looked at him since entering the pub. "What the hell is happening to you?"

"I'm just dandy."

"You can hardly sit straight."

"It happens when you fight."

"When you lose a fight you mean." Ed leaned forward and prodded Jason's forehead. "When's that brain in there gonna get it? It was a fucking accident. Everyone but you knows it."

Ed held his stare for a couple of seconds. A frown creased his brow deeper than usual. The till slammed shut and the barman put Ed's change on the bar. Ed held Jason's stare but his face tightened. Jason could tell his friend didn't want to look away. But Ed was a tight wanker. Loved a pound note.

Trying to ignore the money on the counter was killing him. Ed blinked, slow like, and turned. Took his change and slipped it into his back pocket.

Jason scoffed. Ed – tight as a gnat's chuff. "You been to the hospital yet? Tell the girl who she is?"

"Yeah."

"And?"

"And what?"

"How'd she take it?"

"How'd you think?" Ed picked up his pint and gulped down a mouthful of beer. It left a layer of froth on his top lip and he licked it away. "Anyway, she's no longer our problem."

"Oh?"

Ed glanced at Jason. "Jesus Christ. Now you want to fixate over her? You need to get your shit together, man. I mean, look at you. You're fucking up, and that means you risk fucking me up. I won't let that happen."

"Just showing an interest in her well-being. It hardly makes me Glenn Close." Jason looked away. "And I wouldn't worry. Carter's taking sole ownership of the whole cover-up thing." He stared at the bar top. Dried beer from his previous pints marked the varnish in perfect circles. He reached for his new pint and sat it in front of him. When he lifted it up, it left another perfectly formed circle. He rolled the glass between his palms, destroying the shape and enjoying the freshness the condensation brought to his skin.

"I know you don't want to hear it, but your sister was a junkie."

Jason stopped rolling. His fingers tightened around the glass. "You're walking a thin line, Ed."

Ed leaned in close. "I walked a thin line when I covered up what you did to that dealer, regardless of what shit Carter's spewing out." Ed sat back. He picked up his drink. "Leah's death was a terrible loss to us all. But it was just an accident."

Jason released his grip. He took a deep breath. He knew Ed meant well. He'd had his back these last eight months, after all, and, if the roles were reversed, Jason would probably be giving the same advice. But the roles were not reversed. Ed hadn't lost his sister. Jason had.

"I don't know how to let it go."

"Well, you'd better figure it out because this fucked-up shit of yours is dragging you down a sodding rabbit hole. There's only so long people will stick around putting up with it." Ed swigged another mouthful. "You lost Karen…fuck, you lost your driving license—"

"Me and Karen was never gonna work."

"Maybe. Can you say the same about your job?"

"You heard, eh?"

"Everyone's heard."

"Course they have." Jason gulped back his beer When he placed the glass down, just under half of the drink remained. He wiped his mouth dry on the cuff of his hoodie.

Ed sighed. "You're gonna end up lying next to Leah six feet under. Because, if this obsession don't kill you, the sodding drinking will."

Jason tilted his head back. "Shit."

He closed his eyes. Ed was right. Leah's death was destroying him. "I think the amnesiac girl is involved somehow."

Ed spat out his drink. "Fuck me, Jason."

Jason opened his eyes and glanced at his friend. He'd expected some kind of reaction – just not something so bloody dramatic.

Ed wiped the spilled drink from his chin. "You are so fucking far from reality. The amnesiac girl jumped."

"You're still going with that assumption, eh?"

"Okay. Due to her bag being found some distance away – and there being no purse or ID inside – there is the slight possibility her unfortunate nosedive into the Thames was the result of a mugging. But that is not official."

Jason scoffed.

"Either way – mugging or attempted suicide – the girl is not linked to Leah or her death." Ed took a deep breath and exhaled – slowly – the air almost whistling past his lips. "You need to leave it alone, my friend. If ever there was a wrong tree to bark up, this is it."

"I'm telling you, they're linked."

"And what proof do you have?"

Jason thought about the man in Bethnal Green – there for Leah or for Kate? The bird tattooed across his hand – the blue bird Kate had mumbled about in her sleep. The same man Jimmy the Junkie had described being with Leah near the burger van. He thought about confiding in Ed.

Instead, he said, "I'll have some soon."

"You can't even get back in the office."

"I have friends."

"What friends? I'm your only friend and that's wearing fucking thin." Ed sighed. "Seriously, man. Leave it be."

Jason stared at his beer. Suddenly, the need to drink it no longer consumed him. "I need to clear my head." He pushed his glass across the counter and stood. Winced and reached for his waist. "I'm going home."

Ed turned on his stool. "Don't do anything stupid, Jason. Go home."

"There an echo in here?" Jason pushed open the pub door and walked outside.

There was only one place he was heading – and it wasn't home.

CHAPTER TWENTY-SEVEN

The hospital corridor was strangely empty considering visiting hours were already half an hour in.

Jason rushed to the fifth floor, ignored the nurses at the station, and opened the door to Kate's room.

An orderly looked up at him, a change of bed sheets already laid across the mattress.

"Where's the girl that was in here?" Jason said.

The orderly shrugged and went back to making the bed. He either didn't understand the question or wasn't bothered enough to answer it.

Jason slapped the doorframe and ran back to the nurse's station. One small mercy – the old troll from yesterday wasn't around. He smiled at the younger, much prettier, nurse that now sat in her place. "Where did the amnesiac girl, Kate Caldwell in room seven, go?"

"She's been discharged."

"Already?" *Crap*. Ed must have taken her home before he came to the pub. "When'd she leave?"

"I'm not sure."

"You don't know when one of your patients leaves?"

The girl's face hardened. "I've only been on shift for two hours. She'd already left by then." She held her stare for a second then returned to her paperwork.

"Do you have a forwarding address or a number?" Jason pointed to the array of papers piled on the desk. "You know, something she can be reached on?"

The nurse glared at him. "Do I look like a telephone exchange to you?"

Jason stepped forward. This nurse was worse than the troll. He leaned on the counter – palms spread flat and holding his weight. Time for a change of tactics. "I'm sorry. It's been a long day."

The nurse glanced up. Her features softened and the hatred in her eyes disappeared. "Would you like me to get my manager?"

Jason shook his head. "Thank you anyway." He turned his back on her and pulled out his phone. Ed's number was at the top of his call list. "Come on, Ed. Pick up."

Ed failed to answer. Shit. This just wasn't his day.

Jason started to pace. Where in the fuck had Kate gone? He turned back to his phone. This time he phoned Karen.

It took three long rings for her to answer. "For the love of God, leave me be and I'll find what you want a hell of a lot quicker."

"I'm not ringing about the CCTV. I need another favour."

"No."

"Karen, please."

"Absolutely not."

"This is the last thing. I promise."

"You said that already."

"This time I mean it."

"You said that already, too."

"Karen, please."

"You're going to get me sacked."

"Please." Jason moved towards the lift – away from being overheard – and pressed to go down. "I've been suspended. I can't ask anyone else."

Silence.

"Karen?"

The lift doors parted and he entered. He pressed the ground floor button. "Karen? You still there?"

He heard her sigh.

"This is the last time," she said.

"Are you near a computer?"

"Not right now, no. I'm looking at your bloody street footage and getting chronic eye-strain."

"Can you get to a computer?"

Karen muttered a string of obscenities under her breath. Jason heard her open a door. It closed. Another door opened. A feminine grunt as she presumably sat down.

There was a short silence then she said, "Okay, what am I looking for?"

The lift arrived on the ground floor. Jason exited and made his way towards the lobby. "Check a name for me. Kate Caldwell. DOB—"

"Yeah, I remember. I already gave you her information and you got yourself beat up."

"I actually got beat up before that."

"Jesus Christ." A short silence. Then, "What the hell is wrong with me?"

Jason smiled. "Good girl. I need to know if there's anything else on her."

He heard Karen's fingers tap across the keyboard.

"Okay, I have one arrest record and one address, both of which you already know, and…um…that's it."

"There's nothing else?"

"Nope. Nothing."

"What about the arrest record? Was anyone nicked with her?"

More keyboard tapping. "Umm…yes. A Charlotte Branson. And no. Not related to Sir Richard."

"Is there an address for her? Something south of the river?"

"Hang on…oh, you're going to like this. You got a pen?"

"Yeah," he lied. Karen knew he never carried a bloody pen.

"The Old Hayloft Building in Shad Thames. The Penthouse Suite."

"Shit. Really?"

"Looks like your girl has expensive taste, with friends in all the right circles."

Jason ignored her.

"We still on for later?" she said.

"Absolutely."

"You booked somewhere?"

Shit.

"Just as well I did. Nine o'clock. La Gavroche."

She fucking knew he hated that French shit.

"Don't leave me there waiting."

"I won't." He hung up.

He left the hospital and waved down a taxi. Charlotte Branson was the only lead he had left.

CHAPTER TWENTY-EIGHT

Kate pulled her knees towards her chest and wrapped her arms tight around them.

Nothing looked familiar. Not the white décor. Not the sparse but expensive-looking furniture. Not the array of photographs where her slightly younger doppelganger laughed with people who remained strangers to her.

A cat rounded the chair – completely bald. Not a single hair on his body. He rubbed against the furniture and meowed. Kate stretched her legs and tapped her lap. The cat, a Sphinx, leapt up. Jesus, he was ugly, but she pulled him close nonetheless and hugged him.

Her friend, Charlotte, who apparently owned the property, was due home soon – A friend Kate had no memory of. A friend who was clearly very wealthy if her surroundings were anything to go by. Did that mean Kate was also wealthy? If she was, why hadn't anyone come forward and reported her missing? Didn't she have a family? Friends? Neighbours? She hugged the cat closer. Suddenly, the animal felt like her only ally.

A buzzer broke the silence and a small TV monitor flickered to life displaying a familiar face.

Relief swept over Kate. She lowered the cat to the ground and quickly went to the box. There were two buttons below the screen.

She pushed the one on the left. "Hello?"

"It's Jason Wade…from the hospital. Can you buzz me up?"

Kate pressed the button on the right. It didn't occur to her to ask him what he wanted. "I'm at the top. In the penthouse."

"I know."

She heard the door buzzer and then Jason disappeared from the screen. She glanced around for a mirror, prey to a sudden urge to check her hair. When she found one, she wished she hadn't. Ashen skin, dark circles beneath tired eyes, hair greasier than a chip pan. Holy hell. She looked awful.

Jason must have run up the four flights of stairs because the knock at the front door came quicker than Kate had expected. She paused. This guy was clearly not operating in an official capacity, and her head screamed that she should report his unannounced visit to the police. Regardless, she opened the door.

He stood there leaning on the doorframe, a weary smile on his face, his arm wrapped around his side. He almost looked as bad as her.

Kate returned his smile and stepped aside. "I didn't think I'd see you again."

"I have another question to ask." He entered and began inspecting the room.

From the look on his face, his first impressions of the swanky apartment pretty much mirrored her own. His expression certainly mirrored that of the policeman who'd brought her here. He cleared his throat and continued to glance around, his eyes betraying the admiration he clearly felt. She thought about asking him if he wanted a tour of the place – something she had not yet gone on herself. But what would she show him? She was just as much in the dark about the layout as he was.

He did a full three-sixty until his eyes found her again. The excitement faded and it was back to business.

"Do you think leaving the hospital so soon was a good idea?"

"The hospital seemed to think so."

Jason frowned. "How're you feeling?"

Kate shrugged. "A little tired."

Jason's gaze wandered around the room again, finally settling on the view of Tower Bridge. He walked to the window. "So, your friend is rich, eh?"

"I wouldn't know."

Jason smirked. He regarded the chair she'd been sitting in. "What in the fuck is that?"

Kate reached for the cat and scooped him up into her arms. A tag hung from his collar. "Looks like he's Bastet."

"Is that its name or its breed?"

"His name." At least, she presumed it was.

"Shit. That is one ugly looking cat."

Kate laughed. It was the first time she'd done so since this whole nightmare had begun.

Jason chuckled, the horrified look falling off his face. He looked nice when he laughed. Almost – dare she say it – handsome.

She felt her cheeks warm and turned towards the spiral staircase. "Can I get you something to drink?"

"No. I'm fine."

She paused on the bottom step, a little reluctant to turn and face him again while her cheeks still burned.

"So," Jason continued. "Nothing here looks familiar either?"

Kate glanced at him and shook her head. He moved towards a small side unit on the other side of the room and began flicking through some paperwork. Found a passport and an old photograph and picked them up.

"Is that the question you wanted to ask me?"

Jason opened the passport. He glanced at Kate then back at the book. "Kate Caldwell. That's you, alright – born in the United Kingdom. Not the United States."

"America?"

"Sorry, just thinking aloud."

She noticed he didn't put the passport down, but instead brought the photograph to the forefront. He studied it for a moment then turned it over.

He read out the short inscription on the back. "Helen, Marjorie, and Katie. Ninety-five." He flicked back to the photo. "I know these flats."

"You do?" Kate approached him and looked at the photo. "How?"

"I was there last night. Grew up nearby, in fact." He held the photo up. "These people familiar to you?"

Kate glanced at the photo. Three people – two women and a child – standing on a balcony in front of a door. Kate shook her head. "My friend should be home soon. She may know."

"Uh-huh," he said vaguely. "You mind if I keep this for a while?"

Kate had no idea why he'd want to keep a picture like that, but she shrugged and nodded anyway.

Jason slipped the photo and the passport into his back pocket.

"Why are you taking the pass—?"

At the far end of the room, two doors slid apart – a lift that Kate had failed to notice. A female who looked to be in her mid-twenties stepped out, dragging two suitcases behind her. She spotted Kate, released the cases, and raced towards her.

"What on earth happened to you?" She flung her arms around Kate's neck and pulled her close. "Why did you leave the apartment?"

The cat hissed and the woman leaned back. She looked down at the cat still cradled in Kate's arms and stroked its head.

Kate was at a loss for words. Other than this girl being in many of the photographs that decorated the apartment, she didn't look the slightest bit familiar. She glanced towards Jason for help. He was fast becoming her safety blanket.

Jason stepped forward and held out his hand. "I'm Jason."

The woman tensed and her eyes narrowed. "Jason…?"

"Wade. I'm a crime scene investigator."

His hand remained extended.

"He took my fingerprints," Kate added.

Slowly, the woman reached out and shook Jason's hand.

"I assume you're Charlotte?"

Charlotte stared at him. She slowly pulled her hand from his. "What are you doing here, Mr. Wade?"

"Nothing underhand. Just checking on your friend, is all." Jason stepped back. "Maybe you can shed some light on who Kate actually is."

Charlotte turned to her. "You mean you really do have amnesia?"

Kate nodded.

"Wow. The police said, but I didn't honestly believe it." She took Kate's hand. "You remember me, don't you?"

Kate shook her head. "Sorry."

Charlotte lightly squeezed Kate's hand and offered her a sad smile. She held her stare for a moment before turning back to Jason.

Her eyes narrowed again. "If you don't know who she is, how is it that you know her name?"

"From her prints. Seems she has a record…you both do."

"That's how you found me?"

Jason nodded. "But that's all I can find. The address on her file is…well, it's occupied by someone else."

"The arrest was just for university shenanigans. Kate lives here with me." Charlotte wrapped her arm around Kate's shoulders. "And, forgive me, but I think she needs to get some rest."

Jason straightened, a pinched expression hardening his features. He glanced at Kate, then back at Charlotte. "I need to ask her a few questions."

"Maybe another time." Charlotte walked Kate to the spiral staircase, the cat still in her arms. "I assume you are capable of letting yourself out, or do I need to call building security?"

Jason looked lost for words. "You still have my card?"

Kate nodded.

"Good. Keep it close – just in case."

One last hard glare thrown in Charlotte's direction, and Jason walked towards the lift.

"You can't get out that way. It leads to the garage and is pass-coded," Charlotte called out after him. "You need to leave the way I assume you arrived – by the front door and take the stairs."

Jason rubbed the back of his neck and threw a scowl at Charlotte that would have turned most people to stone.

"If you wish to speak to Kate again, I suggest you call ahead," Charlotte continued. "In case she is resting. I'd hate for you to have another wasted journey."

Jason ignored her and opened the door.

Kate wanted to shout out for him to stay – after all, he was the only person she really knew. But the words stuck in her throat.

As soon as the door closed behind him, Charlotte was upon her. "What did you tell that man?"

"Nothing."

"Did you tell him who you are?"

"What do you mean? He told *me* who I am."

"And who's that?"

Kate was confused. "Kate Caldwell."

"Crap." Charlotte ran her fingers through her glossy, auburn curls.

"It's okay. He works with the police."

"But it was you who told me we cannot trust anyone – especially the police."

"Why would I say that?"

Charlotte sighed. "Oh sweetie. There is so much I need to tell you. But you must not talk to the police."

"He's not the police-police. He's a forensic fingerprint thingy."

"Not the police or any kind of law enforcement. Those were your words, not mine. Am I making myself clear?"

Kate bit her lip. She didn't understand why she couldn't trust the police. It was true that Jason's excess of attention gave her reason not to trust him. But, somehow, she just did.

Charlotte glanced at the floor and sighed. She rested her hands on her hips and seemed to take a moment to compose herself.

She glanced back up and wet her lips. "What exactly happened to you?"

"I fell into the Thames."

"What were you even doing outside?"

"What do you mean? Who exactly am I?"

Charlotte sighed. "Christ, Kate. We need to get out of here." She ran back to her suitcases.

Kate went after her. "What? Wait! Why?"

"Because you didn't just fall into the Thames."

"I don't understand."

Charlotte turned to her and gently cupped her face. "Can you honestly not remember anything?"

Kate shook her head.

"Kate, you came here to hide."

"What do you mean? Hide from what?"

"Go and pack some clothes. I'll explain on the way."

"Where are we going?"

"Far away from here."

Kate bit her lip. "He took my passport."

"Who took your passport?"

"Jason. And a photograph."

Charlotte's eyes widened. "Heck." She glanced back at her cases. "Okay, go and pack. I'll phone Daddy. See if he can charter a boat or a private plane for us."

Kate lingered and scanned the apartment. She had no idea where her bedroom was.

Charlotte nudged her forward. "Up the spiral staircase, on the first floor. Your room is at the front. Overlooks Tower Bridge."

Kate started up the staircase. Through the runs, she watched Charlotte stand one of her suitcases upright and then head for the side table where the phone sat in its cradle. Kate carried on to the top of the stairs. This level of the building was as impressive as the one below, the enormous kitchen and dining area in front of her overlooking St Katherine's Dock.

She turned to the door behind her – the only other door on this floor – and opened it. Inside, an open-plan living area surrounded a small coffee table. Beyond that, a king-size bed overlooked an identical view of Tower Bridge as the one downstairs. Kate walked to the window. Below, tourists crowded the pavements. She saw Jason exit the building and zip up his coat. He started to walk, then stopped and glanced up at the building, but she doubted he saw her.

She closed her eyes and hugged the cat closer, his purring a temporary comfort.

"Kate, are you okay up there?" Charlotte called up.

Kate opened her eyes. "I'm fine."

"Daddy is sending a plane. Grab a quick change of clothes. I'm just taking my cases back down to the car."

Kate put the cat onto the bed. She pulled her top over her head and dropped it beside the cat. What she really wanted was a hot shower. She reached for the clasp on her bra.

The explosion was silent. The sound didn't come until a split second after the bedroom door splintered inward. The force imploded across the living area. The sofa overturned. The coffee table lifted into the air and knocked Kate off her feet, propelling her sideways. She crashed to the floor, the coffee table landing on top of her. The windows shattered outwards and a gust of winter air raced in.

It was the last thing Kate felt.

CHAPTER TWENTY-NINE

It felt like the earth moved.

Jason's feet left the ground and he hit the car in front of him. Pain ripped across his shoulders. His ribs. Glass rained around him and he sheltered beneath his arms, but shards still scratched and sliced every inch of skin found. He struggled to sit. Tried to shake the fog from his head.

Screams broke through the confusion. He tried to get to his feet. Quickly collapsed again. Took a breath, rubbed his eyes, and looked up at the building above him. Smoke billowed from the first two floors of the penthouse apartment, flames licking and caressing the outer frame of the structure.

Kate.

Jason got to his feet. People of all ages fled the burning building, crying and yelling for help. Jason pushed through them towards the entrance. His feet were unsteady and his legs struggled to hold his weight. He gripped his side, entered the lobby, and headed towards the stairs.

Four flights up and Kate's apartment door still hung on its hinges. He hugged his ribs tighter, prepared for the pain, and kicked the door inwards. Heat exploded out and Jason spun back against the wall. Sweat dampened his skin and he wiped his cuff across his forehead. Another breath.

Smoke poured out into the stairway and quickly stole his vision.

Kate was inside and he was fast running out of time if he wanted to get her out of there. He pulled his arms free of his jacket and held it above his head like a piece of tarpaulin. His ribs screamed at the movement and he was left with little choice but to lower one of his arms mid-way. One last breath and he twisted back towards the open door.

Heat engulfed him. Smoke suffocated him and burned his throat. He pulled the coat closer around his face and lurched inside. Overturned furniture blocked his path. The ugly cat shot past him and fled out onto the landing.

Jason turned back towards the room.

He kicked a loose drawer out of his way and climbed over the side table. "Kate!"

Black smoke blocked most of his view and he tried to wave it away. But it just made things worse. Flames danced across the laminate flooring, swallowing the Egyptian rug, hungry for what was left of the decimated sofa. With the growing fire came a more intense heat not even the winter gust could cool.

Jason coughed the smoke from his lungs and ducked closer to the floor, trying to see beneath the smog. Just ahead, lying motionless against the wall, he saw a shape. A body.

Kate? A sour taste flooded his mouth and he struggled to swallow it. He raced towards her. *Please don't be Kate.* She lay face down, her brunette hair fanning the sides of her head. He reached for her shoulders and rolled her limp body over.

But it wasn't Kate. It was Charlotte – her eyes closed, the right side of her face blistered and burned.

Jason swallowed back the guilty elation that raced through his veins and felt for a pulse.

Nothing.

He listened for a heartbeat.

Nothing.

He sat back and squinted. Flames climbed the walls and disappeared into the murky fog overhead. He coughed again, covered his mouth, and tried to filter out the toxic poison as he inhaled. Parts of the ceiling collapsed around him. Curtain rails crashed to the floor. His mind swooned, light-headedness threatened to take him, and he crawled back towards the door. More ceiling disintegrated under the inferno, and he huddled into a ball, leaving his back to take the brunt of the impact. Embers hit his jacket and quickly became flames. He threw the jacket to the floor, slapping the fabric until the fire extinguished. Then, once again, held the coat over his head and continued towards the door.

He paused at the staircase and glanced up into the black haze. "Kate!"

Flames had devoured the far end of the apartment. Jason coughed again and buried his nose and mouth against his bicep. Smoke stung his eyes. This place was minutes from being totally destroyed. He had to get out. But not before finding Kate. He felt for the iron steps and clawed his way up them, visibility worsening the higher he climbed.

"Kate!"

He remained on all fours and crawled beneath the smoke as best he could.

The grey fog rushed towards the new ventilation system caused by the blown-out windows, and he followed it.

"Kate!"

He reached an overturned table. Felt a hand. An arm. "Kate!"

He crawled around the table. Kate lay on her back, only a bra covering her bare skin and the table's legs pinning her against the ground. Jason lifted it and hurled it away. Pain pierced his side and he reached for his ribs.

He turned back to Kate. Touched her neck, found a pulse, and covered her as best he could with the jacket.

The sound of sirens broke through the smoke and wafted in through the broken windows. At least help was on the way. He scooped Kate into his arms, screamed out the pain as he stood, and staggered towards the spiral staircase. The lower level was barely visible. Flames blocked his escape, frolicking around the bottom of the rungs as though daring him to take them on.

Jason glanced back to where he'd found Kate but could no longer see that end of the apartment. "Shit."

There had to be a fire escape or something up here.

He turned, searching for any kind of exit, but smoke dropped around him like a veil, limiting visibility to less than a couple of feet.

He glanced back at the stairwell, repositioned his hold around Kate, and descended the stairs. Flames licked his boots, but he kept going. Heat burned through his trousers, but he kept going until, finally, he had no choice but to stop. Only four or five feet separated him from the first floor, but it was the highest five feet he'd ever seen. He tightened his hold around Kate, prayed to God, and leapt over the flames.

He landed on the other side, both feet hitting the ground with a thud. Pain paralysed his side and his legs buckled beneath him. He fell to one knee. Swallowed back the agony, and stood.

He didn't look back. He just hurried to the door.

Smoke filled the landing outside. Screams and panicked yells echoed from below as residents fled for safety. He started for the stairs, descending just one flight before he collided with several firefighters.

"Anyone else up there?" the nearest fireman said.

"One. Deceased. A female. First floor penthouse."

The fireman patted him on the shoulder. "Get down to the ground floor. Paramedics are waiting."

Jason nodded and hurried down the stairs – past the second floor, past the first floor – and out onto the street.

The cold air hit him and his vision blurred even further.

"I need a paramedic," he spluttered, his legs weakening.

He inhaled best he could, sucking the winter air into his lungs. Kate remained unconscious in his arms, her face and arms blackened by the smoke. He lowered to the ground and pushed the hair off her face.

There was no way this was going to be written off as some fucking accident.

CHAPTER THIRTY

Kate felt as though she were on fire.

She opened her eyes and shot upright. A jacket fell around her waist, exposing her semi-naked body, and it didn't cross her mind to recover herself. Her throat tightened and she fought for air through breathless gasps.

Two hands quickly consoled her and rubbed her back. The coughing lessened, allowing tiny pockets of air to enter her lungs. Pain constricted her chest and she kneaded the ache away. The hands slipped from her back to her shoulders and tried to lower her back down to the ground.

"Just breathe," a man's voice reassured her. "Help is on the way."

The voice sounded familiar but Kate couldn't relax. She frantically searched the crowds. "Where's Charlotte?"

Trying to converse constricted her chest. Her throat tensed and, without mercy, she choked and battled another coughing fit. She rubbed her chest, tried to swallow, and fought to catch a breath.

"Kate, just try to relax," the man said.

The·hands holding her shoulders lowered between her shoulder blades, massaging, soothing. She tried to shrug free, but the grip held her still. Her coughing worsened and she hugged her knees to her chest.

"Kate, the fire services are up there. They'll get her."

Kate resisted the man's embrace. Another succession of coughs and she caught a split-second to suck in some of the smoky air around her. When she coughed again, it was less ferocious. She wiped her eyes and looked up at the penthouse. Smoke billowed from the windows and escaping flames charred the exterior.

Her heart raced and tears blurred her vision. She felt their warmth trickle down her cheeks and wiped them dry with the back of her hand. "What happened?"

The man's hands released her shoulders and lifted the jacket back around her.

She turned to him. It was Jason.

Every thought inside her head froze – apart from one. "I saw you leave."

"I came back."

Light-headedness muddled her thoughts. "Where's Charlotte?"

Jason's lips tightened. Sadness filled his eyes and he lightly shook his head.

"What's wrong?" Itches scratched her throat, but the coughing never came.

"Kate, Charlotte didn't survive."

Kate stared at him, but he offered no more information. Nausea swirled in the pit of her stomach. Shudders rocked her body. She wanted to cry. Not just cry, but bawl and sob and wail – at least, that was the appropriate reaction her brain expected.

"I don't understand." She tried to hug her body warm, but the shudders worsened.

Jason wrapped his arms around her and pulled her close. "You're in shock. It's okay. It's just adrenaline kicking in."

This time Kate didn't try to pull away from his arms. Tremors took over her body and she couldn't halt them.

She closed her eyes and concentrated on the hurried beat of Jason's heart. "I need to get Charlotte." Her voice was a mere whisper.

Jason's hold around her strengthened and she nuzzled deeper against his chest. She felt his chin rest against her head and his hands rub a little warmth into her back.

"You need to get warm," he said.

She sensed another person approach.

Jason's voice came again, only this time not addressing her. "She's in shock. May have a concussion. Nothing broken as far as I can tell. Kate? Can you stand?"

Kate nodded and drew away from his chest. A paramedic knelt beside them. He hooked an arm around her waist. Jason mimicked him, only he also took her hand and hooked her arm around his shoulder. Together, they helped her to her feet.

Dizziness swam behind her eyes. She could hear the paramedic and Jason conversing, but their words were a jumble. Her head lolled forward, a sudden weight pulling her down.

She felt Jason's hand release hers. Someone cupped her legs and lifted her from the ground.

"Follow me," the paramedic said.

She glanced up. Jason carried her through the confusion. It seemed to last forever. Women crying. Children screaming. Voices shouting. People rushing past her. When Jason finally sat her down, she found herself in the back of an ambulance.

The jacket started to slip from her shoulders.

Jason stopped it and lifted it back up. Scratches grazed and bloodied his dirty arms. He pulled away and grabbed a red blanket from the end of the stretcher. Winced and reached for his side.

"You're hurt," Kate said.

Jason took a shallow breath, then flapped the blanket open and wrapped Kate inside it. He pulled the corners together beneath her chin.

"My friend has just been blown up," Kate said. Still no tears came. Not tears of loss, anyway.

"Kate—"

"Why am I not crying? What's wrong with me?"

"You're in shock." Jason settled on the stretcher in front of her, his hands finding a place on her knees. "Just focus on me."

A paramedic climbed in and sat beside him. He gave her a warm but sympathetic smile. "Hi, I'm Ben. And you are?"

Kate tried to speak but choked.

"Her name's Kate," Jason said. "She was in the penthouse when the explosion happened. Was unconscious for approximately ten minutes and has inhaled smoke."

"Okay." The paramedic took a small mask from the shelf and hooked the elastic straps behind Kate's ears. He positioned the mask over her nose and mouth. "This is just oxygen. To help you breathe." He held up a small torch and a beam of light burst to life. He shone it into her eyes. "Kate, I need you to look up…to the left…right…down."

The paramedic leaned closer, flicking the beam from her left eye to her right. "Do you feel sick? Have any headaches?"

"S…sick." The mask muffled her voice.

The torchlight blinked off and the paramedic turned to Jason. "We'll take her to the hospital. To check her out properly."

"Is she okay?"

"Mild concussion as far as I can see." He moved to the open doors and climbed out. "I'll be back in a moment."

Kate pulled the mask from her face. "I don't want to go back to hospital."

She expected Jason to argue the toss with her, but he glanced towards the open doors, his eyes darting across the crowds outside. Whatever he was looking for, he didn't seem happy about it.

He turned back to face her. "It's just a check-up." He shifted position.

He looked uncomfortable. Rigid almost. He took out his phone, held it to his ear, and turned from her. "I need you to come get me…I can't…there's been an explosion." He glanced at Kate – briefly. "Where do you think I am?" His voice lowered to little more than a whisper. "I know…huh-uh."

He turned from her again and Kate struggled to hear him. "Direct hit…yeah, she's fine. No, that won't do. She needs somewhere safe tonight."

He gazed up at the ambulance's ceiling and ran his fingers through his hair, leaving his hand resting on top of his head. "I know, okay." He sighed. "Just do it."

He hung up and slipped the phone into his back pocket.

"What's happening?"

"I need to get you out of here."

"Why?"

Jason seemed hesitant to answer. He bit down on his lip, his hardened eyes penetrating her.

"Tell me."

Jason slowly knelt before her. He reached for her hands. "Because it sounded like an explosion."

"Yes…"

He wavered, holding back what he wanted to tell her.

Kate turned to the open doors. The cries of the public could still be heard, but Kate could hardly see them. Smoke descended upon the area like a misty fog. Only the golden embers from the fire, which floated through the murky air like fireflies, gave depth to the dense atmosphere.

"Was this meant for me?"

"What makes you say that?"

Kate turned to Jason. "Charlotte said I came here to hide."

"Hide? Hide from what?" Jason's mobile began to vibrate. He pulled it from his back pocket, glanced at the screen, and cancelled the call.

He turned back to Kate. "Who are you hiding from?"

"I don't know." Kate shivered and pulled the blanket tighter. "She never got the chance to tell me."

Jason's phone vibrated again. He cancelled the call.

"She said I told her not to trust the police."

"Why?"

Kate shrugged. "Does that mean I shouldn't trust you?"

"What? No—"

The vibrating began again.

He cursed but this time he answered. "Karen, I can't talk right now…what? You found him?" He glanced at Kate then lowered his head. "Give me a couple of hours. I'll meet you at yours."

He hung up and tucked the phone back into his pocket.

"Are you leaving me?"

Jason glanced at her. "Yes. For a while."

"Am I going back to the hospital?"

Jason shook his head. "A friend is taking you somewhere safe."

"Where are you going?"

"Somewhere else. But I'll be back."

"Why can't I go with you?"

"You'll be safer with Ed."

"Ed?"

"DS Price."

"I know him. He was the officer who brought me here."

"Then you know you can trust him."

"No. I don't."

"Then trust me."

Kate gripped the blanket tighter. She sighed and closed her eyes. "Is all this related to the mugging?"

Jason didn't answer. He just stared at her. But it was written all over his face.

"So, where is DS Price taking me?"

"Somewhere safe."

"Do I tell him what I told you – about hiding?"

Jason shook his head. "Keep that between us. Just for the time being. Until I can figure out what's going on."

CHAPTER THIRTY-ONE

The front door slammed shut.

Tav stormed the length of the hallway and hurled his keys across the sparse living room. They smashed against the wall and fell to the ground.

He turned to the nearest wall and punched it. The plasterboard dented and he punched it again. This time his fist broke through. He leaned against the wall, his free hand flat against the plaster, and inhaled. He'd off'd politicians, terrorists, even a Middle-Eastern prince in his time – and been paid handsomely for it. So it beggared belief how in hell one stupid, fucking bitch could prove so bloody difficult to kill.

Tav's shoulders tightened. He inhaled again. Held it. And exhaled slowly. It did little to subside the tremors shaking his shoulders. He pulled his fist out of the stud wall. This contract was definitely not a career highlight. Another deep breath and, finally, his heartbeat slowed. He wet his dry lips, biting the bottom one while he thought. This Wade guy's untimely appearances were either an unbelievable coincidence or he was being fed information. And Tav didn't believe in coincidences. Regardless, his interference could no longer be overlooked.

Tav crossed the room and retrieved his keys off the floor. It was time he and Wade had a little chat – and then he would eliminate him from the picture once and for all.

Tav pulled the net curtain back and looked out of the window.

It was relatively quiet outside considering it was a main road. Signs of the previous snowfall remained everywhere he looked and, if the weather bods on BBC One were anything to go by, more snow was on the way. A car reverse-parked and a man got out. The lights illuminated the alarm and the man negotiated the slushy pavement until he reached his front gate. He fumbled through his keys then carried on up the path to the front door.

Tav's mobile began to ring. The casino. He thought about cancelling the call, but that would bring a whole heap of different shit down on his head. He picked up but remained quiet, just listening while the voice on the other end reminded him of the unfinished job they'd already paid him for.

He heard the man slide the key in the lock. Then the front door banged shut. This was not a phone call Tav wanted to have witnesses for and he let the curtain fall back across the window.

"Understood." Tav hung up.

He turned and waited for the living room door to open.

David Carter walked through from the hall. He threw his coat over the back of the armchair, then caught sight of Tav.

Carter froze. "Who are you? What are you doing here?"

On the surface, the CSI boss looked unfazed at Tav being there. Angry almost. But Tav was an expert at reading people. This guy was smart. This guy was nervous as hell.

"Mr Carter. Please, come in." Tav stepped away from the window. He patted the back of Carter's armchair, his genuine leather gloves slapping against the faux leather seat. "Sit."

Carter swung his keys from his index finger and glanced around the living room. "If you're thinking of doing me harm, you'll get caught. I'm with the force."

Tav smiled. He pulled a knife from behind his back. "I know who you are. And if I wanted you dead, your doorstep would be swimming in your blood right about now."

Tav patted the chair again.

Carter stuffed his keys into his jacket pocket. Still hesitant, he turned and settled into the leather chair.

Tav leaned on Carter's shoulders and lowered himself until his mouth was only inches from his ear. "Tell me about Leah Wade's death."

"What?"

Carter tried to turn but Tav held him still. He remained like that for a moment, then straightened. Releasing Carter's shoulders, he stepped around the chair. Sweat had broken out across Carter's forehead and a slight tremor rocked his arms.

Tav perched on the edge of the sofa opposite. He crossed his arms and stared harder at the man. "Tell me about the autopsy report."

"You need to speak with the pathologist."

"Why? Aren't you the one who authorised the bogus one?"

Carter's eyes widened. "How do you know—?"

"Why were they changed? Was the girl murdered?"

Carter's lips parted. His breathing accelerated. "What are you going to do?"

"Do? That depends."

"On?"

"How you answer my questions." Tav clasped his hands together, the knife between them, and rested his chin on the knuckles. "I'm waiting."

Carter swallowed. "Yes, she was murdered."

"Now that wasn't so hard, was it?" Tav scratched his neck and rested his chin on his hands again. "Who killed her?"

"I don't know."

Tav tilted his head. "See, that I don't believe."

"It's true. I was just asked to sign off on the paperwork."

"Why would a crime-scene knobhead like you sign off on a bogus autopsy?"

"Not the autopsy. Just the forensic stuff."

"Why? What were you hiding?"

"The marks around her neck."

"I saw the pictures. So?"

"Her death had to look like an accident." Carter wiped the sweat from his brow. "I made it consistent with something like a fishing line."

"And? What was it really?"

Carter looked at the door.

"Nothing over there's going to help you. Now, look at me and answer the question."

Carter sighed. "It was a seatbelt."

"Who killed her?"

"I don't know."

"Sure you do."

Carter wiped his brow again. His shirt was wet with perspiration. "I can't tell you."

"You can." Tav stood. "And believe me, you will tell me." He walked back to the window.

Carter's head lolled. His shoulders bounced lightly, and the sound of sobbing followed. "I can't go on like this."

A pad sat on the nearside table. Tav tossed it at Carter. "Write the name down."

"I was blackmailed." Carter began to scribble.

"Tell me more about the brother. He's a boxer, right?"

Carter nodded and looked up. His eyes found the knife and widened. "Quit years ago. Lost his license, so I heard."

Tav motioned for him to continue writing. "He good at the job he has now?"

Again, Carter nodded. "He was. Before the drink took over. Now he's just reckless."

"And that wouldn't have anything to do with your indiscretions, would it?"

Wade's interference with the girl was driving Tav to the point of distraction, but the loss of a loved one fucking sucked. Tav had to respect Wade for not letting go – even though he still had to eliminate the maggot.

"Can you tell me how he happened to be on scene to save the girl tonight?" Tav tapped his hand against his arm. "Did you tell him? Maybe you're playing both sides."

Carter frowned. "What girl? No."

"Then how?"

Carter swallowed. "What girl are you talking about?"

Tav cocked his head to one side. "The amnesiac one."

Carter tried to get up out of the chair.

Tav leapt to his feet and shoved him back down. He placed his hands on the arms of the chair and leaned in. "What is Wade's involvement with her?"

Carter shook his head. "He's forensics. He took her prints. That's all."

"And yet he keeps muddying my waters."

"He's resourceful. Like a dog with a bone."

"Well, somebody is helping him."

"Maybe it's his old girlfriend."

"Name?"

"Karen…something."

Tav walked back to the sofa and took up position on the arm again. "Write it down. I want Wade's address as well."

"I don't think I can—"

"It wasn't a request."

"No. I'm out." Carter threw the paper on the floor.

"You know, secrets are dangerous things in the wrong hands." Tav stood up. From his left pocket he pulled a small bag tied with a red band. "This…" he waved the bag, "will make you feel *real* good – just the way you like it. But this here…" he pulled a syringe from his right pocket, "this could be the death of you."

Carter's eyes widened. "Are you blackmailing me as well now?"

Tav flung the bag at him. At least Jimmy had been right about the guy's need for a high. The bag landed at Carter's feet – beside the notepad – and his body tightened. Every inch of him looked as if he wanted to scoop it up and snort it down in one go.

Tav plucked the biro from Carter's hand and leaned over him again. "Give me an address and thirty minutes from now you can be swimming in heaven." He raised the syringe close to Carter's eye. "Or you can go straight to hell. It's your choice."

Carter nodded. Sweat beaded his face. The guy was one breath away from a heart attack.

Carter bent for the pad. "Are you going to kill Wade?"

Tav smiled and held out the pen. "You just need to worry if I'm going to kill *you*."

Carter eyed the syringe. Gulped. And hastily scribbled down the address. "I wish I never stepped foot in that casino." He bent for the bag of drugs and ripped into the plastic.

Tav took the pad.

"Don't take all those at once," he said over his shoulder as he left.

CHAPTER THIRTY-TWO

The chair was uncomfortable.

Kate shifted position, but it did little to relieve the numbness that had set in during the last thirty minutes. She pulled the paramedic's blanket back around her shoulders and watched the three men through the office window. Two she recognised. Jason and the officer who'd taken her home – what was his name? DS Price. Ed. But, the third man she didn't know. He sat behind his desk. Lots of certificates framed the wall behind him. The cheap gilt plate on the closed office door making it known he was Inspector Waddell.

Inside, tempers were high. Raised arms flapped in the air. Fingers pointed at each other. Every now and again, their shouting made it through the glass - most of it coming from Jason.

He shouldn't have even been in there. By his own admission, he'd other matters he needed to urgently attend to – seemingly so important that they couldn't wait. It was Christmas Eve, after all. The time for families – and she assumed he had a family – to come together and celebrate. But Jason hadn't left her. And now, instead, he argued that she needed a safe place to stay for the night.

In retaliation, DS Price – Ed – continually demanded that Jason deliver some evidence to back up his ridiculous theory.

And now the pair argued their case to Inspector Waddell.

At this point, even Kate didn't know what to think. She'd smelled alcohol on Jason's breath the moment he walked into Charlotte's apartment and it was clear his handling of this unofficial investigation was far from legit. He was a maverick. He'd been beaten to a pulp and didn't seem to be running on all four cylinders. But if it hadn't been for him, she would be dead right now. And he seemed to be the only one who believed she was, in fact, in danger – just as Charlotte had warned.

She tried to stop the tremors rocking her body. Her memory was non-existent and, if Jason was correct, somebody seemed to want to kill her. She glanced towards the door, wondering if she'd survive if she made a run for it – away from the police altogether. Surely other friends would come forward to help her once the explosion at Charlotte's flat hit the news.

She continued to watch, not knowing whether to trust any of these men or run as far from them as she could get.

"The apartment was just blown to shit," Jason screamed.

Ed stepped forward. He addressed his inspector. "Nothing's been determined yet. It could just as easily have been a gas leak."

"You fucking serious?" Jason said.

"It wasn't even her flat."

Jason threw his arms in the air. "I suppose the bridge was an accident too?"

"Fuck, Jason." Ed turned to him. "It was probably just a shitting mugging."

"The evidence shows otherwise."

"What bloody evidence? Fucking finger marks in the snow?" The man slapped his head. "All that says is that she went overboard and held on for dear life."

"There's more."

"Like what? That all this shit is related to your sister?"

"If you'd just stuck her in a safe house instead of bringing her here, I would have fucking found out…" Jason exaggerated a look at his watch, "ten minutes ago."

"This is bollocks." Ed turned away.

Jason glanced Kate's way. His face softened, but the anger remained behind his eyes.

He glared back in Inspector Waddell's direction. "You know what? Fine. Put her in the hospital or back out on the street or wherever the fuck you think she'll be safe. But if something happens to her, I'll make fucking sure your cock-up headlines every front page of the morning's papers." Jason yanked open the office door to leave.

"Okay, that's enough." Inspector Waddell stood. He eyed Jason for a second then turned to Ed. "Sort it out. One night only."

"You can't be serious? He's not even fucking accredited anymore."

"A temporary setback," Jason interjected.

"Enough!" The inspector stepped out from behind his desk. He grabbed his jacket from the coat stand and looked at Ed again. "Just sort it. And stay with her."

"It's Christmas Eve, for fuck's sake."

"And I'm sure your wife'll still be there in the morning."

Ed seethed. He turned to Jason. "Who's feeding this obsession of yours?"

"No one."

"You said someone was helping you. Who is it?"

"A little bird." Jason left the room. He marched across the office to where Kate sat. "Ed's gonna take you to a safe house for tonight."

"Can't you stay?"

"I'm already late."

"He looks really cross. Maybe I *should* go to the hospital."

"He's pissed with me. Not you." He re-tucked the blanket beneath her chin. "I'll be back. I'll bring some clothes."

CHAPTER THIRTY-THREE

Jason reached the top of the steps and pressed the doorbell.

All this rushing about was doing nothing to soothe his ribs.

Karen opened the door – dressed to the nines and ready for their date. The look of annoyance immediately fell from her face. "What the hell happened?"

Jason glanced down at his attire – smoke-covered clothes, burn holes in his jacket, cuts and grazes to his hands. It seemed an age ago that he'd battled the inferno to find Kate.

He stepped past her and headed straight for the fridge. "Tell me you've been to the offy."

"Picked them up on the way home."

Just as she promised, eight bottles of Bud were crammed onto the middle shelf. He slid two out, cracked their caps, and swigged from one. Now, this was exactly the kind of medication he needed.

He wandered back into the living room. Karen sat at the table, her laptop open and already switched on. She slotted a flash drive into the USB port and waited for the file to load.

He passed her one of the beers. "So, what did you find?"

She took the beer but didn't drink any and placed the bottle on the side. "Maybe your man." She opened the file, clicked on a video, and scrolled through a way. She hit pause and sat back. "That him?"

The picture quality was far from clear. In fact, it was downright crap. The stamp in the righthand corner read: 20/04/17 18:04. Jason leaned forward and studied the blurry image of a man.

He shrugged. "Play it."

Karen scrolled back twenty seconds or so and the footage began to play – slightly clearer now it was a moving picture. A man, suited in light grey, exited the casino.

Jason frowned. It could be his guy from Bethnal Green. They looked the same build. The guy on the monitor seemed to be balding. Jason kept watching. The man walked across the narrow street. Just before he disappeared out of shot, a girl approached him.

"Is that Leah?"

"I think so, yes." Jason continued to watch but both people disappeared out of frame. His heart raced. "Is that it?"

Karen moved her fingers across the mouse pad. The screen jumped to another image. Still evening. Different angle of the street – the burger van in the background – and a slightly cleaner image. But no man in sight.

Jason clocked the date, now two days later with the time 23:19. "What am I supposed to be looking at?"

"Just watch."

Jason sipped back his beer. He watched the monitor. Glanced at the time. The seconds ticked by and the same man walked into view. Different suit, this time a darker colour. Shaved hair, definitely balding. "That's him."

The guy on the video slipped his hand into his trouser pocket and pulled out some keys. Pointed them to something out of shot. He neared the camera and then, as before, walked out of frame.

"Tell me you have more."

Karen smiled. "I always save the best for last."

Another angle of the street appeared on the monitor. The date in the corner confirmed it was the same day and time. The man stopped beside a car right in front of the camera.

"He's the guy I ran into last night in Bethnal Green," Jason said.

"Keep watching."

Jason kept watching. The man opened his car door, but didn't get in. Instead, he stared in the direction of the burger van. Various people crowded the area. Leah materialised between them, holding two burgers. She walked towards the man. Handed him a burger, then handed him something else, which he slipped into his pocket. She walked around to the passenger side of the car and got in.

Karen paused the video. She glanced up at him. "So, we know Leah knew this guy. But, how is your amnesiac from Bethnal Green linked to them?"

Jason shrugged. He turned and perched on the table. "First time I saw Kate, she said something in her sleep. *Blue bird.* I didn't think much of it at the time. Then a druggie gives up information about this guy with a tattoo and the next thing I'm brawling with him on a fucking stairwell in Bethnal Green." Jason glanced at her. "He has a tattoo of a blue bird on his hand."

"So, what? This girl's involved in your sister's death?"

Jason shrugged.

"The man, then?"

"Honestly? I have no fucking idea. I don't think so." He sipped his beer.

"Coincidence then?"

"Two girls found in the Thames? The same geezer connected to both?" Jason scratched his eye and swigged again from the bottle. He turned and looked at the monitor. "There a plate to go with that car?"

Karen started the footage again. "Yeah. It's fake."

Jason stood. "He has to be the son of a bitch who pushed her in the Thames."

"You're talking about Leah, right?"

Adrenaline pumped through his veins. "I mean Kate."

"The amnesiac bridge girl?" Karen unplugged the flash drive.

Jason nodded and perched on the desk again. He swigged his beer. Finally, he had some concrete evidence. "Did you send his DNA off?"

"I submitted it, like you said." She got up and went to the kitchen.

From where Jason sat, he saw her open the fridge. She removed the ice tray, put it on top of the fridge, and pulled out a plastic bag. Inside was her passport and some folded papers. She dropped the flash drive inside and zip-locked it back up.

Jason scoffed. "You still hiding shit in your freezer?"

Karen put the bag back, followed by the ice tray. "Keeps it safe."

"You do know that the majority of burglaries I attend have their fridges ransacked?"

"I know. You said last time." She shut the door and walked towards him. She picked her drink up off the table and took a sip. "I found something else."

Jason raised a brow.

"It is probably nothing. You have to keep an open mind."

Jason nodded. "What is it?"

Karen leaned for the mouse. She skated the arrow across the screen and clicked on a file. Another video, similar to the footage they'd just watched, began to play on the monitor. Grainy as hell, the point of view concentrating on the casino entrance.

Jason clocked the date. Different night – a couple of months prior to the footage they'd just watched. "What am—?"

"Shh. Just watch."

Jason did. The blurry picture showed clientele coming and going. He sipped his beer. He was starting to lose interest – then he saw. He lowered the bottle and stared at the screen. Two people – one man and one woman – exited the casino. They descended the steps, side by side. The girl planted a kiss on the man's cheek and they parted ways.

Jason looked at Karen. "What the fuck is Carter doing at the casino? And why is Leah kissing him?"

"It's probably nothing."

"Another coincidence, eh?" Jason turned back to the screen, Carter's image still on it. "That son-of-a-bitch knows what happened to her."

"Jason, he's your boss. Not some criminal."

"Then why has he never mentioned the casino or meeting Leah there?"

Karen shook her head. "Why on earth would he involve you in the bridge case if the amnesiac girl is linked to Leah? It doesn't make sense."

"Maybe he didn't know." Jason put his beer down. He turned back to Karen. "Shit. Nothing makes sense anymore."

"You want another beer?"

Jason shook his head. "I gotta be somewhere. Email that file to me."

"What you gonna do with it?"

"Fuck knows. I can't think straight."

"Then promise me you'll sleep on it, yeah?"

Jason planted a kiss on Karen's forehead. "I'm sorry about missing dinner. I owe you."

"Damn right you do."

He walked to the door, stopped, and turned back to her. "You don't have any clothes I can nick, do you?"

CHAPTER THIRTY-FOUR

Tav slid the tension wrench and pick from the lock and pushed opened the front door.

The inside was cleaner and more orderly than he'd given this Wade guy credit for. After all, he did dress in hoodies and run around the streets of London like a maverick. Tav stepped into the hallway and closed the door behind him. Wade lived alone – that much he'd been told – but he liked to assume the worst in any situation. Less of a surprise when shit hit the fan.

He headed into the living area, immediately clocking the boxing memorabilia and trophies that crowded the wall units. So, Wade had definitely been a professional boxer. Tav smiled. It certainly explained Wade's ability to take and, indeed, deliver a punch – especially the upper cut that had caught Tav off guard on the stairwell.

Tav crossed the room and lifted a trophy from the shelf. Dated a couple of years ago – nothing that would tell him where Wade might have disappeared to now.

He sat the trophy back down and turned to view the rest of the room. Papers were scattered across the coffee table – information on a girl's accidental death in the Thames nearly a year ago. Wade's sister.

He turned towards the kitchen. Magnets held several photographs to the fridge. He moved nearer and pulled one free. A much younger Wade with his arm around a dark-haired girl – Leah, though he barely recognised her. Tav threw the photo on the counter and opened the fridge. He wouldn't find any useful information in here, but at least Wade had good choice in beers. Tav took a bottle, cracked the cap, and headed upstairs.

Much of the same – a bed, made but not totally neat. In the wardrobe, clothes and a couple of jackets – nothing out of the ordinary. Beneath the bed – completely clear. Not even a pair of slippers. Inside the chest of drawers – socks, underwear, and some T-shirts. He searched through them but found nothing of any interest.

He swigged some beer and glanced around the room. Wasting time really. But Wade fascinated him. Old boxing gloves hung from a hook on the back of the bedroom door. Tav had never come up against anyone who wasn't military-trained but who could put up such a good fight.

He headed back downstairs to the living room. In particular, to the photographs that lined the mantle. Again, nothing out of the ordinary. Family photos. Tav smiled bitterly, remembering his own childhood. But, unlike his boxing adversary here, he didn't keep photos to remind him of the horrors he'd endured. He drained the last of the beer, a little jealous of Wade's life, and headed back into the kitchen. As he had at the Shad Thames penthouse, he placed the bomb inside the fridge. He didn't expect Wade to return but, if he did, then his last beer was going to go with a bang.

He closed the door and turned to leave. Stopped. A photograph – magnet pinning it to the fridge and buried beneath a receipt and a takeaway menu – caught his eye. Tav lifted the menu. Behind it was the same young kid standing in middle of the ring, an adult close behind and holding the junior boxer's arms up in victory.

Tav peered closer at the picture – at the name on the wall behind. The Phoenix Boxing Gym.

CHAPTER THIRTY-FIVE

Jason looked at the photograph.

Two women and a child standing outside flat number twenty-nine. Jason recognised it the moment he saw it. He'd been right outside less than twenty-four hours earlier.

He lowered the picture and looked at the flats in front of him – still pretty much mirroring the photo. He tucked the picture in his back pocket and headed for the stairwell. Hard to think he'd got his arse kicked here less than a day before. One thing was for damn sure, when he met the elusive Mr Blue Bird again – and they would meet again – there'd be a different fucking outcome.

He reached the second floor and headed out onto the walkway. It was nearly midnight and a voice inside his head screamed at him not to knock on the door. But what he had to ask the occupant inside couldn't wait.

He lifted the pixie doorknocker and tapped it against the brass plate twice.

Behind the door, he heard movement. "Who is it?"

"Ma'am, my name is Jason Wade. I work for the police. I met you yesterday on the stairs."

"You have any identification?"

Jason reached for his wallet then remembered he only had his business cards on him.

He posted one through the letterbox regardless. "Only this."

"Then you have to leave."

"Ma'am, I'm here about Kate."

There was a moment of silence. "I don't know any Kate."

"Ma'am, she lived on the floor below. Number forty-six." Jason took the photograph from his pocket. A quick glance at it and he posted it through the letterbox as well. "That's her as a child. You are standing behind her."

"Where did you get this?"

"Kate gave it to me."

Behind the door, he heard the lock click. The door opened a crack – as much as the chain allowed.

The old woman peered out. "When did she give it to you?"

"A couple of hours ago."

"She's alive?"

Jason smiled. "Very much so."

The woman closed the door and Jason listened as the chain slid from the latch.

When the door reopened, she had the photograph clasped to her chest and her eyes had glazed over. "Where is she? Is she okay?"

"Actually, I could do with your help. I think she's in trouble."

The woman raised her hand to her mouth. Concern painted her eyes. "Come in, come in."

She ushered Jason into the hallway and closed the door behind him. Re-bolting the chain, she pulled a curtain across the door. "Come through to the living room. It's warmer in there." She scurried past him, the picture still gripped in her hand. "Can I get you some tea?"

"No, please. It's late and I don't want to take up any more of your time than I have already."

"Nonsense." The woman sat down in the chair and motioned for him to do the same on the sofa. "Now, how can I help Kate?"

"Who is the other person in the photo?"

The woman glanced down at the image. "That's her mother, Sarah. Kate must have been five or six when this was taken. Such a sweet girl."

"Do you know when they moved?"

"Not long after this picture. Her mother met a young man, quite wealthy."

"Do you know where they moved to?"

"San Francisco."

"America?" Of course. The American accent the security guard had mentioned made sense now. "Did they live there long?"

"They married soon after arriving. We conversed for a few years, but the letters eventually stopped. You know how it is. Life gets in the way, doesn't it? Before you know it, years have passed by." She laid the photo on the coffee table. "Last time I saw Kate was when she was at university."

"What do you know about her father?"

"Step-father. Oh, he was some kind of businessman. Had a very expensive car. Always arrived with flowers. I think he built houses or something."

"Here in England?"

"Here and in America."

"He was American, though?"

"Yes. Jon Reynolds, I think his name was. At least, that was the surname both Kate and her mother used after her mother married."

Jason took out the passport. "I found this." He passed it to the lady.

She opened it and looked at the picture of Kate, slightly older. "Yes, she certainly grew up to be a pretty little thing."

"Do you know why, when she lived in the States, she would renew her UK passport under her old name and use the flat upstairs as her residence?"

The woman smiled. "She listed that address so her father wouldn't find out about the shenanigans she and her university friends got up to. I assume that's why she also used two names." The woman chuckled. "Oh, her antics were nothing more than what any other university student gets in trouble for. Mainly drinking too much. But she and her friends all came from affluent families who wouldn't have wanted the bad publicity. And, of course, the children wanted to keep their allowances. The old flat upstairs has been empty for years. Perfect address for them to use."

She passed him back the book. "What trouble is Kate in?"

"I don't really know yet." He lifted the photograph from the table and stood. "Thank you for all your help."

"Will you tell Kate to come see me? I heard her mother passed away last year. Cancer. Terrible thing. It would be nice to see Kate again."

Jason nodded. He smiled and retreated to the front door. Waited on the balcony and listened as the old lady bolted the locks on the other side. Then he rang Karen.

She was going to bust his balls for this one, but he needed to know everything about Jon Reynolds. The call went to voicemail, but he declined to leave a message. Shit. He opened the browser and typed the name into the search bar. Reception was a bitch around here – just like everything else. The cog turned middle of the screen but no information came up.

Bollocks.

CHAPTER THIRTY-SIX

The safe house was not how Kate had imagined it would be.

It wasn't out of sight and hidden away from prying eyes, but in a quiet, residential street, where normal families lived in ordinary terraced houses.

DS Price – Ed – parked outside the end house. A wall running beside it held a narrow, wooden gate. You didn't have to be Einstein to know the alleyway behind it probably led to the rear gardens. Ed opened the car door and got out. He hadn't told her to follow him, but he hadn't told her to stay put either. In fact, he hadn't really said much of anything during their drive here. Kate opened her door, watching for any expression on his face that said she needed to remain in the car. Nothing. So she climbed out and joined him by the front gate.

"Now, it ain't the Ritz, but it is safe," Ed said.

Kate didn't care. Anything was better than being back in hospital. She followed him along the short path to the front door. "Is it just the two of us?"

Ed slipped his key into the lock. "No. There are two other officers inside. I'll introduce you and give you a quick tour."

He twisted the key and pushed the door open.

His description hadn't done the house justice. Exposed boards led her through the hallway. The living area wasn't much better. Grubby furniture and dirty, cream walls. Not that the place looked unclean. She searched for any kind of mess – discarded food packaging, dust, dirty plates. The place looked sanitary, at least.

Two officers sat at a small table. They stood when Ed entered.

"This is Officer Butler," Ed said. "And this is Officer Simmons."

Both men held out their hands. Kate shook them but had forgotten their names before she'd released the second officer's hand. She stepped back and stifled a yawn.

"How about I show you to your room?" Ed said. "You must be wiped out."

Kate nodded, grateful for the suggestion. Ed walked her back into the hallway and began to climb the stairs. Kate followed. At the top, a small landing led to only four doors.

"Bathroom's through there if you want a shower." Ed didn't give Kate time to check it out. He turned and pointed opposite – to the door on her right. "Your room is through here."

He crossed the landing and pushed open the door.

Kate thanked him with a smile and headed inside. She heard Ed start back down the stairs and turned. "Detective Price?"

Ed paused. He looked at her through the banister. "Please. Ed's fine."

She smiled again, this one only slight. "I know the timing isn't great – what with it being Christmas – but I do appreciate what you're doing for me."

Ed nodded and a smile found his own lips. It was the first time he'd shown any emotion other than anger; he'd been acting put out ever since leaving the police station.

Kate turned for the bedroom. Surprisingly, the inside wasn't too bad. Nothing extravagant – a bed, a wardrobe, a dated lamp on a small side-table. She closed the door behind her, welcoming the solitude the room offered, and sat on the corner of the bed. Another yawn found her and her eyes glazed over. She hadn't seen a clock since getting out of the car at midnight. What a nightmare she was in. She glanced down at the baggy police jumper she now wore. Clean, but the stench of smoke still clung to her skin underneath. Christ, her eyes hurt, but she was too afraid to sleep.

She peeled back the duvet, switched off the bedside lamp, and crawled beneath the covers. The sound of the television downstairs vibrated through the floorboards. She hugged the duvet tighter and willed some heat to hurry up and warm her body. Thoughts of the last couple of days muddled her thinking. Charlotte's apartment thrust itself to the forefront of her mind – the explosion, the smoke, what had happened to her friend. She tried to push the images away and fill the void with other, happier memories. But all she knew was horror, death, and this safe house.

She tucked her knees tighter to her chest. Her real life was buried somewhere inside her head. If only she could remember it, remember what had happened that had caused this mayhem to come knocking on her door now. Tears filled her eyes and she let them overflow and soak away into the pillow. If only she could remember.

More tears flowed. Jason wasn't telling her everything and she had no idea why. Maybe he knew who she really was. Maybe she deserved everything that was happening to her. She closed her eyes and tried to concentrate on the noise from the TV. She heard voices – all male – but they didn't speak for long and she couldn't hear what was said.

She focused on the TV again – some kind of football match if the chanting was anything to go by – and snuggled deeper beneath the duvet. Sleep hovered but her mind wouldn't relax long enough for it to take her.

She sighed and opened her eyes. The stench of smoke wafted around her – something she couldn't stomach any more. Pushing back the duvet, she got up and went back out onto the landing. The bathroom door was ajar, but she still knocked before pushing it open.

Finding it empty, she bolted it shut and looked in the mirror. Her auburn hair, matted and dull with soot. Her face, drained of all colour. Shadows smeared like war paint beneath her eyes. She drew back the shower curtain and turned the knob. Held her hand beneath the water until she felt it warm, then pulled her jumper over her head.

She stepped beneath the water and the last couple of days washed from her body and dirtied the bathtub. Heat warmed her skin and her body relaxed – a little. Her bruised skin hurt to touch and her head hadn't stopped throbbing since the explosion. She closed her eyes and lifted her face towards the spray, letting the water wash through her hair and cascade over her body like a waterfall.

An image flashed across her mind. Dark. Cold. Water filling her mouth every time she tried to scream for help.

Her eyes shot open and she jumped back from the shower. Her breath quickened, her chest ached, and she reached for the tiled wall. Steam still floated around her, but her damp skin quickly froze in the room's cooling temperature. Kate hugged her body and lowered herself to the edge of the bath. Had she just remembered something? She glanced up at the shower. Had the water triggered a memory?

She turned the water off and reached for a towel. Wet hair dripped down her back and goose bumps pimpled her skin. She quickly rubbed her hair dry best she could and wrapped the damp towel around her body. The house felt colder than when she'd first arrived with Ed.

She poked her head around the bathroom door. She couldn't see or hear anyone – a good thing as she didn't want to meet any police while wrapped in just a towel. Her bedroom door was four strides across the landing. She glanced down at the police jumper and jogging bottoms lying in a heap on the floor. Maybe she should ignore the smell and put them on again. Truth was, every time the smell of smoke found her, she thought of the apartment and what happened to Charlotte. Kate didn't remember much of her life, and she sure as hell didn't want that sad, horrific incident defining it.

Tiptoeing across the landing, she hurried inside the bedroom and closed the door behind her. The room lay under a cover of darkness and she felt for a light switch. Unable to find one, she felt her way along the bed towards the side table.

Crawling beneath the covers, she finally closed her eyes.

CHAPTER THIRTY-SEVEN

Karen was bloody good at her job.

Shame the detection work she was currently doing now wasn't her job.

"I had to hack the military database for this," her friend said.

"And I appreciate it. Really."

"Just make sure it doesn't come back to haunt me."

Karen hung up the phone and went to her computer. As promised, sitting in her inbox was an email containing the analysis of the fingerprints she'd lifted from the clasp on the baseball cap. She printed it off and collected the pages from the tray. Jason owed her big time for this. She'd neglected to tell him she'd submitted the cap for fingerprinting – a little white lie – but this idea of hers had just saved him two weeks waiting for the DNA results. The man's prints had him labelled as a soldier.

She glanced at the pages. In the top left corner was a picture – Tavish Finley. A good looking man – ignoring the fact that he was possibly a criminal of sorts. The rest of the papers didn't hold much on him in the way of information: Scottish with no previous convictions. In fact, the lack of information explained why the police database hadn't churned out anything on him. But it was definitely the guy on the CCTV footage. For now, at least, Jason had a name to go with the face.

She opened the fridge, pulled out the ice tray, and slipped the pages inside the plastic wallet. Grabbing a beer, she closed the door.

Tavish Finley slouched against the kitchen doorframe, arms folded, looking both calm and menacing.

Karen froze. She recognised him immediately. "Who are you? How did you get in here?"

"Front door."

Karen swallowed. Out the corner of her eye, she spotted the knife rack. "What do you want?"

Finley smiled and straightened. He lowered his arms, the bulk in his biceps denying them the ability to touch his sides "I think you know." He stepped forward.

Karen gripped the bottle. She backed away, as far as the counter would allow.

Finley stopped in front of her and leaned in. "I know you're helping the copper guy."

His breath warmed Karen's cheeks and the leather of his jacket invaded her nostrils. She waited for him to step back, but he remained close.

"I…I was just doing my job."

"Hmm." Finley tilted his head and lightly traced his finger down the side of her face. "Tell me. What does he know?"

Karen shook her head. "Nothing. I haven't found anything yet."

Finley traced the outline of her jaw and tutted. When he finally glanced up, his brown eyes bore straight into hers. "Is he worth dying for?"

"W…what?"

Finley lowered his fingers to her throat.

A tear rolled from Karen's eye. She swallowed again and turned her face from him.

He clasped her neck and squeezed. "Look at me."

When Karen didn't, he twisted her to face him.

A sob choked in the back of her throat. "He doesn't know anything."

"He knows something."

"I looked but couldn't find anything."

Finley studied her for a second. His eyes narrowed. "I almost believe you."

He stared at her for the best part of a minute. Then smiled. "Tell me about him."

"W…what?"

He held up a photograph. "Who is the man in this picture? His father? Uncle?"

Karen glanced at the photo. She'd never seen it before, or the man standing beside a much younger Jason. "I don't know."

Finley tutted and his fingers tightened.

Karen felt her neck contract. Each short breath became harder. She clawed at his arm with her free hand, the neck of the beer still clasped in her other. Then smashed the bottle against the side of his head.

The glass broke and large pieces sliced into her palm.

Finley released her and stumbled back. He reached for the counter, red droplets bloodying the surface, and shook his head. Karen shoved past him and raced into the living room. Didn't get far. Felt him grab a clump of her hair.

She jerked backwards.

Finley hauled her back and pressed against her, one hand still entwined in her hair, his other clasping her neck. "Feisty little bitch, ain't ya?"

He shoved Karen across the room. She struck the cabinet. When she tried to straighten, Finley took her by the hair again. He yanked her back and ran her towards the glass-panelled hallway door. His fingers pulled free from her hair and Karen plummeted through the glass. She collapsed on the carpet, broken glass raining down around her. Blood, sticky and warm, oozed down her face and arms.

Finley's footsteps crunched across the glass. Karen glanced up. The blurry hallway looked almost unrecognisable to her. She clawed at the carpet, her arms feeble and unable to pull her to safety.

Two shoes stopped in front of her and blocked her from going any farther.

Finley grabbed hold of her hair again – his fingernails scratching her scalp – and hauled her off the ground so she stood before him. "Last chance to save yourself, honey."

Karen struggled to focus. He was a blur in front of her. She spat a pool of blood from her mouth. "I don't know…"

Her legs weakened, but the fingers in her hair held her up. She swallowed and coughed up more blood. Finley released her hair and repositioned his hand around her throat. Karen reached for his grip but her weak arms felt weighed down.

"I hope he appreciates you," Finley said, and started to squeeze.

Karen struggled for air. Breaths spluttered past her lips. She glanced through the broken door towards the computer. The flash drive. He couldn't get the flash drive.

Finley's grip loosened. He followed her gaze and turned towards the computer. "Good girl."

He dragged her back into the living room, her feet trailing lines through the carpet behind her, and released her.

Kate collapsed to the ground beside the desk and clasped her neck. Every sharp breath burned her chest.

Finley switched the computer screen on. He pulled out the chair and sat. Slid the keyboard towards him and tapped his fingers across the letters. Found the email attachment and sat back. "You print this email out?"

Karen glanced up. Finley's military record sat open on the screen. Not to be caught out again, she forced herself not to glance towards the fridge and shook her head.

Finley pushed the chair away and knelt before her. "Are you sure?"

Karen reached out in an attempt to keep him at bay but Finley took her arm, palm up, and stretched it out across his knee. He applied a little pressure to her hand.

Karen cried out, her arm bending backwards.

"I asked you a question."

Her tears overflowed. "Please. Don't."

Finley pressed down.

Karen's arm snapped and her screams filled the house.

Finley's hand covered her mouth. He glared down at her and grimaced, giving a disappointed shake of his head. "Do you want to die?"

The stench of stale cigarettes clung to his fingers. Karen clasped her arm and struggled for breath.

"Then tell me. Did you print this out?"

Her muffled cries bawled past his fingers. She squeezed her eyes shut and shook her head again.

Finley released her. "See, that wasn't too hard, was it?"

Karen collapsed to the ground and curled into a ball.

Finley knelt in front of her and lifted her head. He smiled. "I think we got off on the wrong foot."

CHAPTER THIRTY-EIGHT

A silent vibration woke him.

Jason opened his eyes and, for a moment, he couldn't remember where he was. He cracked the stiffness from his neck and waited for his eyes to adjust to the darkness. The outline of the bed materialised and then Kate – sleeping, her back to him.

He sat up. Again, tried to stretch the ache from his neck. Couldn't. And reached inside his jacket pocket for his phone. The screen's brightness momentarily blinded him and he squinted and turned away. Blinking the dots from his eyes, he dimmed the glare. Now he saw the text from Karen.

Shit. He was supposed to call her before he crashed.

Found something. Meet me at Battersea Power Plant.

His thumb hovered above the screen for a moment. Why the hell did she want to meet at Battersea for? Uncertain, he hit call and listened while her phone rang. Finally, it went to voicemail and he hung up without leaving a message. His gut churned. Something wasn't right. He glanced at the time in the corner of the screen. Twenty-five to three. Something definitely wasn't right. Reluctantly, he rubbed his brow and tapped back a message that he was on his way.

He got up from the chair and stretched. Waited for the numbness in his arse to fade, and picked up Karen's sports bag from the floor. He placed it on the end of the bed – somewhere Kate couldn't possibly miss it – and walked to the door. When he glanced back at her, he saw the outline of her legs curled towards her chest. She looked almost childlike. He'd wanted to wake her when he'd first entered the bedroom but reasoned she needed sleep far more than he needed his questions answered – especially at such an early hour in the morning. Instead he'd taken to the chair and settled in for the night. Now he wished he'd just woken her.

He reached for the door handle, chewed on his lip, and thought about waking her now.

Bollocks. She'd still be here in a couple of hours when he returned.

Having his license suspended sucked. He hated having to rely on black cabs and Ubers every time he wanted to get somewhere sharpish.

Ed was gonna be pissed when he saw that Jason had taken – no, borrowed – his Jag for a couple of hours. But he was a big boy – old and ugly enough to deal with it.

Jason pulled up outside the main entrance to the Battersea property. A mash of steel railings and high, brick walls bordered the old, coal-fired power station. Still, an uneasy feeling sat in the pit of his stomach. Through the gates, he saw construction materials stacked high in carefully-sought-out plots, heavy equipment parked alongside the perimeter – everything in sight covered with a fresh blanket of snow.

Karen's car was nowhere to be seen. Jason glanced up at the gate – a good eight to ten feet in height, with cameras watching him from either side. He looked down at the lock, expecting to see a padlocked chain. But there was nothing.

Where the fuck was Karen?

In the yard, no lights. No security guards. No movement.

The nervousness – no – perturbed feeling inside his gut expanded into his chest. It was just too damn quiet. He took out his phone and dialled Karen's number. It rang twice before he heard the tinny sound of the Rolling Stones (*I can't get no) Satisfaction* echoing across the building site.

Jason hung up. Keeping hold of the phone, he pushed one of the gates open a little and stepped inside. Still no sign of a watchman. Surely someone was monitoring the security cameras? He thought about calling out but, deep down, he knew his presence hadn't gone undetected.

He phoned Karen again, waited for the Stones to chime, and followed the melody farther into the property. Every inch of his being screamed at him to back the fuck out and call Ed. Get the Calvary down here, pronto. But this itch in his gut told him Karen didn't have that much time to spare. Bile rose in his throat at the thought and urgency found his step. He reached the power station, its walls supported with scaffolding and mesh, and entered. Inside, more building materials sat beside a loader and a forklift. Water dripped from steel girders. Weeds pushed through the decaying, concrete floor. Karen's phone went to voicemail and Jason redialled. Again, Jagger's voice rocked out and Jason followed it through the building and out to the wasteland on the other side.

Some twenty yards away, a yellow Fiat 500 – Karen's Fiat – sat facing the River Thames. The engine wasn't running and condensation misted the windows. Jason hung up and slipped his phone back inside his jacket. He stepped backwards, letting the doorway conceal him, and looked up. No floors. Just a derelict building above him with nowhere to hide. Back outside, he glanced around the area. In the snow, tyre marks led to Karen's car. And from the driver's side, a single set of footprints walked to where Jason stood now – way too big to be Karen's dainty shoe size.

Jason kept his eye on the car, his other senses scanning for everything else. Finally, he approached the passenger side. Karen's phone sat on the roof, six of Jason's missed calls on the screen along with his opened text.

He glanced over the car. Darkness hindered his vision, but he crouched low and checked beneath it. After what had happened at the Shad Thames apartment, he had to assume the possibility of another explosive device. He stood and leaned closer to the window – still the conscious effort not to touch the car. Someone was inside, slouched in the seat, their head lolling forward. Karen? Jason reached for the handle, inhaled, and pulled open the door.

Karen sat slumped in the seat. Blood coloured her hair, her clothes. He felt for a pulse and found one. Just. Reaching behind the seat, his fingers felt their way along her arms until he touched the broken radius protruding through her skin just below her elbow. He grit his teeth. The wanker had snapped her bone. Jason moved to her wrists – zip-tied together. Fuck. He sat back and glanced at her feet. Her ankles looked to be tied to the seat adjuster beneath the seat. She had no shoes on or coat. Just the clothes he'd last seen her in.

He cupped her face. "Karen? It's Jason."

Scratches sliced her face. Bruises coloured her swollen eyes. A faint groan whispered past her lips. She was barely conscious.

"I'm gonna get you out of here, okay, sweetheart?"

He reached behind her again, careful not to knock her arm, and pulled on the ties. They wouldn't break – unsurprisingly. He crouched in the front footwell and tried for a better look under the seat. The floor felt wet and sticky, and when he lifted his hand he saw that blood painted his palm. He looked at Karen again. Her torn clothes were splashed with blood consistent with the beating she'd clearly taken. But there shouldn't be nearly enough blood to soak the floor as much as it had.

He lowered himself into the footwell again. Ran his hands around her bare feet, her ankles, her shins – all wet with blood. Slid his hands higher, cupping her calves.

He froze.

Felt a single cut at the top of her left calf. A neat downward slice through her saphenous vein.

A million thoughts whirled inside his head. He glanced up at Karen again – this time seeing the paleness of her skin beneath the bruises. Fuck. He pulled on the ties again. Opening the glove box, he routed around for something sharp. Nothing. Fuck. *Fuck!*

He slammed the little door shut, got to his feet and hurried to the boot. No fucking jack or tools or anything.

He searched the yard. There had to be something sharp here. He looked at the wing-mirror and kicked it. It broke free from the mount and dropped to the ground. The mirror cracked and Jason pulled a piece free. He crouched back in the footwell, found the ties around Karen's ankles, and started to cut through them. It took two seconds for the plastic to sever. Jason pulled off his fleece, raised Karen's feet onto the dash, wrapped her leg, and applied as much pressure as he could. He needed to get her out of this car. He released her leg and pulled the fleece tighter, securing it in a knot. Then, reaching behind the seat, he cut the ties from her wrists.

He threw the mirror on the ground and cupped her face. "Karen?"

She looked up at him through partly closed lids. Her voice was barely audible. "Blue bird."

"What?"

She tried to speak again. "Blue…"

"Karen?" He felt for a pulse.

Nothing.

"Karen?" He lifted her lids.

Dead eyes looked back at him.

His hands clasped her throat, his fingers searching for her pulse. Still nothing. He pulled her from the car. Lay her flat on the snow. Tilted her head. His lips found hers and he breathed into her mouth. A moment, then he started to pump her chest. A second breath, then back to her chest.

He felt for a pulse. Nothing.

A third breath. A fourth. No pulse.

He shook her shoulders. Grabbed her hands. Nothing woke her up.

He sat back and stared down at her, her once warm body now motionless and pale. He wanted to scream. He wanted to kill the bald-headed fucker who'd done this. Instead, he wiped the tears from his eyes, swallowed back his anger, and took out his phone.

"This is Jason Wade. With SOCO. I have a colleague down." The words caught in his throat. "Need a crew out to Battersea Power Station. One vic. Female."

He shook his head. Why had—?

He froze.

Fuck.

Kate.

CHAPTER THIRTY-NINE

Kate opened her eyes and listened.

Silence. Not even the sound of the TV filtering through the floorboards. She rolled onto her back and stared up into the darkness, trying to cough the dryness from her throat. Tiredness lingered behind her eyes, but recent events already buzzed inside her head. She rubbed her eyes and closed them again, but the thoughts remained.

Shit.

She opened her eyes and leaned for the bedside lamp. The room brightened and she saw a glass of water on the side. It hadn't been there when she'd gone to sleep. Nevertheless, she sat up and gratefully drank. Wiped the dribble from her chin and put the empty glass back down. Then noticed the sports bag on the end of the bed. Now, that definitely hadn't been there when she'd fallen asleep. She dragged it towards her and pulled back the zip. Inside was a hairbrush, toothbrush, leggings, socks. No underwear, but the softest jumper she'd ever felt.

Jason.

He'd been here. While she slept. Did that mean he was downstairs now?

She pushed back the duvet, threw the towel to the floor, and slipped into the clothes. Nipping across to the bathroom, she quickly brushed her teeth and pinned back her hair using a band that was wound around the brush handle. Finally, she felt a little more human again.

The woolly socks kept the low temperature from freezing her feet as she walked downstairs. The living room was empty, the coffee table littered with foil take-away cartons, and the TV turned off. She listened for voices – for any kind of movement. Nothing.

The downstairs toilet flushed, and Ed opened the bathroom door.

Kate moved towards the kitchen.

Ed caught her movement. "Jesus Christ!"

A moment to compose and he lowered his hand from the ASP hooked on his belt. He smiled away his embarrassment. "Can't sleep, eh?"

Kate shook her head. "Where is everyone?"

"Butler's checking outside. Simmons is upstairs in the front bedroom." He sat at the table. Laid out in front of him were lines of playing cards. He picked up the small deck, added another card to the line on the right, then placed another line on top of that. Laid another card. It was clear a conversation was not on the cards.

"Was Jason here?" Kate said.

Ed glanced up and frowned. "He's not upstairs?"

Kate shook her head.

Ed slammed the cards down and stood. The chair toppled backward – his jacket with it – and he stormed towards the living room window. He was heavier than Jason, and shorter by about six inches.

He pulled back the curtain. "Son of a bitch."

When he marched back towards the kitchen, Kate saw his jumper could have done with being a size larger, and his trousers a little more loose-fitting around the groin area.

He took out his phone, tapped the screen, and held it to his ear. Waited a few seconds then threw it across the table. "That little prick." He punched a nearby cupboard door and leaned on the counter.

A little over the top, but Kate remained quiet. Whatever Jason had done to annoy him, she wasn't about to step into the middle of it. Ed's hostility towards her was bad enough without her making it worse.

Ed glanced at her and closed his eyes. His shoulders slumped forward. "He stole my Jag."

"Where did he go?"

Ed shrugged. He turned to her and forced a smile. "He's a loose cannon."

"What do you mean?"

Ed walked to the table, stood the chair up, and motioned for Kate to sit.

She did. "Is he coming back?"

"Who knows?" He picked up his coat, found his cigarettes in the pocket, and threw the jacket on the table. "You know you don't need to be here, right?"

"You don't think I'm in danger?"

Ed shook his head. He took a cigarette out of the box and slipped the filter between his lips. "All this is in his head." He threw the box on top of his jacket and patted down his clothes. He stopped at his trouser pocket and pulled out a red, plastic lighter.

"What about the bridge? And tonight, at the apartment?"

"After finding your bag, it appears you probably went over the bridge during a mugging that got out of hand."

"And tonight? That explosion."

"Trumpton thinks it was a dodgy fridge." A flame burst from the lighter and he lit the end of his cigarette.

Kate stared. Charlotte had died because of a faulty refrigerator? That didn't seem right.

A line of smoke wound around her. "Why is Jason convinced otherwise?"

Ed sighed. He dragged on his cigarette again and another line of smoke surrounded her. "Eight months ago, his sister fell in the Thames and died."

Kate sat up.

Ed waved her back down. "She was full of coke and booze. It was an accident he's convinced was a murder."

"Why?"

"Because of some marks he saw around her bloody neck. Thinks she was strangled."

"Isn't that his job, though? To determine those things?"

"Fishing line caused it." Ed sucked on the cigarette again.

Kate readied herself for the fresh stench of smoke to reach her. She held her breath until it passed. "What does all that have to do with me?"

Ed scoffed. "I ain't no sodding doctor, but I reckon you're a substitute."

Kate frowned. None of what he said made any sense.

"Leah – that's Jay's sister – started going off the rails after their mum passed away. I think he blames himself for not being there, or some shit like that."

Kate's heart sunk. "And he can heal that guilt by saving me?"

Ed shrugged. "I don't know." He shifted position, dragged on his cigarette again, and puffed blue circles into the air. "You know he was suspended yesterday?"

"For helping me?"

"He broke someone's hand and held a boiling kettle over their head."

Kate clasped her hands together. Her palms felt clammy and she rubbed them together. This did not sound like the Jason who'd pulled her from the burning building only hours ago.

"You don't believe me?"

Kate glanced up.

A smirk smeared Ed's lips. "He nearly killed someone once. Beat 'em to a pulp so even their own mother couldn't recognise them. All because of his obsession with blaming someone else."

Kate shifted in her seat, prey to a sudden need to leave the kitchen. "I thought you were his friend."

"I am. Christ. I'm his best friend. I was Leah's friend too." He paused for a second. "I don't mean to sound harsh, but I'm worried about him. He is a good guy. Really. But where his sister is concerned…he needs help. His brain's fried."

Kate looked at the playing cards. She slid the three of clubs over to the four of hearts and forced a yawn.

Ed checked his watch. A light sweat broke out across his forehead and he paled. He clasped his stomach. "Goddamn vindaloo. Been squirting out of me all night."

He backed up towards to the toilet. "I'd better see where Butler is. You head up to bed. Grab as much sleep as you can."

Kate didn't need telling twice. She stood up, gave him an obligatory smile, and quickly retreated to the stairs. She paused on the bottom step and turned to the front door. Maybe she should leave. This house made her feel uneasy. Ed thought of her as nothing but an inconvenience and appeared to have no qualms about hiding it. And Jason – the one person she thought she could trust – was a nutcase.

"You okay?" Ed stood at the living room door. "Something wrong?"

Kate turned from the door and shook her head. "Night," she said, and headed up the stairs.

Simmons exited the bathroom. He stood aside and smiled as Kate passed him on the stairs, but offered no conversation. She watched him jog the rest of the way down, then headed into the bathroom herself and bolted the door behind her. Without bothering to look in the mirror, she splashed a little water on her face.

The thud was loud. Like a sack of unopened potatoes dropping on the ground. Kate turned the tap off. Stilled. And listened.

No other noises followed. The house was quiet – deathly quiet.

She dried her face on the towel, opened the bathroom door – just a little – and peered out at the landing. No one there. Regardless, her body remained frozen to the spot – her legs refusing to step outside.

She silently cursed. What the hell was wrong with her? Ed had explained that she wasn't in any danger. But something inside screamed for her not to open the door any farther.

Another thud – what sounded like a chair toppling over.

Kate hovered, unsure what to do. Damn Jason for making her feel this insecure. Heck. It was probably Ed standing up from the table again. She massaged her forehead and tried to rub the ache from her head. Sleep called her. The tiredness she felt was probably the cause of her paranoia. Tomorrow she'd leave this house and find somewhere else to live.

Footsteps, slow and careful, started up the stairs. A floorboard creaked and the footsteps stopped.

A white cord dangled beside Kate. She slowly pulled it, muffling the *click* as the light switched off. The bathroom was plunged into darkness and Kate peered out at the landing again. From her position, she could just see the top of the stairs. The footsteps started to climb again. Kate slowed her breathing and watched. A shadow climbed the wall, followed by the darkened figure of a person.

Not any of the police officers.

This person, broad-shouldered and muscular, was dressed in dark clothes. A balaclava covered his face. He reached the top of the stairs and raised his arm, a long sort of gun thing clasped in his hand. Kate stepped away from the door. Her heart raced. Terror shook her fingers, her arms, her legs. Would she make it outside if she bolted for the front door? She glanced around the bathroom. No scissors, no razors, nothing she could use as a weapon. She saw the window and crept towards it, the woolly socks silencing her steps. As quietly as she could, she climbed onto the toilet seat and opened the window.

The drop was significant. Still, she climbed onto the sill and glanced down at the garden. Fresh footprints patterned the snow-covered grass. Outside on the landing, she heard footsteps again. She had no choice.

She jumped.

- 247 -

CHAPTER FORTY

Tyres squealed and the Jag skidded to a halt in the middle of the road.

Jason kicked open the driver's door and rushed towards the house. The front door was ajar – no signs of forced entry – and he pushed it open. Darkness shrouded the hallway. He cautiously stepped over the threshold and saw Simmons lying at the bottom of the stairs, face down and motionless.

Jason paused, holding his breath until his lungs ached. He couldn't hear anything. Not a sound. He crept towards Simmons and rolled him over. The officer stared up at him, his eyes wide and lifeless. A single hole the diameter of a pencil punctured the flesh just below his left cheekbone. Jason felt for a pulse but wasn't surprised when he couldn't find one. He glanced up towards the first floor. Still no sound.

He took the stairs one at a time, sticking close to the wall.

The freezing temperature numbed his hands. Even with the front door ajar, it was still far colder than it should be. Two-thirds of the way up, he paused eye-level with the first-floor landing. Colder still. The icy air dried his eyes and chafed his skin as it swept past him.

An open window maybe? But where?

Light from Kate's bedside lamp filtered out through her open door. Jason saw the corner of the bed, but not much else. Dread gnawed at his gut and his chest tightened. Images of Karen flashed in front of him. His jaw tightened and his hands clenched into fists. This blue-bird guy was gonna pay for what he'd done. Jason would make sure of it.

He climbed the rest of the stairs. There were three other rooms on the landing – two bedrooms, their doors open, seemingly empty. The bathroom door was pushed to, but not closed. Cold air raced through the gap. With his senses alert to the quietness surrounding him, Jason crossed the narrow landing. The closer he got to Kate's bedroom, the more of the interior he saw. The sports bag lay on the floor at the foot of the bed, open and empty. The drained water glass sat on the bedside table. The bed itself was vacant.

He didn't know whether to feel relieved or panicked at not finding Kate there.

A stair tread creaked. Jason spun around, his fists raised. In the dim light he saw the barrel of a gun aimed his way. Ed behind it.

"Downstairs is clear." Ed lowered the firearm. "She in there?"

Jason shook his head. "What the fuck happened?"

"I was in the Jon having a shit." Ed climbed the rest of the stairs. He paused at the top. Blood reddened the right side of his face. He didn't re-holster the gun. "Fucker fired at me as I came out. Nicked my fucking 'ead."

"You okay?"

Ed nodded. "You seen Simmons?"

"Yeah."

"Butler's in the kitchen. Same fate." He felt his stomach. "Guess I got lucky with that vindaloo after all."

"He gone now?"

"Our mystery visitor?" Ed nodded and his eyes narrowed. "You know who it was?"

"Not his name." Jason turned back to the bedroom. Where the fuck had Kate gone? "You call it in?"

"Yeah." Ed joined him on the landing. "So, where's Kate?"

Jason turned to the bathroom, marched across the landing, and pushed the door open. It felt colder in here than outside in the snow. He darted to the open window and leaned out. Below: footprints and a whole heap of messed up snow. He raced back onto the landing.

"She in there?" Ed said.

Jason ignored him. He charged downstairs, jumped over Simmons's body and ran through to the back of the house. Just as Ed had said, Butler lay in the kitchen surrounded by a puddle of his own blood. Jason leapt over him and headed out to the garden where he studied the disturbed area of snow directly below the bathroom window. The marks certainly looked consistent with a fall. And a bloody big fall at that. He glanced up at the bathroom. Shit. How had she landed and managed to get away?

Ed came up behind him, gun still clasped in his hand.

"She got out," Jason said.

Ed glanced up at the window, then at the snow piled below. "You think she's close by?"

Jason turned towards the garden. Footsteps – embedded deeper at the toes – led to the end of the garden and disappeared into the darkness beyond. "No. She's running."

"Maybe our visitor took her."

Jason shook his head. "Only one set of prints." He continued to scan the area. "What's our timeline?"

"I was only in the lav for five minutes. Eight tops."

"There a torch inside?"

"Drawer under the microwave."

Jason rushed into the kitchen. Sure enough, a police-issued torch – right where Ed had said. He flicked it on, the beam of light confirming it worked, and headed back outside.

"She's gonna be long-gone, mate." Ed said.

"Maybe." Jason shone the light across the snow.

"Fuck, Jason. Wait for the boys to get here."

"I need to know she wasn't followed."

"You just said it – one set of prints. She's running, mate."

Jason looked up from the snow. "Karen was murdered tonight."

Ed's eyes widened. "What?"

Jason nodded. "I got her killed."

"You roped her in to helping you?" Ed slipped the gun into its holster. He stepped forward and motioned like he was going to offer comfort.

Jason straightened. That was not what he needed. What he wanted was for Ed to get back to doing his job, and let Jason crack on with his. He rubbed his neck and cracked away some of the anxiety. "Someone's playing both sides."

"Whoa. That's quite a leap you're making."

Jason turned to him. "Someone knew she was helping me."

"Who'd you tell?"

"No one."

"Then what the fuck?"

Jason turned for the garden. "Look, I don't have time to explain now."

"Then give me the edited version." Ed pulled him back.

Jason chewed on his lower lip. Every minute that passed, Kate got further from him. He stared at Ed and tried to read what his reaction would be. "I think it's Carter."

Ed scoffed and cocked his head, his eyes fixed on Jason's. Slowly, the wheels turned. His eyes hardened and he turned away. He paced into the garden, stopped after a couple of metres, and turned. He kept his focus on the snow piled around his feet for a moment then booted it away.

"The guy who came here tonight. I've seen Leah with him."

Ed looked up. Finally, Jason had his attention.

"And I've seen footage of Carter at the casino. I think Carter's the slag who's talking."

"Bollocks." Ed ran his hands through his hair. "I mean, I'm not Carter's biggest fan, but what you're saying is mental. You know that, right?"

"A cop on the take isn't uncommon." Jason glanced out across the darkness, at Kate's lone footprints disappearing towards the back of the garden. She hadn't been followed – at least, not from here. But that didn't mean to say this shit-head blue-bird prick hadn't cut her off somewhere on the other side of the boundaries.

"Carter ain't the police."

"He's close enough. How else would he have known where Kate was?"

"Carter wouldn't have known that." Ed swallowed. Now he was thinking. "Maybe Karen was forced to spill the beans."

"Karen didn't know."

Ed stared at him. "How're you going to prove it?"

"Karen already has." Jason took off into the darkness of the garden before Ed could slow him further with his questions.

The torch light led the way to the back fence where a gate swung open on its hinges. Even with the light, Jason knew he stood little chance of finding Kate. The snow still held only one set of prints. This was good. But, the gate led through to an alley. The alley to the end of the road. The road to the high street. And, the high street to just about every-fucking-where.

Shit.

Where the fuck was Kate?

CHAPTER FORTY-ONE

Kate pulled her knees in close and hugged them.

Wet socks froze her feet and the warm jumper she'd put on inside the house was no match for the wintery morning outside.

In the distance, sirens wailed through the air, and she couldn't help but wonder if they searched for her or if they were on a mission to save some other poor soul whose Christmas was just as horrific as hers.

A flurry of snow whirled around her and she buried her face in her hands, squeezing the cold from her cheeks until the gust passed. But each time she tensed, her arms grew heavier. She'd long since lost control over the tremors that rocked her body, chattering teeth ached her jaw, and her unfocused vision struggled to discern the objects around her.

She closed her eyes and rocked back and forth. Still, warmth eluded her. An orange glow started to light the dark night. Early morning had arrived, but how early she didn't know. She continued to rock, the movement almost hypnotic, and prayed someone would find her soon.

"Miss?"

Kate lifted her head. It took every last ounce of energy she possessed. Someone stood before her, but she couldn't make out who.

"What are you doing here?" the person – a male – asked.

What was Kate doing here? She couldn't remember coming here. She didn't even recognise where *here* was.

She felt the warmth of a coat drape around her shoulders. "Let's get you inside."

Two hands clasped her arms and helped her up from the ground. Now she saw her helper was some kind of security guard. He wrapped an arm around her waist and guided her towards the gallery entrance. It occurred to her to refuse his help. To fight him off and flee. She didn't know him. He could be the man she'd seen back at the house wearing the balaclava. But her uncontrollable shuddering numbed her mental ability to make any kind of decision. She hobbled on, held by the guard, every pained step cramping her frozen feet.

The guard gripped her tighter, pulling her close and almost lifting her from the ground. They reached the door and his arm left her. She heard the jangle of keys and then the door opened inward.

He walked her inside and closed the door, shutting the cold out with it. "We need to get you warm."

Kate ground her teeth and tried to stop the chattering long enough to thank him, but her ability to talk was lost to her.

The guard lead her through a foyer towards a huge staircase. "Normally I'd take the lift, but they're shut off when the gallery's closed."

He helped her up the stairs – one at a time, and so slowly she felt like she hardly moved. When they reached the top, he walked her through a succession of rooms. Breath-taking art work hung from the walls. Kate was frozen to the core. She had no idea where she was or why she'd come here. But, as she glanced around at the passing walls, something made her feel safe.

The rooms came to an end and the paintings disappeared. The guard opened a grey door and led her through it. He sat her down in the small room on the other side, switched on a tiny, electric fire, and closed the door. He rubbed his hands together, knelt beside her, and took her hands.

The warmth from his palms melted her fingers. But they didn't stop her frozen body from quivering. The guard peeled off her wet socks, pulled the scarf from around his own neck, and wrapped it around her red, swollen feet.

He rubbed some more warmth into her hands. "Do you want to explain to me what's going on?"

Kate managed to swallow. She forced her dry lips apart and tried to lick some moisture into them.

"Is there someone I can phone for you?"

The only person Kate knew was Jason. He'd told her to keep his card close and now she wished she had. As it was, she had no idea how to reach him.

"There was a man here the other day looking for you. He left a number."

Kate's body stiffened. Her breathing quickened. It had to be the man in the balaclava. He'd found her. She pulled her hands from the guard and tried to stand.

The guard held her still. Worry etched his face. "It's okay. You're safe."

Kate didn't feel safe. She scanned the room. No windows and only one door – the one they entered through. Was she a prisoner? She needed to get out of here before the man came looking for her again.

The guard took hold of her hands again. "You're not in any danger here."

Kate glanced up. He looked sincere. Kind. Trustworthy. "Are you?" she croaked.

"Am I what?"

"Trustworthy?"

He smiled and any doubt about his motives for bringing her here melted away. "I am."

He stood and went to the notice board. Lifting some paperwork, he pulled the pin from a business card.

He passed it to Kate. "He's the guy who came looking for you."

Kate stared at the name typed across the front of the card. *Jason Wade. Scenes of Crime Officer*. She glanced up at the ceiling and exhaled. He'd found her.

"Can you phone him?" Kate said.

The guard smiled. "I can."

CHAPTER FORTY-TWO

Jason stood in the middle of the room.

He wanted to go to the kitchen. He needed to go to the kitchen – but his feet wouldn't move. Broken glass spread the carpet like spilt sugar and, around the room, furniture lay overturned and in pieces. Only the Christmas tree seemed to have survived the attack. Jason glanced at his feet – still unmoving. It was obvious what had happened here – Karen had put up one hell of a fight.

Ed entered the room. "Forensics are on their way." He rested his hand on Jason's shoulder. "You okay?"

Jason clenched his fists. Karen had been his friend. His confidante. "I'm gonna make that bastard pay."

"We both will." Ed's hand left his shoulder and he walked to the desk. "What we s'posed to be looking for?"

"So, you're on side now?"

Ed turned to him and swallowed, seeming a little hesitant to answer. "I admit there may be something more untoward going on. Does that make you feel happier?"

It didn't make Jason feel happier. Ed was his friend and should have believed him from the very beginning. But it was a conversation for another day. He watched Ed turn back to the desk. It remained upright – about the only thing in the room that was – but the computer screen had been smashed and was void of the flash drive. Jason glanced towards the printer. No papers sat in the tray. Karen was a clever girl. She must have hidden everything.

Jason left Ed searching the desk and hurried to the kitchen. He opened the fridge and pulled out the ice tray – the plastic wallet still where Karen had hidden it. He took it out and closed the door.

Ed turned from desk. "What's that?"

"Evidence and information."

"On what?"

Jason opened the wallet and took out the paperwork – stills Karen had printed from the CCTV. "This guy killed Karen."

Ed took the copy. "Is that Leah with him?"

"Uh-huh."

Jason flicked through the other the paperwork. Pages he hadn't seen before – a military record for one Tavish Finley. His body stiffened and he closed his eyes, cutting off the tears that threatened. Karen had actually found the bastard. And died for it.

He dropped the paperwork on the counter. Wiped his eyes and tilted his head back. She'd be alive now if he hadn't dragged her into his mess. When he glanced back down, he saw his hands were still stained with her blood. He stared at them, turning them palm up. Red everywhere – in the creases of his skin. Underneath his fingernails. Karen's blood – on his hands. Literally. Vomit rose in his throat and he rushed to the sink. Heaved, puked, and turned on the tap. He remained like that for a moment, not wanting to look at his hands again.

Ed clasped his bicep but made no attempt to pull him from the sink. Instead, Jason remained bent over the basin while the water hit his hands and washed the last of Karen from him. Then, finally, the tears came.

Ed stood back, giving him space. Crying wasn't a manly thing. Certainly not something that Jason had been encouraged to do while growing up. His father was old school. Swap the tears for a punching bag and work your shit out.

Shit. Jason looked at his hands – now clean – and splashed some water onto his face. "Fuck." He turned off the tap and stood. "Need to let SOCO know what I've touched out here."

Ed nodded. Leaned past him and collected the papers from the counter. "Tavish Finley." He looked up. "Is this the guy?"

Jason nodded.

"Okay, so what now?"

That was the million-dollar question. Other than his run-in with Finley at the Bethnal Green flat, Jason couldn't place him anywhere other than the casino and the hospital.

He slid the paperwork back inside the wallet. "I'm going after him myself." He turned from Ed and headed through the lounge to the hallway.

"We're going after him."

"No." Jason stopped short of opening the front door.

"You still think Carter's the mole, don't you?"

Jason said nothing. He didn't think Carter was the mole. He *knew* Carter was the mole. Carter knew he and Karen were tight. Carter would've been able to find out where Kate was hidden. Carter had been caught on camera with Leah at the casino – the same casino Finley frequented. It had to be Carter.

His mobile began to vibrate and he slipped it from his pocket. An unrecognisable number lit the screen and he answered.

"Mr Wade?" the voice asked.

"Yeah."

"I'm a security guard at the National Gallery. You came in looking for a young woman the other day."

"Yeah."

"Well, she's here. At the gallery."

Jason's heart beat faster. "Can you repeat that?"

"The girl. She asked me to call you."

Thoughts scattered through Jason's mind. Kate was alive. Finley hadn't killed her. "Is she hurt?"

"No. Just cold."

Jason's fingers trembled, and he gripped the phone tighter. "I'm on my way."

"You found Kate?" Ed said.

Jason hung up and opened the front door. "I need you to go question Carter. Find out what you can on this Finley guy – an address, phone number, where he drinks…anything."

Jason paused. "Press him about Leah, too."

Ed nodded. "Where're you going?"

"Trafalgar Square to look at some paintings."

CHAPTER FORTY-THREE

Jason still had the phone in his hand even though it had run out of juice a good ten minutes back.

He pulled the Jag up onto the pavement – just let the fuckers try and clamp him – and raced across Trafalgar Square to the gallery, taking the steps two at the time. His ribs still hurt like hell and he gripped them tight, but this time they failed to slow him down.

The security guard, the same old boy he'd spoken to the day before, was at the entrance before he reached the top. He unlocked the door and pushed it open.

Jason rushed into the foyer. "Where is she?"

The guard locked the door. "In our staff room." He turned from Jason and hurried towards the main staircase.

Jason followed.

The guard walked at a hasty pace, but it wasn't quick enough. Jason wanted to run. To sprint. To get through the rooms as quickly as possible and see for himself that Kate was unharmed. Hundreds of paintings passed him by. Still no Kate. He wanted to scream at the guy to hurry up but held his frustrations back. Where in the hell was the guard taking him anyway?

Finally, the man stopped outside a door. "She's in here." He started to search the keys that hung from his belt.

"You locked her in?"

"She insisted." He unlocked the door and stepped aside.

Jason gripped the handle. Paused. He'd hurried to get here but now he was nervous at what he might find. He opened the door – just a little – and peered inside. Kate was asleep, curled up in a chair. A coat draped over her.

"She was frozen to death," the guard said.

"She say anything? About what happened?"

"She was incapable of speaking. You know, shivering and all. It took a while for her to calm down." The guard licked his lips. "There is something, though. When I met her a couple of days ago, she had an American accent – like I told you. Tonight, though, she spoke the Queen's English. Perfectly."

Heck. Jason had forgotten all about Jon Reynolds and the American connection. He turned to Kate. She looked peaceful for the first time since he'd met her and guilt tightened his chest – because now he had to wake her and pull her back into this nightmare. He glanced back at the guard, nodded his appreciation, and entered the room.

He knelt in front of Kate, dropped his phone on the floor, and lightly shook her shoulder.

She stirred and her eyes fluttered open. At first, horror filled them. She bolted upright and scanned the room. Jason waited for her to find him.

He smiled. "You okay?"

Kate nodded, but her body remained rigid.

"Gonna tell me what happened?"

"A man. In the house. I jumped out of the window." She started to lightly rock in the chair. "Did I do wrong?

"No, you did good."

"Who was he?"

Jason thought of Karen and glanced at his hands. Even though he'd washed them clean, he still saw her blood covering them. "He murdered a friend of mine tonight."

Kate's eyes widened. A breath caught in her throat. "Because of me?"

Jason shook his head. "Because of me." He inhaled and fought back the tears that wanted to flow again. "The guard here says you spoke with an American accent the other day."

Kate frowned. "I was here?"

"Uh-huh."

"What was I doing?"

"Looking at a painting," the guard chimed in.

Kate frowned. "*Chalets at Rigi?*"

"Yes." The guard remained in the doorway. "Said your grandmother liked it."

"Wait. Do you remember?" Jason interrupted.

"I saw a painting at the hospital. It looked familiar." Kate's eyes flitted between the two men. "Am I American?"

"English." Jason stood and stretched the cramp from his legs. "You moved across the pond when you were younger."

"How do you know this?"

"Your old neighbour." He handed Kate the photograph and pointed to the older woman. "Other woman's your mother."

Kate glanced at the photo, then handed it back. "I don't remember them." She lifted her feet back onto the chair and pulled the coat around her. "Do you know why someone wants to kill me?"

"Not yet. But we're gonna rectify that right now." Jason turned to the security guard. "This place have a computer or something with a search engine?"

"There's an iPad in the drawer there. The guys use it to watch the racing."

Jason took out the iPad – no password protecting it – and opened Google. He typed in Jon Reynolds and hit the search button. Way too many choices – from Facebook to lawyers. He added US to the search bar. Still those bloody Facebook pages. He remembered the neighbour mentioning property and added that to the search.

Top of the results: *The death of construction millionaire Jon Philip Reynolds*. Jason clicked through to the New York Times page. Headlined in big, bold letters – *Murdered Tycoon's Daughter Missing*. Reynolds, in his mid to late fifties, was pictured top right. Dark hair, blue eyes. No suit – just a casual jumper. The typical, good-looking, rich man.

Jason enlarged the picture and turned the screen to Kate. "He look familiar?"

Kate bit her lip and shook her head.

Back on the screen, Jason scrolled through the article. "Says here he was in construction. Lived in San Francisco. Was married to Sarah. Had a daughter, Kate." He looked up. "Which would be you." He paused. "Kate, I'm sorry, but he was murdered."

Apart from the confusion clouding her eyes, she showed little emotion.

He glanced back at the screen and continued to scroll through the snippets of information. The businessman's body had been discovered shot and half-buried in the foundations of a new casino project in San Francisco. Reynolds's daughter was wanted for questioning. He'd left a tidy fortune behind for her. His wife had died of cancer…

Jason swallowed. How much could he lay on her? How much could she take?

"Your mum's gone too," he said gently. "Cancer."

He scanned down more headlines and stopped.

"What is it?" Kate said.

"There's a strong possibility you witnessed your father's murder."

"That's why all this is happening?"

"Maybe." Jason continued to read but there wasn't much else of interest.

He put the iPad down and turned to the security guard. "You have a phone charger I can use?"

The guard pointed to the plug socket in the corner of the room.

Kate's dirty, bare feet poked out from beneath the coat. "We need to find you some shoes."

"I can help with that," the guard said. "People leave all sorts of things unclaimed in lost property."

"Could you find her some warmer clothes? Maybe some gloves?"

"I'll look." He glanced at Kate's feet. "Size five?"

Kate stared at him. It was obvious she had no idea.

The guard smiled. "I'll be back in ten."

Jason headed straight for the charger. He plugged in his phone and waited for the screen to brighten. Then he called Ed. "It's me."

"You okay? Do you have the girl?"

"Yeah. Listen, do a check on Jon Reynolds. He's an American businessman who was killed a few months back. He's all over Google."

"What am I checking?"

"See if he's linked to this Finley guy or my sister." Then, as an afterthought, "even the Mayfair casino. Anything."

Ed sighed. Jason could read his thoughts – Wade chasing shadows at the casino again.

"Okay," Ed said. "I'll put it through. You still at the gallery?"

"Yeah."

"Good. Stay there till I get back to you."

Jason hung up. He turned to Kate, patting his thighs while searching for something to say. Truth was, there wasn't anything to say. In less than thirty seconds he'd revealed both her parents were dead – one to cancer and one to murder. To make it worse, she'd apparently witnessed the latter.

"Are you okay?" he said to her, knowing he sounded like a dick.

"Honestly? I feel nothing." She looked up. Sadness clouded her tired eyes. "How do you mourn people you don't even know?"

Another question he didn't have the words to answer. He knelt beside her again and placed his hands on the wooden armrests. "Are you up for leaving here soon?"

"Can't we stay here?"

Jason shook his head. "I think we have a mole. In fact, I'm certain of it. If I know you're here, there could be a chance they know you're here as well."

"How? You were the only person I called."

"I haven't the foggiest. But I do know this Finley guy has known our every move so far."

"Finley? That's the man who was at the house?"

Jason nodded. "Tavish Finley. He's ex-military. SAS is my guess."

"Did he kill my father?"

Jason shrugged. He didn't have a bloody clue. "Once you get some shoes, we'll leave."

"And go where?"

That was another million-dollar question. Carter knew all of Jason's friends and hangouts. There wasn't anywhere Jason could hide.

Well, there was one place.

The security guard opened the door to the main entrance.

He wasn't happy about them leaving. He'd wanted to call the police, but Jason had stopped him. Charlotte had warned Kate the police couldn't be trusted – something Jason now agreed with. And then there was Carter's alleged involvement.

Outside, the frosty Christmas morning had brought with it a sprinkle of people. Kate moved to the pillars and looked out over Trafalgar Square. Jason heard the security guard lock the door behind him and wondered if he *was* doing the right thing in leaving. Kate wasn't equipped for this weather. The guard had given her his own coat, and the trainers he'd found were a size too big – although better than no shoes at all. But was she even strong enough to run?

Jason moved beside her. "Ed's car is over there." He reached across her chest and turned up the collar of her jacket.

A sudden pain hit his shoulder and the force whipped him back against the stone pillar. The sound of the gunshot followed a split-second later. He lunged for Kate and hauled her out of plain sight. Screams pierced the tranquil morning. Jason held Kate low and peered out across the square. People fled in every direction – some for the protection of surrounding buildings, others cowering behind the square's plinths. He scanned the buildings. The windows. The rooftops.

"You're hurt."

He felt Kate pull open his jacket and a second pain intensified the first. He bit back the string of obscenities he wanted to scream and continued to watch the area. He couldn't see anyone resembling a sniper. But he knew Finley was there. Somewhere. Watching. Waiting.

In the distance, sirens broke through the commotion – a sound Jason would normally have been relieved to hear. But he didn't know if Carter was acting alone or if there were others on Finley's payroll. He wiped the sweat from his forehead and inhaled. He had a decision to make. He either dealt with the bullets or dealt with the police. Neither option jumped out as a good idea. He swallowed and exhaled. Wanted to check out his shoulder but instead continued to survey the buildings. No other shots had been fired and he was sure the shooter would have moved from his position the moment the sirens sounded.

Jason glanced at Kate. If the police found them, there was the chance they'd move her into safe custody – and that had worked out so well before. No. They needed to make a run for it. From now on, Jason worked alone.

Ed's car waited for him on the west side of the square, but with no cover, they'd be running ducks if they tried to reach it.

"We need to get out of here," Jason said.

Kate looked up. To his relief, she didn't contest it. She got to her feet, clasped hold of his hand, and took his weight as he stood.

"Is it the man from the house?" she said.

"Probably." Jason's legs trembled and he leaned back against the pillar. He wanted to close his eyes. Wanted to crouch down and wait for the pain to subside.

"How did he find us so quickly?"

"Someone talked."

"The police?" Kate's grip tightened. "Where are we going to go?"

"Charing Cross is just across the way. We'll be less exposed there." Of course, he had serious doubts he would make it that far before passing out.

"Maybe we should go to a hospital instead."

"I'll be fine." He wiped his forehead again and glanced around the pillar one last time. The police lights illuminated every window in Whitehall.

It was now or never.

CHAPTER FORTY-FOUR

Tav watched the front of the gallery from the rooftop across the way.

He'd had the girl in his sights. The odds of anyone blocking that bullet were a million to one – if not more. But that East End fucker had managed to accidentally pull it off. And now Tav couldn't get a clean shot.

The sirens arrived pretty much straight away. Tav had expected nothing less than an immediate response from Britain's finest – being that he was only minutes from both the Royal Palace and Westminster.

Fuck it. He couldn't wait any longer for his target to re-appear. He had to move out, pronto. He packed the rifle into the duffle bag, collected the bullet casing, and shoved both into one of the ventilators. Re-attaching the steel casing, he headed for the stairwell. With his hat pulled low over his face, he stepped out onto the pavement.

What people remained on the streets continued to flee the area. Tav pushed and dodged his way through them, his view of the gallery his primary concern. This Wade guy wouldn't be stupid enough to stay hiding up there. So where would he go? Tav scanned the square. Caught a glimpse of them – together, hand in hand, hurrying east across the square towards the Strand. Wade didn't look in terrific shape. His shoulders were hunched forward, his movement was sloppy at best, and the girl looked to be holding him upright.

This was good news for Tav. His speed far out-weighed theirs and, when he caught them, Wade didn't look to be much of a problem for him to handle. Tav fastened his pace. Now he sprinted across the square, pushing the last remaining individuals from his path. Wade copped a look around and it occurred to Tav to duck for cover to keep his pursuit covert. But given his previous diagnosis of Wade's health, reaching the girl swiftly was more important than maintaining a clandestine chase.

Wade clocked him immediately. The guy's eyes widened and his whole stance straightened. He glared at Tav with the look of a fighter ready for another round. Then he faced forward and bolted, his ailment convincingly masked.

Tav chased hard, making up ground with every step he hammered out across Trafalgar Square. Wade fled across the road, his hand still clasping the girl's. A white van screeched to a stop, clipping Jason's shoulder. It spun him off balance, but not off his feet. The girl caught him and pulled him to the other side of the road. The driver blasted his horn, yelling and swearing and screaming for Wade and the girl to return. But Wade and the girl didn't look back. They headed for the train station and vanished from sight.

Tav leapt across the road after them. The van inched forward, jolting to a stop for a second time. Again, the driver screamed at the top of his voice. But Tav kept running. He descended the stairs, jumping the last half a dozen steps. Ahead, Wade had made it to the ticket barriers. He climbed over – nowhere near as elegantly as he'd done with the gate at the flats – then helped the girl over. Tav leapt the barrier, fast and clean. He barged through the morning crowd, gaining on them all the time. Wade and the girl reached the bottom of the escalator and headed into one of the four passageways. Tav took the moving stairs two at a time. He reached the bottom, trailing by just a couple of metres. He was almost within touching distance.

A gust swept through the tunnel as a train arrived. The doors opened and a crowd exited onto the platform. Tav fought his way through to the train. Wade and the girl tumbled into a carriage. The doors started to close and Tav dived towards them. Forcing his hands between the doors, he curled his fingers around the edges. Momentarily halted the doors from closing but couldn't re-open them. He pulled until his arms shook and his biceps felt ready to pop.

Wade turned to face him. He was breathless, the left side of his jacket soaked in blood. He moved the girl behind him and positioned his feet ready to attack.

Tav glared at him through the gap. "Give me the girl and I'll give you your sister's killer."

Wade cocked his head to one side and the fight in his eyes waned. "What did you say?"

Tav couldn't hold the doors any longer. His grip weakened and the doors slammed shut.

Wade pounced on the door. Now it was he who tried to re-open them. When he couldn't, he whacked the window and stared at Tav through the glass. "Who killed my sister?"

The train slowly began to rock forward.

Tav smiled. He'd found the bastard's Achilles Heel.

Wade whacked the window again. "Who killed my fucking sister?"

Tav marched along the platform; Wade rushed back through the carriage – both men refusing to break eye contact. The train sped up, but Tav didn't. He glared at Wade through the passing windows and watched the carriage disappear into the tunnel.

He turned and walked away from the platform, across the foyer, and onto the platform on the opposite side. He'd dangled a carrot for Wade to bite on. Now he just had to wait.

The first train pulled in to the station, but Tav was unbothered by it. Not enough time had passed for Wade to reach the next station and grab a tube to double back. But, the second train…this train had Tav's attention.

Carriages raced by, each one easier to see into as the train slowed to a stop. The doors opened and its occupants descended onto the platform. Tav stood on a bench and scanned the people. There was no sign of Wade or the girl.

Tav rubbed his head, the short bristles furry under his palm. Maybe he'd misread Wade. The train pulled out and Tav clocked the information board. Three minutes to the next train. It was a gamble to wait but wait he did. The next train arrived but, unlike the two before it, the carriages raced through the station and didn't stop. No surprise really. The shooting would have closed off half of London by now. He scanned the crammed carriages as they rushed past him. Impossible to make out the blur of people inside.

A voice crackled over the Tannoy system informing the public of the station's immediate closure. Shit. Tav hopped down off the bench and headed into the foyer. The police had worked quickly; their presence would soon swarm the station and surrounding areas. He headed up the escalator and back out onto the street.

Although pretty sure Wade would come looking for him, he made the call to Jimmy. "It's me. They've run. Find out where they'd go."

He hung up.

CHAPTER FORTY-FIVE

Ed parked his borrowed car a few doors down from Carter's house.

He blew the last cloud of cherry-flavoured vape smoke through a tiny gap at the top of the window. This was not a visit he wanted to make, but he got out of his car and headed towards the house. Hinges creaked when he pushed the gate open and he winced. The thing was louder than a burglar alarm.

At the top of the steps, he heard the TV on in the living room. He scooted across the front garden and peered in past the net curtain. No sign of Carter at all.

Ed glanced at the white Mondeo parked alongside the kerb. Carter's vehicle. He had to be home. Ed reached for the doorbell, then decided better of it. What was he going to say if Carter was home? Was he just going to lay the accusation of being a mole at Carter's feet? Jesus. Carter would never roll over and go for that.

Ed stood there imitating a spare dick at a wedding, then pressed the buzzer. When no one answered, he crouched and looked through the letterbox. Seeing nothing but an empty hallway on the other side, he stood again.

He sighed and pressed the buzzer again, this time holding his finger on the button longer than was needed. An ache niggled away in the back of his head and he rubbed his neck. Tensed until his jaw ached and his stomach hardened, then whacked his fist against the door.

"Carter," he shouted. "Open this goddamn door now."

Screw this.

Back out on to the street – and five houses up – he reached the alley. Running – even jogging – was out of the question. The large Big Mac meal he'd scoffed down earlier was lying on his stomach and giving him gip. At best, all he could manage was a walk, and a slow one at that. He headed along the alley. Overgrown grass formed bushes along the garden fences and any shingle that had once paved the ground now lay buried beneath a couple inches of snow.

At the back of the houses, he counted five gardens until he reached Carter's home. He lifted the latch and pushed on the gate. It was bolted from the other side. He stepped back and stared up at the fence. Well over six feet. Normally, not that big of a problem. Right now, however, he stood no chance. Bollocks. A dustbin lay overturned a little way along. He dragged it the couple of feet to the fence, struggled to climb on top of it, and peered over the fence.

The garden was empty, the back door closed. No lights were on and he couldn't see the living room from here, either. He gripped the top of the fence, hauled his McDonald's-bloated bulk up higher, and hooked one knee over the boundary. His shoulder tightened and he balanced on top of the fence for a moment to catch his breath. Shit, he really had to start eating more healthily.

He inhaled, held the breath, and lowered himself down into the garden. Clouds congregated in the sky, threatening to dump a shit-load more snow on him.

Shit. This just wasn't his week.

He made it to the back door, relieved that lady luck had at least unlocked it for him, and entered the kitchen. He heard the television – some naff quiz show – playing in the living room.

"Carter? It's Ed."

He walked through to the hallway, popped his head into the lounge – no Carter – and started to climb the stairs.

Only two bedrooms and a bathroom on the first floor. He checked them all. Bathroom – empty. Bedroom one and two – both empty. To his left, another flight of stairs led up to a second floor. He reached the top and walked into the only room up there.

Turned out it was Carter's office. Fully furnished with a desk, shelving, and a body hanging from a beam in the centre of the room. For the best part of a day by the look of it.

Ed covered his nose. No matter how many deaths he'd been called out to, that initial smell of a deteriorating body always caught him off guard. Carter's body was no different. His neck – slightly stretched – had started to bloat. His head was shaded purple. His open eyes had rolled to the back of his head. One shoe lay on the floor beneath him – surrounded by a whole heap of drugs. The other shoe was still securely laced on his foot. Faeces and gut fluid leaked from his sphincter and stained his corduroy trousers, the stench polluting the air.

Ed scanned the room. The windows were closed. He felt the radiator. Lukewarm – must be on a timer. An overturned chair lay beneath the body – the kind that swivelled and were a git to stand on and maintain your balance. Fuck knew how Carter managed it with the lard he carried round his waist.

Ed glanced at the body. "You got off lightly, you son of a bitch."

CHAPTER FORTY-SIX

"I need to go back," Jason said.

Kate frowned. "You can't be serious."

"He knows who killed my sister."

"And you trust him?"

"I can't afford not to."

"Then that bullet has muddled your brain."

The train pulled into London Waterloo East, one stop on from Charing Cross. The doors slid apart and a handful of travellers exited. Jason turned towards the platform, but Kate held him back.

Her eyes hardened, a spark of fight still left in them. "What do you expect to gain going back alone? He wants to trade information for me. Why would he even know what happened to your sister? He's taunting you to get to me. He wants you to go back."

Jason glanced at the open doors.

"Jason, you're not thinking straight." Kate's grip didn't weaken. "He's pushing your buttons. He's going to kill you and then he's going to kill me."

"Not if you go to the police—"

Kate scoffed. "After what happened at the safe house?"

The doors began to beep and close, taking away Jason's last chance to jump ship.

"Jason, he's trying to lure you away from me. Or he's banking on you returning with me," Kate continued. "Either way, you can't go back. I need you here…to keep me alive."

He turned to her. She suddenly seemed smaller, her eyes wide and pleading. Behind him, the doors closed. He'd searched for answers to his sister's death for the best part of the year, losing all his credibility along the way, and now he was turning his back on the golden ticket to finding out what could have happened to her.

He looked at Kate – still warm and alive. Then thought of Karen, the weight of her limp body still heavy in his arms. Finley had played him. He'd lured him to Battersea so Kate would be alone – easy prey – and Jason had fallen for it. Was this alleged information on his sister just another of Finley's bluffs? Could Jason survive another innocent death if this fool's errand of his ended with Kate's murder?

The train shunted forward, beginning its journey to the next station.

Jason reached for the handrail. "I won't leave you again." He wobbled towards a seat and collapsed into it. Blood soaked his shirt and when he tried to do up his jacket, his trembling fingers couldn't manage the simple task.

Kate knelt in front of him, her hands quickly replacing his. She zipped up his jacket and settled in the chair beside him. "So, what do we do now?"

Jason had no idea. He just knew he needed to let go of the dead if he was to save this girl before him. Dizziness swam inside his head and his vision blurred. He lay back, letting his head tilt until it rested against the back of the chair, and closed his eyes.

The rocking carriage jolted his shoulder and he bit back the pain. "We need to find somewhere to hole up."

When Kate didn't respond, he opened his eyes. She still sat beside him, staring.

"What?" he said.

"You need a hospital."

Jason shook his head. "Then you're bringing in the police."

"You've been shot. You're going to bleed to death."

"Let's ease up on the melodrama." He shifted position and tried to sit up and give the illusion he felt better than he really did. She did have a small point – he did need to get his shoulder looked at before he passed out.

He sank back into the chair. "I know a place we can go."

"Is it far?"

Jason shook his head.

"Can this madman trace us there?"

Jason shook his head again.

"Are you sure? Going to a place you have a link with seems a little stupid."

"I don't have a link to this place."

"But—"

"Kate. The link's with a person who disappeared from my life a long time ago."

He hadn't spoken about his past with anyone. Not even Karen.

Kate paused. Behind her eyes, he saw the mountain of questions she wanted to press him on.

"How far away is it?" she said instead.

Jason shrugged. "An hour. Give or take."

"An hour? You're not going to last—"

"No hospitals."

"But—"

"I'll get it looked at in an hour."

Kate pursed her lips. She looked ready to blow.

"Please." His voice was weak no matter how hard he tried to inject some kind of strength and authority into it. "Just trust me."

He didn't have the energy to argue with her. Fact was, he was struggling to stay lucid.

"Can you at least tell me where we're going?"

The train rattled into Oval Station. One more stop and then they'd change lines.

"Finsbury Park."

Kate's voice broke through Jason's haze. "We're here."

He opened his eyes and saw a flash of words whizzing past as the train pulled into the station. The carriage slowed and the words cleared. Finsbury Park. He reached for the armrests and pushed himself up out of the seat. Kate's coat slipped from around him and fell to the floor, but he didn't try to pick it up. Couldn't.

She grabbed it and quickly wrapped it around him again. "Your blood was soaking through your jacket. People were looking."

Jason gripped the metal handrail – partly to hold him steady and partly to stop him collapsing back into the chair. Only when the train had come to a complete stop did he release it. He headed towards the door. Fatigue weighed on his legs and his vision blurred. The carriage began to swirl around him and he reached for the metal bar again.

Kate wrapped her arm around his waist and held him steady. The carriage darkened and he closed his eyes. Kate's hold on him tightened.

"Do you need to sit down?" Her voice sounded surprisingly calm.

"I'm fine," he lied, and opened his eyes.

The darkness lightened to a fog, still distorting his vision but not enough that he couldn't see the doors.

Kate helped him out onto the platform. "I know you don't want to discuss a hospital—"

"Then don't mention it." He let her take his weight.

She sighed. "Where are we going?"

Jason reached for the wall. He inhaled, wiped his cuff across his forehead, and clasped a hand to his shoulder. The jacket was damp with blood. "Just help me to street level."

Kate helped him. At the barriers, he readied to pass one of his cards to the inspectors and blag his way through – after all, there was no way in hell he'd be capable of climbing the blockade. To his relief, all the gates were open.

He shuffled forward, Kate still supporting him, and let the escalator take him to street level. Outside, the cool air hit him, sparking his senses, albeit briefly.

A line of taxis queued in the rank and Jason nodded towards the front one.

"Abney Park," he directed the driver, then crawled into the back, leaving Kate to close the door behind them.

He got out his phone and relaxed into the seat. The screen was a blur and he struggled to focus as he tapped Ed's name. "Tell me you got something?"

"Forensics are still searching Karen's. Haven't found anything to get excited about yet. This guy is good, I'll give him that."

"You spoken to Carter yet?"

"I'm with him at the moment."

"He say anything?"

"Not a fat lot. No." A moment's silence. "He's dead."

Jason paused. "How?"

"Bastard hung himself. Looks like he was into all kinds of shit. Found some bank statements on his desk. Guy liked the gee-gees and had one hell of an overdraft. Certainly gives him reason to sell our secrets."

Jason swallowed and wiped his forehead again. A sick feeling lodged in his throat and wouldn't budge. "Finley was at the gallery."

"You okay?"

"Yeah."

"Then your bastard boss got his just desserts."

Jason glanced at the traffic behind him. No other taxis. Just a line of cars. "Thing is, Carter didn't know where I was."

"He must have."

"Did you call it in?"

"No. Course not."

"Then how'd he know?"

"My inspector put a call through to him after the to-do in his office. He had to have spilled about the safe house." A short silence. Then Ed said, "I found Karen's address on his desk – scribbled on some scrap paper."

Shit. Carter had to be the mole. So why did this doubt still nag at him?

His silence must have alerted Ed. "So, what else? You think you were followed to the gallery?"

"Maybe." Suddenly, the mobile weighed heavy in his hand. Traced?

He leaned forward, winced at the strain on his shoulder, and tapped the screen that separated him from the driver. "Hey, mate, pull over a sec."

He waited for the driver to stop.

"I'm ditching my phone," he said to Ed.

"Well, how am I supposed to—?"

"I'll call you later."

Jason hung up. He removed the SD card and dropped the phone out onto the pavement. He tapped the window again and signalled for the driver to continue.

He sensed Kate watching him, but right now he needed rest. The traffic steadily worsened and Jason leaned against the door and closed his eyes. Five minutes' shut-eye and he'd be right as rain.

CHAPTER FORTY-SEVEN

Kate lightly shook Jason awake.

His lids flickered open and his eyes found her.

She leaned over him, her hand resting lightly on his good shoulder. Dark shadows ringed his eyes and his skin had paled to ghostly white.

"We're here," she said.

"Here? Here where?"

He tried to straighten but collapsed back against the door. He waited a second then tried again. Shaking his head, he glanced around the inside of the cab, then looked outside.

The taxi had parked directly outside the entrance to Abney Park. Kate's door was open – she'd already been inside and found a caretaker in the small building on the other side of the gates. She gave Jason a minute to take in his surroundings while the caretaker – a man well into his sixties – leaned in through the passenger window and handed the driver some cash.

Once done, he stood behind Kate. "Here, let me get him," he said.

Kate backed out of the cab and allowed the man to climb in. His blues eyes were as bright as a twenty-year-old's, and his physique unashamedly toned.

"Alright, son?" he said, hooking an arm under Jason. "Looks like you've been mixing with the wrong crowd again."

Jason's voice was a mere whisper. "Jeff?"

"Who else?"

The man hauled Jason from the cab with little effort and pretty much carried him through the park gates and towards a small building.

"Open that door for me, luv," he said to Kate.

The smell of paint and white spirit hung in the air. A small scaffolding plinth ran the length of the far wall and blue paint splashed the white sheet beneath it.

Jason's feet started to drag and Kate hurried to take his other arm – not that Jeff seemed to need the help.

"Over there." Jeff pointed to a worn, leather couch. He laid Jason down, peeled open his jacket, and sighed. "What happened?"

"He was shot," Kate said.

Jeff pulled Jason's jacket free, dropped the bloodied garment on the floor, and ripped apart the sleeve of Jason's jumper. Examined Jason's shoulder. "Okay, the bullet went straight through."

"Is that good?"

Jeff nodded. "You'll find a first aid box top drawer of the desk. A bottle of scotch in the bottom one."

Kate hurried to the desk and found what the man needed.

He unscrewed the scotch and poured it over the wound. Jason didn't flinch. He'd passed out long before they'd reached the hut.

"Is he okay?"

"He's fine. There's a small bowl in the cupboard above the sink. Fill it with lukewarm water."

Kate did as she was told.

"Okay, pretty lady." Jeff glanced up. "Kate, you said?"

Kate nodded.

"Kate, inside that box, you'll find a needle. I need you to thread it."

Again, Kate did as she was told. She passed the needle to the man, who promptly doused it in scotch.

"You look like you've done this before," she said.

A slight smile curled the old man's lips, but quickly disappeared. He focused on the laceration just beneath Jason's collarbone and began to sew. "Who did this to him?"

"A man who's trying to kill me."

The man didn't look up. "And why would that be?"

"I think I witnessed something."

"You think?"

"I can't remember."

The man cut the thread. He pulled a small packet from the first aid box, ripped back the seal, and removed a square piece of lint. One last douse of alcohol over Jason's shoulder and he wiped the wound clean, covering it with the plaster.

"Help me turn him over." He reached for the scotch and poured it over the exit wound. He doused the needle and set to work sewing up the back of Jason's shoulder.

"I think that's it." He covered the wound with lint, turned Jason onto his back, and lifted him forward. "Hold him steady."

Kate held one arm around Jason's waist, the other around his neck.

Jeff expertly wound a bandage around Jason's chest and shoulder, then gently laid him back down. "Let him sleep it off."

"Is he okay now?"

"He's lost a lot of blood. He needs to rest."

"How'd you know how to do all that?"

Again, the man smiled. He got up from the couch and moved to the sink. "I used to run a boxing gym in the east end of London. Dealt with much worse than this, I can tell you." He glanced at her. "Is trouble following you here?"

"Jason said it wouldn't. That the link to you is in his past."

Jeff nodded. "One thing I've learned over the years about hiding the past – there's always one sod who knows about it."

"So, we'll have to leave then?"

"Not until he's rested." He glanced at Jason and a look of love warmed his eyes. "He was a small boy when I first met him. His mother had just died. He'd run away from home taking nothing but his toothbrush. All of Bethnal Green's finest out looking for him – and I find him curled up under my desk, fast asleep, this little kid I'd never laid eyes on before in my life."

"That's how you met?"

Jeff nodded. "Hid beneath that desk for two days. Refused to come out. Screamed the place down if anyone so much as got within ten feet of him."

"How'd you get him to come out then?"

"I didn't. Boxing did. He could see the fighters sparring and it piqued his interest." Jeff got up from the sofa. "Yep, he left that room a boxer – like he had something to prove. Was bloody good too. Went pro for a while."

"What happened?"

"His sister got involved with an idiot." Jeff glanced down at his sweater, now red with Jason's blood. He pulled it over his head. "The junkie twat hit her so Jason hit him – a lot. Beat the bastard to a pulp. Cost him his boxing license." He grabbed a hoodie from the hook by the door and walked to the window. "So, why aren't the two of you at the police station right now?"

"Jason thinks someone is passing on information."

"A mole, eh? Well, it wouldn't be the first time a copper took a back-hander."

Kate yawned. She hadn't slept since the safe house and even then it had only been a couple of broken hours. "How long do you think Jason will be asleep?"

Jeff shrugged. "I doubt too long. Why don't you try and get your head down while you can?"

The activities of the last couple of days had exhausted her. Her arms ached, her legs ached, her head ached. Dryness scratched behind her eyes. But she didn't think for one moment she'd actually be able to sleep.

"It's fine," Jeff assured her. "I'll lock up the gates and keep watch. Nobody will get in."

He grabbed a set of keys from the desk and walked to the door.

Kate waited for the man to leave, then crouched beside the sofa. Jason looked white as a sheet. Shallow breaths passed his slightly parted lips. When she stroked his face, light tremors rocked his body.

He stirred and Kate quickly retreated to the uncomfortable-looking armchair opposite. She remained still, watching him. Hoping she hadn't woken him. He'd been to hell and back over the last forty-eight hours – they both had. When he didn't wake, she curled her legs up onto the chair, ignored the blood that covered her clothes, and tried to find some comfort.

It wasn't long before she too fell asleep.

CHAPTER FORTY-EIGHT

Tav walked to the vending machine in the corner of the room and dropped some coins into

the slot.

He pushed for a Coke, retrieved it from the tray, and turned to survey the scene around him. Men trained – some shadow boxing, others sparring. The pitter-patter of skipping ropes slapped the floor. The fluent pounding on speed balls rocked them back and forth on their iron swivels. The stench of sweat fought through the room and polluted what was left of the air.

Not a single person took any notice of him.

He drew back the ring-pull and gulped down some Coke. The fizz exploded on his tongue. The gym wasn't that dissimilar to the one he'd frequented back in Glasgow – at least in décor. The gym back home had been a shithole and every fighter in it was as rough as houses. You had to learn to fight, not just to survive the beating you'd take sparing with the big boys, but to walk the Glaswegian streets on your way home.

Tav stepped away from the drinks machine. In the corner, a youngish kid repeatedly lost momentum on a speed ball. Tav had been a natural on that thing. An older guy wheeled out a yellow bucket and mop. He stopped a couple of metres from Tav and slapped the mop on top of a spillage.

"Hey," Tav called to him, the photograph he'd swiped off Jason's fridge already in his hand.

The old boy glanced up, the look of a fighter still evident in his stare. He didn't say anything.

Tav held out the picture. "You recognise him?"

The guy eyed the picture then stared up at Tav. *If looks could kill.*

Tav smiled. "I used to train with the kid. Not a kid anymore, though. Joined the Met. Can you believe it?"

The man's eyes narrowed. "You know him?"

"Wade? Course I do."

"Then why you asking if I do?"

"It's the other guy I'm after. For Wade's surprise thirtieth." Tav didn't know how old Wade was. Thirty seemed about right though.

"Wade already reached thirty, eh? Time flies."

Tav chuckled.

The man turned back to the photo. "That's Jeff. Used to run this place. Trained Wade as a kid."

"Yeah, I know," Tav lied. "But I need to find him."

The man scratched his chin. "Well, he ain't been around here for years – you know, after what happened."

Tav nodded. He didn't have a clue what the guy was on about.

"Last I heard, he was in Stoke Newington. Not sure if he's still there, though. Was a while back now."

"You know whereabouts?"

The man shook his head. "Was a groundsman for some park, I think."

Tav thought about touting the photo around the rest of the guys, but most didn't look a day over twenty. And the older ones might not be as gullible about the whole surprise party cobblers.

He reclaimed the photograph and slipped it back into his pocket. "Cheers, mate."

The man waved him off and turned back to mopping the floor.

Tav marched to his car. There were at least four parks in Stoke Newington that he knew of. Finding this Jeff guy wasn't going to be a quick or easy process – that was for damn sure. And who was to say Wade and the girl were even with him?

Tav opened his car door but didn't get in. He looked at his last dialled numbers and hit the third one down. "You found anything yet?"

"No, man," Jimmy the Junkie said. "My contact can't get a handle on them."

"Well, you'd better find something out quick. I'm chasing my fucking tail out here."

Tav hung up. Stoke Newington it was then.

CHAPTER FORTY-NINE

Jason sat up.

His waist cramped, his shoulder burned, and he didn't know which to reach for first. He opted for the sofa cushion, his fingers gripping the hell out of it, and his silent curse came out not so silent. He bit back the call for help only a spineless prat would utter, and slowly exhaled until the pain simmered down and his trembling limbs stilled.

He glanced around the small room, but nothing looked familiar. A small window – the outside view shrouded by trees – allowed a little daylight to filter through. That was good. Daylight meant it wasn't night, so he hadn't spent the best part of the day passed out cold.

Abney Park was an amazing yet strange place, a cemetery encased inside a small forest. What had come first – the woods or the cemetery – Jason didn't know. Didn't care either if he was totally honest.

He slowly swung his legs over the side of the sofa, grimaced for the second time in as many minutes, and inhaled again. Kate was curled up on the chair opposite him. She looked like hell.

The door opened, allowing more light to brighten the room, and Jeff entered. He shook fresh snow from his coat and closed the door.

He saw Jason awake and smiled. "How you feeling?"

Jeff hadn't aged much – the younger Jeff had always looked older than his years. But so much time had passed since they'd last spoken that suddenly having to converse didn't come as easy to Jason as he'd have liked. In fact, he was at a loss for words.

"You want to tell me what's going on?" Jeff said.

Jason looked down at his torn and bloodied clothes – then at his bandaged shoulder. "You do this?"

Jeff nodded. "And a hospital visit wouldn't be a bad idea." He glanced at Kate. "For the both of you."

"We can't." Jason lowered his head and ruffled some energy into his hair. Pain burned across his shoulder again. Jeff watched but didn't come to his aid, and Jason was glad of it. He exhaled, taking a couple of seconds to compose himself.

"The girl said someone may be coming for you. This someone have a name?"

"Yeah. Finley." Jason cast a glance at Kate, still covered in his blood and still curled up asleep on the chair.

"So, who knows you're here?"

Jason looked at Jeff. "No one. But someone's been talking."

"You have any ideas who? Narrow it down maybe?"

Jason shook his head. "It's looking like it was my boss. And he's just hung himself."

Jeff stepped away from the door. He wheeled out the desk chair, spun it to face Jason, and sat. "So, this Finley's leak has been plugged then?"

"So it would seem."

Jeff's eyes narrowed. "You don't think so?"

Jason closed his eyes. He didn't know what to think anymore. Thoughts scrambled around inside his head: contract killers and police informants – it was like a bad episode of the Sweeney. "I know I can't stay here."

"Where you gonna go?"

Jason shrugged. He slowly got up from the sofa and clasped his side, his broken ribs hurting more than the bullet hole in his shoulder. He shuffled toward the door.

"Where're you going?"

"We'll leave first thing in the morning. Right now, I'm gonna check the grounds."

"In that state? You won't last five minutes."

"I need to know we're safe."

Jeff stood. He moved Jason back towards the sofa and sat him down. "Everything is locked up tight. Nobody can get in here."

Jason scoffed. Enclosures were good – but they were made to be climbed and conquered.

"I got some clothes you and the girl can change into. No trousers, but a couple of jumpers." He pointed to a door Jason hadn't noticed just left of the sofa. "You can clean up in there."

Jason nodded. He was covered in blood – both his and Karen's. It was a sight he wouldn't miss.

"I'd suggest some more sleep first, though." Jeff turned to the door.

"Where you going?"

"This place don't run itself. I'll be back and then we'll check the grounds – like you wanted."

Jason caught an hour's kip, maybe two. It was broken by the sound of a siren wailing along the high street just outside the park's entrance.

Kate remained asleep on the chair, in exactly the same position as the last time he'd checked. What the hell was he doing dragging her out here? What the hell was *he* doing out here? Carter was dead. Finley was in the dark. Another safe house, surrounded and protected by the police, was what Kate needed – not to be dragged around London by a washed-up boxer who couldn't protect shit at the moment. He hated to admit he needed help, but even he was smart enough to know a hospital wasn't the worst idea he'd heard today.

He sat up, yawned, and shook the grogginess from behind his eyes. When he tried to stretch some life into his arms, his muscles spasmed and forced him to quickly lower them again. He waited for the soreness to simmer down, stood – slowly – and shuffled to the door just left of the sofa. Just as Jeff had promised, on the other side was a small bathroom – well, a tiny sink you could just about fit your hands into and a toilet. On the back of the door were a couple of hoodies and a rain mac – all blood free.

Jason leaned on the sink. He ran the hot water, which was lukewarm at best, and splashed his face. There was no mirror – probably just as well if he looked as bad as he felt – and no towel either. He didn't bother shaking the excess water from his hands.

Bruising covered his torso. How on earth did he expect to go another round with Finley – should he show up – while he was in this state? He felt his ribs. Not the first ones he'd ever broken. And not the first time he'd have fought with them busted. Maybe he could take on Finley and survive – if he treated this scenario like a ten-round fight. He scoffed. And maybe the bullet hole in his shoulder wouldn't make any difference either.

"Fuck," he muttered, leaning on the sink again. Who was he kidding?

He glanced at the hoodie hanging on the back of the door – the old Phoenix Gym's boxing logo plastered across the front – and pulled it free. He didn't know exactly how long it took him to try and slip his injured arm into it and pull it over his head, but it was time he didn't have and he quickly gave up.

He opened the door and threw it on the sofa.

Kate was awake.

"How do you feel?" he said, reaching for the sweater again.

Her eyes lingered on his bareness. A slight smile touched her lips, but she didn't speak.

"There's a bathroom back there. A clean top hanging on the door." He pointed to the room behind him.

Kate sat up. "You need some help with yours?" She got up, not waiting for him to answer, and took the jumper from his grip.

She ruffled one of the sleeves together then held it towards him. "Here, put your arm through."

"I can do it myself," Jason protested.

"Then why haven't you?"

He stared at her, no answer coming to mind. This was not how he normally rolled. He was usually the protector – the strong one. He glanced at the floor. Swallowing, he slipped his injured arm through the woollen fabric.

"I can take it from here." He reached for the jumper.

"Nonsense." She stretched the jumper's neck.

Jason remained still while she slid his other arm into the sleeve, then let her slip the jumper over his head and pull the jumper down over his torso.

"There. Your masculinity remains intact." She stood back and glanced up at him. "It's okay to accept a little help once in a while."

Jason stood rigid, unsure how to respond.

That same light smile curved her lips. "Does it still hurt much?"

"It's better than earlier." He tried to look away. Tried to focus on anything else in the room, but he couldn't. The sight of her captivated him – the room's low light filtering across her matted hair. Her eyes, soft and warm, watching him, studying him. A rush of guilt caught in his chest and Karen's lifeless body pushed to the forefront of his mind.

He cleared his throat and stepped aside. "I'll let you freshen up."

Again, that faint smile that warmed his insides. She moved past him towards the bathroom and he reached for her hand. He hadn't meant to. Hadn't even realised he'd done it until she turned to face him. His lips dried and when he tried to swallow, he found his throat had too.

"Thank you," he said, the words scratching over his tongue.

"For what?"

He tried to swallow again, this time with a little more success. "For getting us here." He glanced at his newly donned jumper. "And for this."

Kate nodded. She smiled again and glanced at her hand.

Jason immediately released it. He straightened, grabbed the chair Jeff had previously used, and pushed it back under the desk. When he looked back up, Kate was just closing the bathroom door behind her.

CHAPTER FIFTY

Kate heard voices outside.

Jeff was talking to Jason – something about checking the grounds alone, which Jason was having none of. Then the inevitable knock on the door came.

Kate opened the door just a slither. She'd removed her soiled top but hadn't yet dressed in the clean one.

Jason stood there, a thick coat covering his clothes and a beanie pulled down over his ears.

His gaze briefly lowered, then found her again. "I'm heading out to check the grounds with Jeff. The entrance is locked and everything is safe, but I want you to lock the door behind us."

He held out a key.

Kate reached through the gap and took it.

"I'll be gone ten minutes, okay?"

Kate nodded. There was no point arguing with him. She'd just listened to Jeff unsuccessfully pointing out the obvious to him – that he was injured and needed a hospital. And that walking the grounds would just drain what little energy he had left.

"Also, take this." Jason held up a small radio. "If you need me, just press this button and talk."

Kate opened the door a little farther and took the radio. She watched the two men head towards the front door, Jason glancing back one last time.

"Lock this door as soon as I close it."

Then they disappeared outside and closed the door.

Kate looked about the room – basically four brick walls and a ceiling, with a threadbare carpet that had frayed so much it resembled more of a rug. An eerie feeling fell across the place, even though two lamps had been switched on, giving light to the darkest of corners. A quiver shook her insides and she drew in a deep breath. She rushed to the front door, a split-second thought in her head that she could stop the men from leaving – or at least make them wait for her to join them. But she stopped short of opening it.

Instead, she slid the key into the lock and turned it. Hearing the latch click, she walked to the window. Putting the radio on the desk, she cupped her hands around her eyes and pressed against the glass. The afternoon was already turning into night. With the office lit up inside, she just made out the figures of Jason and Jeff heading into the woods.

Goosebumps pricked her skin and she tried to rub them away. She stepped back from the window and headed into the bathroom. Unhooking the jumper from the back of the door, she slipped it over her head. The oversized fleece brought instant warmth, and she pulled the long sleeves down over her hands and scrunched them tight.

Back in the main room, she settled on the sofa. An old paperback had been shoved down the side of the cushions – a horror by Stephen Laws by the look of it. She glanced about the room. No TV or radio that she could see and tiredness eluded her. Staring at the front door waiting for Jason to return – well, time may as well stand still.

She looked back at the book. Did she even like horror? She flicked open the pages to the first chapter and started to read.

She'd just started on chapter two when she heard the noise outside. Nothing big. More of a crunch, really. On the other side of the window, darkness had eaten away all remaining daylight. So, she listened. Hard. But, other than the light murmur of traffic, she couldn't hear anything.

She lay the book down and stood. Walking to the door, she checked it was locked then moved to the window. Only her reflection stared back at her. She cupped her face and, like before, pressed against the window, hoping to catch a glimpse of Jason returning.

Tavish Finley stared straight back at her.

He raised a gun, its long barrel aimed at her forehead. Voices screamed inside Kate's head – to move, to duck, to yell for Jason – but her paralysed body wouldn't move.

The two stared at each other. Then Finley fired.

Kate screamed and dropped to the floor. The window shattered and glass fell from the frame. Another shot cracked through the air. Kate covered her head, biting back her cries for help.

Cold air swept down upon her, but no more shots came. Outside, heavy footsteps retreated from the window. Was Finley leaving? Had he assumed he'd killed her? She crawled beneath the desk and wrapped her arms around her legs. Scrambled thoughts muddled her thinking. Then she remembered the radio. She lifted her head, but the desk blocked her from seeing anything.

Shit. She was a sitting duck like this. All Finley had to do was jump through the window and shoot her. So, why hadn't he? Had someone interrupted him? Was someone outside? Was Jason outside? Maybe he *had* left – like she thought. But, even with that sobering thought, she remained quiet and stayed put, listening to the eerie silence outside the building.

Tremors rocked her body. She inhaled, closed her eyes, and tried to calm down. With little choice, she edged out from beneath the desk. Still, other than the murmur of traffic, she heard no other noises. No movement outside or in. She peered over the top of the desk, clocking the broken window. Nobody waited for her. Spotting the radio, she reached across the desk until she felt it brush against her fingertips.

A muffled pop hit the front door and a section of wood just to the right of the lock fractured inwards. A second pop punctured the door, and more wood splintered free.

Kate got to her feet and grabbed the radio. She clicked the button. "Jason! Jason!"

A foot stamped against the wood and the door burst open.

Finley stormed into the room and raised the gun. "Put it down."

Kate lowered the radio and froze.

"On the desk," Finley ordered.

He edged towards the bathroom, the gun still trained on her, and quickly popped his head around the door. "Where is he?"

"Not here."

"I can see that. Where is he?"

Kate shrugged and glanced around the room, looking for a way out. There was only the door or the window.

"You'll never make it, luv."

"Why are you doing this? I don't remember anything. Can't remember."

"I know. I read your hospital file."

"So, whatever I saw – I can't remember it. You don't have to kill me."

Finley cocked his head to one side. "Afraid it don't work that way, sweetheart." He steadied the gun.

"Wait. Please. You don't have to do this." Tears streamed down her face. "At least tell me why I have to die. Did I see who killed my father? Was it you?"

"There wouldn't have been any witnesses if I'd done it."

"So, I did witness it? And the killer…he hired you?"

Finley smiled. "See. You do remember."

Her light sobbing turned heavier. "But I don't. I swear I don't."

Finley crossed the room in two strides and grabbed a fistful of her hair. "But you could – at any time."

He pressed the nozzle against her temple.

Kate's breath caught in her throat. She tried to scream but couldn't find the breath. The room around her began to blur.

"It's nothing personal, luv, even though you've been an annoying fucking thorn in my side."

"Please don't kill me." The hoarse words scratched her throat.

The nozzle pressed harder against her head.

"Oh god, please—"

Footsteps charged across the snow outside and a darkened figure leapt through the broken window. The nozzle lifted from her temple and she fell backwards, hitting the desk. When she looked up, she saw Jason wrestling Finley for the gun.

He glanced her way, his face straining under the obvious pain he was in. "Get out," he shouted at her.

The path to the door was clear. Finley saw it too. He released the gun and punched Jason in the stomach. Jason hunched over and Finley hit him again. He reached for the gun, but Jason caught him with a swipe to the temple, knocking him off balance.

Kate ran to the door. She glanced over her shoulder. Finley kicked Jason away and rushed after her.

Jason grabbed the gun. The bullet missed Finley by inches, but the distraction was enough to slow him down.

Kate fled across the fresh snowfall. She heard another pop of the gun and glanced over her shoulder. Finley hadn't emerged and neither had Jason. She hovered on the edge of the forest, not knowing what to do. Should she run or go back?

Two hands pulled her back.

Kate swung around, her fists raised and ready to lash out.

"It's me," Jeff said in hushed tones. He pulled her into the trees and out of sight of the office. "Is Jason in there?"

Kate nodded. "We need to help him."

"How many others?"

"Just Finley. He has a gun."

"Okay, I need you to follow this path. You'll reach an old chapel. Inside is a staircase. Follow it to the top. There's a tiny window up there that leads to a ledge. You'll just about squeeze through it. The guy that's after you won't. Now go."

"What about Jason?"

"I'll help him."

CHAPTER FIFTY-ONE

"Okay, you piece of shit," Wade said. "Turn and face me. Slowly."

Tav wasn't far from the door. A couple of steps away, in fact. He'd easily be able to dive outside before Wade got a shot off. But he'd never make cover before Wade had him in his sights again – and something told him that Wade wouldn't hesitate. He'd shoot first and asked questions…never.

Tav turned, his hands raised chest height and within reach of disarming Wade of the gun – if he stepped close enough.

But Wade didn't. He remained by the desk, one hand holding his waist, the other pointing the gun straight at Tav. He displayed surprising steadiness too, considering he looked to hold it in his non-dominant hand.

"You have a high pain threshold, Wade."

"That annoy you?"

Tav grinned. It did annoy him. Wade's play in the game should have been over the moment the bullet hit his shoulder. He was proving one hell of an adversary. Unfortunately, Tav didn't have time to take on the challenge. He glanced at the door. He'd spotted the girl running for the trees and now another male hurried towards the hut.

Wade called for his attention again. "Hey."

Tav turned back to face him. Still that distance between them and the gun pointed towards him.

"Tell me who killed my sister."

Tav grinned.

Wade's face hardened and his grip tightened around the gun.

"I laid out the terms. Give me the girl – I give you the killer."

"That ain't gonna happen."

Tav shrugged. "Then we have no more business to conduct."

Wade took a single step closer. "You think you have a choice?"

"You think I don't?"

They locked eyes. The gun wavered a little. Sweat dampened Wade's face and hair. All he needed was a little more coaxing.

The old man reached the door, a little out of breath. At his age he wasn't someone Tav would usually consider a threat. But Jeff – like Wade – was an East End boxer. Tav would never underestimate a man with that background again.

"You called the police yet?" Jeff said.

Wade shook his head. "He's got something to tell me first."

Tav widened his grin. "I ain't telling you shit. You know the deal. Take it or shoot me."

"Was it Carter?"

Tav shrugged. "If you like."

Wade took another step closer. He was right on the edge. Just a little nearer and Tav would have him disarmed within a second; Wade and his friend would be dead two seconds after that.

Tav glanced over his shoulder. Jeff was his second option.

He spun on his heel and reached for the man. Jeff was quick to react. He raised his arm and blocked Tav from wrapping his hand around his neck. He followed through with a punch. The first Tav didn't expect. It clocked him on the side of the face. The second punch found air, pulling Jeff off balance. Tav side-stepped, catching Jeff as he plunged forward. He hauled the old man close, one arm wrapped around his throat, the other a lever across the back of his neck.

He locked his grip and spun Jeff to face Wade. "Drop the gun."

Wade wavered but the gun didn't lower.

"I'll snap his neck quicker than you can blink."

"And you'll be dead before he hits the floor."

Tav tightened his grip but he knew Wade wasn't bluffing. "So, what now?"

"You let him go."

"Try again." Tav edged towards the door, dragging Jeff back with him like a shield.

"There's nowhere for you to go."

Tav grinned. He pushed Jeff away from his chest and launched him towards Wade. Then he ducked out of the door and sprinted towards the trees.

CHAPTER FIFTY-TWO

Kate ran.

Snow hadn't settled beneath the trees and the path was a mixture of mud and fallen leaves lined with a mishmash of headstones and monuments four or five deep.

She followed the path – just as Jeff had instructed – until she hit a clearing. In the middle sat a chapel, relatively small as far as chapels went, its spire reaching high into the night and silhouetted by the moon. Some windows were boarded up, others open to the elements.

Behind her, the path was shrouded in darkness that not even the moon could reach. She listened. No sound. No footsteps. No Jason calling her name. *Shit*. She never should have left him. She turned back to the chapel and just about made out a ledge some thirty feet above her. It was high. Much higher than she wanted to climb.

Shit.

She scanned the building, searching for a way inside. The front gates were padlocked. Bars secured the windows. Why would Jeff have sent her here knowing it was locked up and she couldn't gain access?

She rattled the gates and tried to pull them apart as much as the chain binding them would allow. Still not enough of a gap for her to squeeze through. She gave up and stepped back. What was she missing?

She looked down and saw the gap where the gate didn't quite meet the ground. Not a big space, but it was a way through nonetheless. Lying flat on her back, she hauled herself underneath the gate, the bottom of the bars scraping against her chest, her thighs. On the other side, darkness shrouded the majority of the area. She paused a few metres in, the nagging doubt that gnawed at her insides too strong to ignore.

Was Jason hurt? Was he dead? He certainly wasn't in any fit state to take on Finley. She should have headed out to the street and returned with reinforcements instead of fleeing into the woods.

Even with these thoughts racing inside her head, she headed to the rear of the chapel where a narrow opening hid a rickety staircase – and began to climb. Each wooden step creaked and groaned beneath her weight. She kept going, her hands gliding across the rough, stone walls for guidance and security until, near the top – just like Jeff had said – she saw a tiny window. No glass, no boards – just the cold, wintery night sweeping through and freezing her to the bone.

Kate hoisted herself up, wriggling through until she rolled out onto the ledge. No wall or railings protected her from falling – or from Finley. All he had to do was look up and he'd see her.

On all fours, she edged along the ledge to the other side of the roof and crouched beside the spire. This was not safe. She did not feel safe. Another gust of wind rushed through her hair and she clung tight to the tiles. Where the hell was Jason?

Below, a shadow emerged from the trees. Jason? She opened her mouth to call out in relief. But the words stuck in her throat. Her heart pounded against her chest until her mouth dried and her lips chapped and hardened. The shadow wasn't Jason. It was Finley.

She glanced at the tiny window – it was too late to vacate the ledge now, and she wished she'd hidden somewhere else. She hugged the spire, trying to shrink against it and let the night hide her. Below, Finley stepped away from the trees, careful and cautious. He scanned the area, the trees, the chapel windows. Then he disappeared around the front of the building.

Kate wanted to move, but fear held her close to the spire. The iron gates rattled – Finley trying to find a way inside? She squeezed her eyes shut. She was sure he'd never fit beneath them as she had done, but maybe he'd manage to break them open…

Silence again.

She kept her eyes closed, finding invisibility in the darkness.

"I see you, Kate," Finley called above the wind.

Kate opened her eyes. Finley stood below her, looking up. Her breath caught, but she didn't move. Could he see her or was he calling her bluff?

He walked to the corner of the building, clasped a stone that jutted out, and began to scale the wall.

Kate scurried across the ledge back towards the window.

"That's it. Come back down. Make my life easier."

Kate froze. He was right. If she climbed back through the window she would be trapped inside the chapel. How long before Finley broke through a boarded window or found another way to get inside?

She hovered where she was. Finley waited below, killing time to see what her next move was going to be. When she didn't move, he started climbing again. If he reached the top, could she kick him back off, or would he grab her and pull her off with him? She edged closer to the window. If he made it to the ledge, she'd have no choice but to climb back through. And if he found a way into the chapel, she'd just climb out on to the ledge again – do the same all night until morning if she had to. It was a crap plan, but it would keep her alive.

"Finley!"

The sound of Jason's voice warmed her eyes with tears. Kate glanced over the edge. Finley still clung to the stones halfway up the wall.

He swung out, gripping the wall one-handed, and glanced down at Jason. He shook his head. "Give it up, mate. You're half dead."

Jason aimed the gun at him. "And so will you be if you don't slide your arse down off there. Nice and easy like."

Finley swung back against the wall and rested his forehead on the stone. He remained that way for what seemed the best part of a minute. Then he slowly descended the chapel. He landed in the long grass with a thud. One last glance up at Kate and he waded through the weeds until he was back in the shortened grass.

"Hold it right there." Jason stopped him at a distance of fifteen feet – give or take.

Behind Jason, Jeff jogged out of the trees. He seemed a little out of breath but held a shovel and looked ready to do battle.

"So? What now?" Finley sounded impervious to the firearm pointed at him. "You gonna shoot me while Alf Garnett here sticks me six feet under?"

"The police are on their way, son," Jeff said.

Finley chuckled. "And you think I'm gonna wait for them?"

Jason ignored him. He looked in a bad way. One arm was wrapped around his waist and the other trembled so uncontrollably that Kate could see the gun wavering in his grip, even from her elevated position.

Jason looked up at her, the moonlight painting his face paler than it'd been earlier in the office. "You okay up there?"

Kate shifted position and nodded. She didn't know if he could see, but a verbal acknowledgement stuck in her throat and just wasn't forthcoming.

Finley took a step towards Jason.

Jason fired the gun.

Finley's leg buckled below him and he fell to one knee — a string of *fucks* cursing the night air. He remained that way for a second and didn't try to stand.

"You're one lucky son of a bitch." Finley glanced up at Jason, his back still hunched and venom poisoning every word he spat. "Or did you mean to shoot my toe?"

He struggled to his feet and limped forward. "You'd better put one of those shells between my eyes if you want to stop me." He tapped his forehead.

Jason pulled the trigger. An empty *click*. Jason squeezed the trigger again. The same *click* – over and over.

"Oops." Finley hobbled closer. "Looks like you've got trouble."

Finley stretched out his arms and shook his hands. He rolled his shoulders, cracked his neck side to side, and threw a couple of upper cuts to the wind. Jason remained still. He seemed to be sizing Finley up. Looking for a weak spot. When Finley finally finished, he turned to Jason and flashed a smile.

Jeff stepped between the two men, the shovel raised to chest height, and Finley paused. Even from this height, Kate could see Finley was a little hesitant when it came to the old man.

The three of them held their positions. Jason looked close to collapse and it frightened Kate that Jeff – the sixty-something cemetery caretaker – appeared the more competent of the two.

Finley limped another step closer but Jeff stood his ground. He swung the shovel, but Finley blocked it. Hooking the handle under his arm, he pulled Jeff close. Jeff appeared ready for the move. He gripped Finley by the collar and headbutted the bridge of his nose. Swinging upwards, he caught Finley with an uppercut that sent him staggering backwards. By some miracle, Finley remained on his feet, but the shovel fell from under his arm. He shook his head and glanced up. Jeff stood, fists raised, ready to fight. He looked every inch a boxer.

Blood trickled down Finley's nose and he wiped it clear. A quick glance at his reddened hand and he flicked a respectful salute towards Jeff. He bent for the shovel.

Straightened and, balancing extremely well on his good foot, began to whirl the implement between his hands like a copter's blade.

Jeff backed up, his arms outstretched, shielding Jason. Finley swung the shovel towards Jeff like a pickaxe. Jeff dodged – the blade missing his head by inches. Finley pivoted on his good foot, rounding the shovel three-sixty through the air, like he was some kind of ninja. Jeff moved with the speed of a much younger man and dodged the tool again. But Finley was quicker. He jabbed the blade forward, socking Jeff in the stomach, then scooted upwards, cracking it beneath Jeff's chin. He jutted forward again, swift and clean, the blade hitting Jeff in the throat. Jeff gasped and clasped his neck, his fingers unable to stop the flow of blood.

Kate cried out as Jeff collapsed to the ground.

Jason leapt forward. Finley turned the blade towards him, but Jason parried the attack away. He parried a second time, knocking the shovel from Finley's grip. But each movement took its toll and Kate watched his defence grow weaker. Finley, balancing on one foot, looked the more superior of the two by far. His injury didn't appear to be hampering his ability to take on Jason's assault.

Finley was going to kill Jason if she didn't help him.

The two men circled the unmarked space between them. Finley jolted a fist forward. Jason bobbed in anticipation of the punch. The next punch Finley threw was for real. Jason parried it, ducking the next swing that followed.

Finley smiled. "So, you are a good boxer."

Jason didn't respond. He remained focused on Finley.

Finley came at him, throwing punch after punch. Jason took one on the chin. Dodged another. Caught Finley with an uppercut and followed it with a gut punch. Finley stepped back. A moment to catch his breath, then he planted a side-kick into Jason's stomach.

Jason doubled over. Finley raised his leg straight out and hammered his heel down onto Jason's shoulder, forcing Jason into the snow.

Kate climbed back through the window and hurried down the rickety steps. The chapel seemed darker and smaller now than when she'd first entered. She ran to the iron gates and slid herself beneath them.

The men were still doing battle. She edged to the corner of the building and peered round. Both men now had hold of the shovel, each gripping an end. Jason swung at Finley, his fist hammering the side of his temple. Finley responded with a kick to the side of Jason's thigh.

Jason staggered back, his hand still keeping a tight hold on the shovel's handle. Finley dropped to one knee and rolled forward, swiping Jason's legs out from under him. Jason landed with a thump and Finley hammered his foot down into Jason's groin. Jason curled forward and Finley kicked him in the head.

Kate's mouth dried. A ringing shrilled inside her ears. Her vision blurred. The park disappeared from view and a construction site appeared in its place. Still under a night sky, she watched three men through a windscreen, the wipers intermittently erasing the rain from view. One of the men held a shovel, levelling out concrete as it poured from a truck's discharge chute. The next man stood and watched, the third man lying at his feet.

Then they glanced up. Saw her.

"Kate," Finley called.

The men and the construction site blurred and Finley came sprinting across the clearing towards her.

Behind him, Jason lay on the ground. Unmoving.

Kate backed away from the chapel. Turned. And ran.

CHAPTER FIFTY-THREE

Jason opened his eyes.

Clouds hid the moon and a gloomy darkness shadowed the clearing around him.

He tried to sit up, didn't get far, and crashed back down onto the snow. He curled his knees toward his chest and rolled onto his side. His tight chest struggled to draw breath and it took a good minute before the ache died enough to roll back. He stared up at the sky. Even though fresh snowflakes flurried down onto his face, stars still littered the night above. He waited for the pain to lessen a little more, then tried to sit up again. And failed again.

He inhaled and lifted his head. Jeff lay just to his right. He reached for him but Jeff didn't move – not when Jason shook his shoulder, nor when he called him by name.

Jason tried to sit up again. His stomach tightened and he fought the pain. Now he saw Jeff clearly, his head lying on a pillow of crimson snow. Jason scrambled towards him, searching for a pulse, his hand trembling as he took his friend and mentor's wrist. Faint palpitations throbbed under Jason's fingertips and relief washed over him. He pulled off his coat, then his jumper and wrapped it around Jeff's throat. It stemmed the blood flow a little but Jeff needed help. He needed a hospital.

Jason looked up at the chapel. Kate was gone and Finley was nowhere to be seen. His body tightened. Rage burned in his gut and he grabbed the jacket and staggered to his feet. His ribs still hurt like hell, but the pain and adrenaline were now his friend. He bit back the agony, redonned the coat, and waited to regain his balance.

Then he headed towards the path.

CHAPTER FIFTY-FOUR

Kate fled through the forest.

She thought she heard Finley's footsteps pounding the dirt some way behind her. How he managed to move so fast after being shot in the foot was beyond her. Her brain screamed that he gained on her with every step and her frightened imagination envisioned his breath hitting the back of her neck. Thought she felt him grab her shoulder.

The broken headstones and wildly overgrown foliage were hard to make out in the dark. She could only just about see the path and had no idea if she was even heading in the right direction for Jeff's office and the park entrance. Regardless, she quickened her pace, doubtful she'd reach it before Finley reached her.

The forest either side of the path called to her with the offer of greater protection, and she diverted her route, leaping between the graves and racing for cover – ducking and diving between the trees and heading farther into the woods. Twigs and dried foliage snapped and crunched under her weight. Ivy tangled her feet and tried to pull her over. Crumbling headstones lay toppled, blocking her route. But she ran on until the forest parted and she found herself on another path.

Shit. The place was a maze.

She turned left. Behind her, she heard someone tramping her way. It had to be Finley, his footsteps uneven and irregular.

She paused, not wanting her own footsteps to give her away, and listened. Finley sounded close, but she couldn't see where he was. Every inch of her quietened – her shallow breaths no more than a whisper. He was close. Too close. She searched around, desperate for somewhere to hide. Trees offered branches to climb and headstones something to cower behind. None of them would fool Finley, though. The guy was way too smart.

Kate started running again, but the path only led into further darkness. She thought about turning back. To find Jason and the chapel again. But then she saw the lights of the high street through the park gates. She escaped from the trees and raced towards them, the snow muffling her steps.

Her heart raced. Hurried breaths wheezed past her lips. She gripped the iron railings and pushed but a padlocked chain secured them together.

Outside, cars passed by. She called out for help. Nobody heard her.

Shit. She glanced up at the gates, certain she could scale them. Caught the sound of footsteps crushing snow behind her and turned.

Finley stepped out of the trees. Moonlight shone down on him like he was some kind of angel. But he wasn't an angel. He was the devil. And he was here to kill her.

His first glance was towards the office. Kate held her breath. Had he not seen her? He remained where he was and slowly scanned the area.

Her rapid breathing started again, escalating when his eyes finally settled on her.

"There you are." He limped towards her, his injured foot starting to drag a little.

Kate rushed for the office. Finley quickened his pace. Even with his injury, he gained on her. Kate fell through the door and kicked it shut, holding it closed with her feet.

Finley whacked the wood. Kate scanned the room. Her gaze landed on the bathroom door. But with no window to climb out of this time, she'd be cornered.

The hammering stopped and she heard footsteps crunch through the snow until a shadow approached the broken window.

Kate leapt up, grabbed the fire extinguisher from the wall, and edged towards the window.

She waited.

Finley was just on the other side. She could hear him. Her grip tightened around the extinguisher and she raised it shoulder height, ready to swing.

Finley's shadow seeped across the floor. She heard him breathing. The shadow moved again. An arm reached through the window and Kate swung the extinguisher. It whacked Finley's arm and he quickly withdraw it.

She raised the extinguisher again, ready. But Finley didn't materialise.

The door behind her burst inward. Kate raced at him. She swung the extinguisher. It didn't get anywhere near Finley – only opened her up for attack. She whirled off balance and Finley struck her across the back. Kate sprawled across the floor and the extinguisher rolled from her clutches.

She turned onto her back and glared up at him. He towered over her, his chest rising with every heavy breath, his eyes hard and looking for blood. She kicked out, catching the side of his injured foot.

Finley crumbled back, struggling to remain upright. He hopped, trying unsuccessfully to distribute his weight evenly between his two feet.

Kate rolled. She grabbed the fire extinguisher and scrambled to her feet. Finley's face hardened. His eyes widened and he swung for her. Kate leaned out of his reach, then followed through with the extinguisher. She bashed it against his shoulder. Finley's lopsided balance let him down and Kate swung again. The metal cracked his skull and he fell to the floor.

He lay there, motionless.

Kate watched him for a second then shifted a little closer. She stretched her leg and nudged him. No groans. No expletives. Nothing. He was out cold. Or dead.

Now she had to help Jason – if he was still alive. She turned for the door.

Finley's hand wrapped around her ankle and pulled her down to the floor. Kate rolled away but Finley dragged her back. He straddled her, his knees burying into her sides, pinning her to the floor. Blood dripped from his head and wet her face.

He glared down at her, his eyes struggling to focus. He didn't speak. He clasped her around the throat and started to squeeze. Kate squirmed and struggled. She kicked her legs. Gasped for air. She reached for his face and pressed her thumbs into his eyes until he screamed and released her. He leaned back, the palms of his hands rapidly rubbing his sockets. A string of obscenities spat past his lips and, when he finally glared down at her, death was all that filled his eyes. He held that stare for a second, his hatred for her intense, then he punched her in the face.

Kate's head snapped to the side. She saw the open door – the snow-covered ground just beyond it. High-pitched ringing shrilled inside her head. And then Finley's hands were back around her throat, crushing every last breath from her body. She pushed at his chest, but he was too heavy for her to move. She clawed at his hands but he was too strong. She stretched for the extinguisher. Out of reach. Her arms flailed across the floor above her head. She touched something metal. Felt a handle, grabbed it, and swung.

The paint pot smashed against Finley's head, knocking him clean off her.

Kate gasped for breath. Rolled onto her front and crawled towards the cluster of building materials. Within seconds, Finley was on her again. But his strength had weakened, and she kicked him off. She grabbed a bottle of white spirit, pulled the top free, and turned to him. He was on his knees, looking incapable of actually standing. He reached for her again, his determination to get her not waning like his strength seemed to be. Kate cast the white spirit at him.

The liquid sprayed from the bottle, showering his clothes, his hair, his face.

Finley yelled and reached for his eyes.

Kate threw the whole bottle towards him and rushed for the extinguisher once again. Finley tried to stop her but his movements were slow and sloppy. Kate lifted the red cylinder and swung with all her might. Its base cracked Finley between his shoulders and he fell to the floor. Kate swung again, this time clobbering him in the back of the neck.

She raised the extinguisher again.

Two hands grabbed her and she cried out.

"It's okay. It's me," Jason said.

Her grip loosened and Jason took the extinguisher from her. He hobbled towards Finley. The killer's eyes were open, staring blankly across the floor.

Kate massaged her throat. Tiny breaths wheezed past her lips. "Have I killed him?"

Jason shook his head. "Think you've broken his neck."

He limped back towards her, settling the extinguisher by his feet. His hands moved to her shoulders and he held her steady. His withered body looked ready to drop. Blood streaked down his nose and across his cheek to his ear.

He clasped her shoulders. "Are you okay?"

Kate swallowed. Nodded.

Her throat itched and she rubbed it. "I remember everything. I saw who killed my father."

"Was it Finley?"

"No. It was another man."

"Do you remember who you are?"

She shook her head.

Jason squeezed her shoulders. "Find the phone. Call 999. Can you do that?"

Kate nodded.

CHAPTER FIFTY-FIVE

LONDON
Ten Days Later

Jason stood on the bridge and looked out across the water.

This river had taken his sister from him. And it had tried to take Kate.

The busy public trundled back and forth behind him, but they didn't distract him. It had been a day short of a week since Kate had fallen from this exact spot – and where this whole nightmare had started for him. But, sad as he was, he couldn't hate the river – for it had also brought them together.

He hadn't seen her since the night at Abney. He and Kate had been rushed to hospital, both had given statements, and then some bigwigs had swept in, flashed some paperwork, and scooped her away.

And boy, did he miss her. He'd asked about her. Tried to find out where she'd been taken. Was she coming back? Every door had been slammed in his face. *Protective custody* and *MI5* had bounced from copper's lips. Truth was, nobody really knew.

Someone approached but Jason didn't turn. Even when his visitor leaned on the railing beside him, Jason didn't glance their way.

"Not thinking of jumping in, are you?"

Jason wasn't in the mood for one of Ed's jokes.

"I went to the hospital to see you. Nurses said you checked yourself out – against their advice." He remained quiet for a moment. "You been home yet?"

"Nope." Jason thought about leaving it there. Instead he said, "I might go and see the Doc."

"Didn't think you liked her."

"I have to if I want my job back."

"And?" Ed glanced at him. "Do you want it back?"

Jason shrugged.

Ed sighed. "A guy's been arrested." He held out a late edition of a newspaper.

Jason already knew but glanced at the headline: *TYCOON'S MURDER CAUGHT ON CAR'S CAMERA*. The black and white picture of a face – unknown to Jason – plastered below it.

"Turned out our girl's dashcam recorded and uploaded the whole thing to the cloud."

"The Met bods know why he did it?"

"If they do, no one's spilling. But, it's out of our hands."

"Oh?"

"Yanks have taken it. Ongoing case, blah, blah, blah." Ed scoffed. "Good fucking riddance, I say."

"What about Kate? She coming back?"

"Come on, Jason. You know how this shit works. She's long gone, mate. Swallowed up in some stateside witness protection shit no doubt." Ed sighed. "Brave girl though, testifying and all. Whoever wanted her father dead looks to be high-profile."

Jason scoffed but said nothing. He knew she was brave. What he didn't know was if he'd ever see her again. Was she even safe? "You know if her father was in any shenanigans over here that'd get him killed?"

"Shenanigans?"

"Business dealings?"

"Fuck." Ed groaned. A defeated groan. "I swear, if you mention that fucking casino."

"I'm just thinking, is all."

"I know you're upset about Leah." Ed seemed a little hesitant to continue. "You know, not getting the answers you wanted from Finley."

"Finley played me."

Ed's surprise was evident in his tone. "So, you've dropped this pursuit with him?"

"It's time I stopped chasing ghosts." Jason lied. Fuck Ed. Finley was the link. He had been hired to kill Kate and he knew something about his sister. And, even though rumours had Finley tagged as under armed guard at an unknown hospital (and Jason most likely wouldn't get within fifty feet of him), Jason was sure as fuck going to make him talk – one way or another – even if he had to beat the fucker to a pulp first.

And Jason would find him. And he would make him talk. Jason intended on getting to the bottom of his sister's death. And heaven help the bastard who'd killed her when he did. Ed just didn't need to know. Nobody did. "I was right about the amnesiac girl not jumping, you have to give me that now.

But Leah's death was a tragic accident – that one, I'll give you."

Ed straightened and turned to him. "Man, you don't know how good it feels to hear you say that."

Jason glanced at him. "I guess you could say we're now even."

"So," Ed smiled. "How's Jeff?"

"Still alive."

Ed chuckled. "Blast from the past, that one. I thought the old git had snuffed it years ago."

"It'll take more than a shovel to the throat to kill him." Jason returned his gaze to the water.

And thought of Tavish Finley.

THE SACRIFICE

By Donna Collins

"Asmospheric, beautifully-written, and compelling, this book scared me to the core."

J. Carson Black

From the author of the DEAD series, Donna Collins, comes a thriller series with a difference.

When Cornish nurse Eliza Hamilton is mugged on her way home from work late one evening, the mysterious Roman Holbrook appears out of the darkness and fights off her strange attacker. He quickly disappears into the night before the police arrive, leaving a semi-conscious Eliza questioning if he was, in fact, a figment of her imagination.

That is until he shows up on her doorstep one rainy night – and all hell breaks loose again.

But is this man her hero or does he have a more sinister motive for wanting her kept alive?

www.ingramcontent.com/pod-product-compliance
Lightning Source LLC
Chambersburg PA
CBHW072203130726
47910CB00011B/1796